"A coming-of-age story that vividly encapsulates the complexities of the modern encounter between China and America . . . in many ways the quintessential 'Chimerican' novel for the millennial generation. Disarming in its candor, addictively readable."

—Niall Ferguson, author of *Empire* and *Civilization*

"Compelling and authentic . . . a story of China as told by an outsider. Through the perspective of a young American, we can see a different side to our country and ourselves—one that is unfamiliar, but real."

—Yu Hua, winner of the James Joyce Award and the Grinzane Cavour Prize

ALSO BY J. R. THORNTON

Beautiful Country

PRAISE FOR *LUCIEN*

"A crisp, twisting tale in the hands of a writer in the bloom of his abundant talents."
—Graydon Carter, author of *When the Going Was Good* and award-winning former editor of *Vanity Fair*

"*Lucien* is thrilling in every way—the propulsive narrative, the knife-sharp prose, the nuanced and multi-faceted characters, the unflinching exploration of class, ego, art, and authenticity. J.R. Thornton has married *Succession* with *The Secret History*, and the result is an utterly original and deeply affecting novel that lays bare the pressure and perils of privilege."
—Bret Anthony Johnston, author of *We Burn Daylight* and *Remember Me Like This*

"Fine art, forgery, young friendship, and the perils of greed—*Lucien* is a closely observed and finely crafted campus thriller."
—Nick McDonell, author of *Quiet Street* and *An Expensive Education*

"J.R. Thornton writes with precision and honesty about the fragile math of male friendship, where violence and love are pals, and vulnerability is the harbinger of rage. In a time when men are not supposed to feel anything, Lucien feels everything. It's an explosion of captivating, haunting, and utterly real emotion."
—Patrick Somerville, creator of the HBO series *Station Eleven* and author of *The Cradle*

PRAISE FOR *BEAUTIFUL COUNTRY*

"Simple but wonderful . . . authentic, pure, and heartbreaking . . . [Thornton] is an exceptionally gifted young writer."
—Mo Yan, 2012 Nobel Laureate in Literature

"An amazing piece of work, well written and clever but most of all, deeply honest and unvarnished."
—Fareed Zakaria, author of *Age of Revolutions* and host of CNN's *Fareed Zakaria GPS*

"*Beautiful Country* is, in a word, beautiful. A novel with morality at the center, but absurdity all around."
—Gary Shteyngart, author of *Our Country Friends* and *Super Sad True Love Story*

"A compelling story of innocence and experience, of East and West, of sport and pastime. Thornton is a writer of formidable talent and deep heart, and this nuanced and moving novel marks his arrival as a significant new voice in contemporary fiction."
—Bret Anthony Johnston, author of *Remember Me Like This*

"This unsettling book about the moral encounter between America and China is a study of privilege, innocence, and risk. It is a tragedy of manners and a portrait of Beijing—amplified and torqued and unmistakable."
—Evan Osnos, author of *Age of Ambition*, winner of the National Book Award

LUCIEN

J. R. THORNTON

MAGPIE
BOOKS

A MAGPIE BOOK

First published in Great Britain, the Republic of Ireland and Australia
by Magpie, an imprint of Oneworld Publications Ltd, 2026

Text copyright © J. R. Thornton, 2024

The moral right of J. R. Thornton to be identified as the
Author of this work has been asserted by him in accordance
with the Copyright, Designs and Patents Act 1988

All rights reserved
Copyright under Berne Convention
A CIP record for this title is available from the British Library

ISBN 978-1-83643-257-9
eISBN 978-1-83643-258-6

Book design by Jen Overstreet
Printed and bound in Great Britain by Clays Ltd, Elcograf S.p.A.

This book is a work of fiction. Names, characters, businesses, organisations, places and
events are either the product of the author's imagination or are used fictitiously. Any
resemblance to actual persons, living or dead, events or locales is entirely coincidental.

No part of this publication may be reproduced, stored in a retrieval system, or transmitted,
in any form or by any means, electronic, mechanical, photocopying, recording of otherwise,
or used in any manner for the purpose of training artificial intelligence technologies or
systems, without the prior permission of the publishers.

The authorised representative in the EEA is eucomply OÜ,
Pärnu mnt 139b–14, 11317 Tallinn, Estonia
(email: hello@eucompliancepartner.com / phone: +33757690241)

Oneworld Publications Ltd
10 Bloomsbury Street
London WC1B 3SR
England

Stay up to date with the latest books,
special offers, and exclusive content from
Oneworld with our newsletter

Sign up on our website
oneworld.co.uk

For my parents

PROLOGUE

No one calls me Atlas anymore. Lucien gave me that name the first time we met. I haven't used it since the night he disappeared.

It took me a long time to piece together exactly what happened that night. My own memory is limited to a handful of isolated flashes: Lucien handing me a glass of whiskey, the stench of vomit on my sweatshirt, an argument. I remember being pushed into a taxi. I remember falling—the way the ground rushed up to meet me. I remember the shock of seeing blood on my fingertips.

I remember moments, images, sensations, but no context in which to place them and no sense of the order in which they occurred. Days later, when I woke up in the hospital with two cops at the foot of my bed, I had no idea that Lucien was missing or how I'd ended up there.

I've carried this story with me for years without ever telling it to anyone. Not in its entirety. I've told bits and pieces of it but never the full story. I've kept that to myself—a secret—because I wasn't prepared to go through it all again. Rather than relive those ups and downs, those triumphs and traumas, it felt easier to sequester the memories behind a padlocked door.

But a secret is an awful burden, and I'm ready to be free of mine.

CHAPTER 1

We met on the first day of our freshman year at Harvard. It was the summer of 2010, and we were roommates—not by choice but by chance. The housing office assigned us a small two-room suite in Greenough Hall, a quiet three-story brick dorm overlooking Prescott Street. Had we not been paired through the random act of a computer, I very much doubt we would have met.

I arrived late on that first day. We were supposed to check in by twelve, but my bus didn't pull into South Station until the midafternoon and it was nearly four by the time the Red Line rattled and screeched into Harvard Station, coming to a stop with a long hiss. I stepped off the subway car and onto the platform. The station was a relic of brutalism plucked straight from the 1970s, a subterranean ocean of fossilized concrete. The walls were plastered with rows of yellowed enamel tiles the color of unbrushed teeth and the air tasted warm and stale. I was tired from the journey, and my back ached under the weight of my bags. I found the turnstiles and rode the escalator up two flights, emerging in the center of the Square.

A summer breeze carried with it the lively buzz of a crowd, the gentle grumblings of cars idling in traffic. Hundreds of people coursed through the Square in every direction. To my left stood a stone and brick building, atop which floated red neon letters spelling out CAMBRIDGE SAVINGS BANK. A nearby Starbucks spilled customers out onto the pavement, drinks in hand, and across the street parents and students revolved through the doors of the Harvard Coop.

I'd visited Harvard once before, in the ice-crusted dark of December, when the days shrank down to just a few hours and the street corners puddled high with gray slush. It was a strange trip. I made the mistake of visiting during finals and had left with the impression of an austere and lifeless place, a puritan outpost perched on the very edge of darkness.

But now, in the warm light of a late summer day, the campus felt transformed. Once-barren trees now heaved with rustlings of green and yellow leaves. The red-and-white brick buildings in the Yard soaked up sunshine and beamed color back into the afternoon light. Everyone seemed happy. No one looked down. I wandered through the Square in a kind of daze, swept along by a heady current of newfound possibility. *This* was my new home.

I found my way to the freshman dean's office, where I collected my room key and ID card and then lugged my bags the short distance to Greenough Hall. A sap-green Range Rover with dark tinted windows turned onto Prescott Street and double-parked right in front of the dorm. It looked so new, I wondered if it had been driven off the lot that very morning. A family of four climbed out, looking just as neat and perfect. They began unloading the car aided by a pair of nearby volunteers in matching orange T-shirts.

I rested for a moment to watch. The Range Rover appeared to be a kind of Mary Poppins carpet bag on wheels. Out of it came a flat-screen TV, a mini-fridge, a beanbag chair, a microwave, clear plastic tubs holding snacks and goodies, a desk lamp, large white shopping bags from Bed Bath & Beyond stuffed with brand-new linens and towels, a Tempur-Pedic mattress pad, a laundry hamper, and a brown cardboard box marked *Xbox*. Atop the Range Rover was a mountain bike. That, too, came down and was wheeled to the bike rack at the back of the building. I noticed how the entire street was lined with cars parked bumper-to-bumper, and I felt suddenly self-conscious of the two suitcases by my side packed with everything I owned.

My room was at the end of a long corridor on the first floor. The door was ajar.

Lucien was sitting by the window, reading, legs kicked up on a desk. He glanced over his shoulder. "You're here! At last," he said, smiling. "Amazing. I was beginning to worry you might not exist."

He sprang to his feet and extended a hand. "Lucien," he said. He was tall and tanned, with long blond hair held back by a pair of sunglasses pushed up on top of his head. He had on skinny blue jeans and a white linen shirt open to the third button, the sleeves rolled up to his elbows. A cigarette was tucked behind one ear, his eyes a stark blue.

"I'm Chris."

"Ah," he said, frowning. "So you do go by Chris. Are you sure? It's a bit dull, isn't it? *Chris.*"

I stared at him, confused.

"Oh, no, I've offended you! I'm so sorry," he said. "*Dull* is too harsh. *Common.* I meant to say *common*. It's rather a common name, don't you think? You must be the fifth Chris I've met today."

"Really?"

"Yeah, there's Tennis Team Chris. There was Fat Chris in Annenberg. There are at least two Chrises on the crew team, and I'm fairly certain there's one more just down the corridor."

"I guess it is pretty popular," I said.

"We should think about changing it."

"Changing what?"

"Your name," he said, smiling.

I assumed he must be joking. "Yeah, okay," I said, playing along. "Why not? I've only had it my entire life."

Lucien laughed. "You're funny. That was good." He looked directly into my eyes when he spoke. There was something intensely intimate about that blue-eyed gaze. I found myself looking away.

"I think you should do it," he said. "We can come up with something better than *Chris*, surely. And now's the time to do it, too. No one knows you yet. What do you think of *Christo*? That's a bit better, isn't it?"

"You're serious?"

"No, you're right. I don't love it, either. Hmm . . . What's your middle name?"

"Dude, I can't change my name."

"Why not?"

"Because it's my name."

"Have you read Nietzsche?"

"Have I read what?"

"You should. He's excellent. Anyway, do you know what he says about identity? *Identity is nothing more than a logical fiction*," quoted Lucien. "And in this case, I'm arguing it would be highly logical for you to make a slight edit to that fiction. Nothing major. Just a tweak. So, what's your middle name?"

I shook my head. "I don't have one."

"That's no good," Lucien tapped an index finger to his lips. "What about a nickname? Any good nicknames growing up?"

"Not really," I said.

"Okay. Hang on, I'll come up with something." Lucien was silent for a few moments, and then he clapped his hands together. "I've got it. What about *Atlas*?"

"*Atlas*?"

"Yes," he said. "Like the chap from Greek myths. Were you ever into those? I used to love them as a kid. I'd fall asleep listening to them on tape every night."

I searched his eyes for any trace of mischief but found none. He wasn't kidding. I hesitated, bewildered by the suggestion.

"But why *Atlas*?"

"Well, number one: it's a cool fucking name. Girls are going to *love* it. Two: it's memorable. I mean, how many people have you ever met called Atlas? And three: you seem quite serious . . . You sort of look like you're carrying the whole weight of the world on your shoulders," said Lucien. "You're not always this serious, are you?"

"Oh. No. I didn't—"

"Thank God. Otherwise I'd have to call you *Eeyore*."

I looked at him in horror. "Don't call me Eeyore," I said.

"So, what do you think of Atlas?"

"As a nickname?"

"No, as a hat. Yes, as a nickname."

"It's better than *Eeyore*."

"Agreed."

"What's wrong with *Chris* again?"

"Let's stick with *Atlas*," Lucien said cheerfully. "Trust me, Atlas. This is a good move. The world has enough people named Chris. An unusual name makes you stand out. It makes you seem more interesting, you know? Even if you're not." He winked.

Lucien produced a Sharpie and went to the name tags stuck on our door. Without giving me time to protest, he crossed out CHRISTOPHER and wrote ATLAS in bold, black letters. He stood back and admired his work.

"Much better. Right, what's next?" He snapped his fingers. "The beds. Let's take the top bunk down and move it into the other room. Bunk beds aren't going to work. I mean, Christ, we're not six, are we? Come on, Atlas, give me a hand."

The next thing I knew I was helping him carry my bed into the smaller of the two rooms. He convinced me the smaller room was the better option because it would be easier to keep tidy. That's how he was: overpowering in a way that made it impossible to say no to whatever he was suggesting. But he managed to make it feel as if it had been my idea all along.

Lucien was everything I was not. He was charming and sociable, handsome and confident, brilliant, rich, and enviable. He spoke five languages and carried himself with a sophistication and elegance that came from a childhood spent in elite boarding schools. During his first year at Harvard, he was a crew team walk-on and won the prize given to the top freshman student in economics.

He spoke with an accent that was hard to place: not quite British but clearly European and upper-class. It was the kind of accent I knew only from films, having never encountered anyone who spoke that way myself. He told me his father was a diplomat and they had lived all over the world. He had been born in Stockholm but lived there for only a year. They moved first to Paris, then to Pretoria, then to London, and finally to Madrid. They summered at a villa in Tuscany and spent winters in a chalet in Gstaad.

"What's Gstaad?" I asked.

"It's in Switzerland. You haven't heard of it?"

When Lucien was eight he was sent to a Swiss boarding school where his best friend was a Saudi prince. At twelve he was accepted to a boarding school in England called Eton. At Eton, he was captain of the rugby team, a King's Scholar and Captain of the School, which he said was like student body president but more important. When it came time for university, Lucien's father had wanted him to go to Oxford. He won a place to read history of art at Christ Church but turned Oxford down to go to Harvard because "it felt less stuffy."

Where Lucien had four names (Lucien Alexandre Orsini-Conti), I had just two: Christopher Novotny. I was not the only member of my family to have an American name. On arrival to the United States, my father, Frantisek, adopted the name *Frank*. My mother, Marenka, told people her name was Mary. They saw their new names as a commitment to their new life—a symbol of their determination to assimilate—and so when I was born they gave me the name *Christopher*, after Christopher Reeve, because he was the most American person they could think of.

After dinner on that first day, there was a short orientation meeting with the other students on our hall. Our proctor had us play an icebreaker. Rather than introducing ourselves to the group, she asked us to introduce our roommates instead. Lucien went first. He stood up and told the whole room that I was Atlas from Baltimore. And that was all it took. From then on everyone knew me as Atlas.

When the meeting ended, Lucien struck up a conversation with a pair of girls while I hovered by the door waiting for him. Sara, a middle-distance runner from San Diego, was tall with long, athletic legs and blond hair that hung to her shoulders. Her roommate, Emily, was shorter, with dark eyes and large white teeth. She had thick dark hair raked backwards into a bushy ponytail and was wearing an oversize T-shirt stamped PHILLIPS EXETER. Emily had been voted "Most likely to live on Mars" by her fellow classmates in their senior class poll. I'd learned this detail during the meeting and spent ten minutes trying to work out if it had been intended as a compliment or a slight. I hadn't yet decided.

Lucien asked the girls if they wanted to come to a party that night. It was an upperclassmen party, he told them, thrown by his friends on the crew team.

"Perfect," said Sara, beaming. "Give us an hour."

I followed Lucien back to our room where he magicked up a bottle of Grey Goose and a stack of red cups. He poured two cups of vodka and thrust one into my hand.

"Right, let's do this," he said.

I took the cup. It was a third full.

"Cheers," he said, raising his own cup.

I hesitated. "Do you have any chasers?"

"You won't need one. This is top stuff. It goes down like water. Trust me," he said. He lifted his cup again. "Cheers," he repeated.

"Cheers."

We touched our cups together and then I tipped mine back and poured the liquor down my throat. It was a large shot and I wasn't ready for it. I retched and coughed, spluttering droplets of vodka into the air. Lucien burst out laughing. For a second I thought I would be sick, but it passed.

"You all right, champ?"

I nodded and tried to compose myself, wiping my eyes and clearing my throat.

"Sorry," I said. "It went down the wrong way."

"Clearly," he said, still laughing. "Have you never done a shot before? You should have told me."

"No, no, I have. Tons of times."

"It's all right if you haven't."

"It just went down the wrong way, that's all."

"Right. Ready for round two?"

I looked up in alarm. "I need a minute."

"Relax. I was fucking with you."

"Thank God," I said, smiling weakly.

"Hang on. I'll get you something to wash it down with," said Lucien. He returned with several sodas from the vending machine.

"By the way," he asked when he returned, "have you come across a guy called Xander something-or-other?"

"Xander? I don't think so."

"Hmm, his name keeps popping up," said Lucien. "City kid. He sounds quite jokes. Apparently, he turned up to school with a suitcase full of drugs."

"A *suitcase*?"

"An exaggeration, I assume. But in any case we should try and meet him. He's probably a good time."

I hesitated. "That's not really my scene."

"Never would have guessed." Lucien laughed. "Don't worry. It's not mine, either. I haven't touched any of that shit since my druggie phase."

"When was that?"

"Oh, ages ago. Back at Eton," he explained. "I was like fifteen or sixteen. My friend and I, we'd sneak out at the weekends and catch a train to London. There were these epic underground parties in Brixton where they'd text you the address a few hours before. We'd get fucked up and stay out all night and get the six a.m. back from Paddington. Our housemaster was fucking ancient and practically senile, so he had no idea what we were doing. Anyway, it all got a bit out of hand. One night I took a bunch of fentanyl, thinking it was K. Ended up in hospital with a bunch of tubes shoved down my throat."

"Whoa . . ."

"Yeah. I was technically in a coma for a bit. *No bueno.* Had to leave school for a year. That's why I'm a year older than you." He paused. "It was a bit of a wake-up call."

"Jesus, man," I said. There was a short silence, and I mumbled something about how I was glad that everything worked out in the end.

"Me too, mate," said Lucien. He stood up and dragged his chair over to beneath the room's smoke detector and jumped up and began unscrewing it from the ceiling.

"What are you doing?"

He waved me off. "It's fine. Ten years in boarding school taught me a thing or two. I know my way around these things." The smoke detector was now detached from the ceiling and had begun beeping loudly. I looked around nervously. Lucien fiddled with it for a few seconds. The beeping stopped. Lucien looked at me brightly. "You see?"

"What if they notice?"

"It'll be fine. I'll just tell them you did it." He laughed. "Kidding. I'm kidding." His work complete, he went over and opened the window, kicked back in his chair, pulled out a lighter and a pack of cigarettes, and lit one up. "What were we talking about again . . . oh yeah. My OD. I guess I was just trying to get back at my dad. Original, right? But I'll tell you: he can be a real fucking dick when he drinks."

"Oh."

"He's been sober for a few years, but it was bad when I was younger. Like, really bad. He broke my arm when I was five. Christ, why am I telling you all this? I mean, we just bloody met." Lucien let out a breath. "I'm sorry, mate. I'll shut up now." He took a long pull from his cigarette and blew a cloud of smoke out the window. "You seem like a good person. Someone I can trust," he said. "On that note . . . I feel as though I've told you nearly everything about me, and yet I still know so little about you."

"Where should I start?" I asked.

"Hang on," he said. "Let's try something. I'll guess and you tell me if I'm right."

"You'll guess?"

"A little party trick I've been working on."

"Okay."

"You're an only child."

"Is it that obvious?"

"Am I right?" he asked.

I nodded.

"One for one," he said. "Okay, let's see . . . so *Novotny* . . . That's Czech, right? Or Slovakian?"

"Czech. My parents moved here just before I was born."

"So Czech immigrants. Came over in the late '80s, early '90s. Right around the fall of the Iron Curtain. I'm guessing your parents are educated. Intellectual. Put an emphasis on academic achievement."

I nodded.

"Educated professionals but not motivated by money. I'm guessing public sector. Maybe work for the government. Doctors? Engineers? Teachers?"

"Uh, kinda, yeah. I mean it's a long story. But you're not far off."

"And I'm getting the sense that you're particularly close with one of your parents."

"Yeah."

"Your mother?"

"How'd you know?"

Lucien winked at me. "Call it intuition," he said.

"It's been just me and my mom for a while," I said. "My dad died when I was really little."

"Oh, shit, man. I'm so sorry. I had no idea."

"It was a long time ago. I never really knew him."

"She didn't remarry, your mother?"

I shook my head. "Never wanted to. That's what she says, anyway."

"How about you? How's your love life? You have a girlfriend. Wait—never mind. No girlfriend, but you want one."

"I don't have a girlfriend."

"Really? A handsome guy like yourself?" he asked. I blushed at the compliment. I'd never been called handsome before. "We'll change that," he said. "The girls here are going to love you."

"I don't know about that," I said.

"Are you blushing? You are! You're blushing!" He pointed, delighted. "It's all right, mate. You know, you remind me a lot of how I used to be. Shy. Quiet. Lacking a bit of confidence. I think we're actually a lot more similar than you'd believe."

"Really?" I asked, surprised.

"Tell me how far off I am here. Ready? Okay. You're shy but you open up once people get to know you. You're creative. You're an independent thinker but sometimes you enjoy having structure in your life. At times you can be very self-conscious and critical of yourself, but you also have a strong belief in your own ability. You're not good at receiving compliments. You don't like being the center of attention. You're thoughtful, loyal to your close friends, and—although this will be hard for you to admit—you're more sensitive than you let on."

"Wow," I said, stunned.

"Pretty good, right?"

"That was amazing," I said. "How'd you do that? Did you, like, google me before or something?"

Lucien smirked. "Nothing so nefarious. It's just a trick. It's called cold reading. It's what fortune tellers do. I read a few books on it for fun."

"How does it work, though?"

"Well, some of what I said I just picked up on since meeting you. You're obviously shy, and shy people tend to be sensitive. You blushed when I called you handsome, so it was easy to guess that you're not good at taking compliments. But the rest of it was what they call Barnum statements. They seem specific to you but, really, they could apply to just about anyone. You say something like *You enjoy freedom, but at other times you like having structure in your life.* I mean, who would disagree with that? Or *Sometimes you can be creative.* Everyone can think of a time when they did something creative. It works the same way as a horoscope."

"Oh," I said.

"Good party trick, though, right?" Lucien drained the contents of his drink and waved the empty cup in the air. "Another one?"

"Sure," I said.

"There we go! He's loosening up a bit. I love it! I knew you had it in you." He waited for me to down my drink and then took my cup and refilled it alongside his. He handed it back to me with a broad smile on his face. I couldn't help but smile back. "This year is going to be epic," he said. "I can already tell that we're gonna get on super well. It's going to be a fun year, man. A really fucking fun year."

I felt a rush of euphoria. *Fun.* That magic word—the promise of carefree joy. There'd never been much room in my life to just have fun. High school had been one long, unending grind, a constant barrage of assignments and papers, standardized tests and AP exams. When I wasn't in school or the library, I was in my studio painting late into the night. My weekends were spent babysitting and teaching art. Fun was something that other people had. I envied them for it, of course. But I told myself it was a worthwhile sacrifice—the price to pay to end up where I wanted to be. But now I was here, and I was ready to have some fun.

We met the girls outside Greenough a little after ten and walked with them to the shuttle stop by Lamont Library. We passed a gaggle of chatty freshmen returning from an excursion with cups of frozen yogurt. I felt the vodka drift through my veins, anesthetizing me with a kind of calmness I wasn't used to, but I didn't mind.

We found four empty seats at the back of the shuttle. Right away Lucien made himself the center of attention. He told the girls a story about the time he met the queen of England when she visited Eton and how he had tripped and almost fallen on his face in front of her. The girls bubbled with laughter.

As Lucien put on a show, I felt myself receding into my seat, shrinking smaller and smaller until I was just a speck in the shuttle's rearview mirror. I wondered how different my life would be if I were more like him.

The shuttle came to a stop outside Pforzheimer House and everyone got off. Lucien led the way with Sara and Emily at his side while I trailed behind like a forgotten balloon tethered to his belt.

We went through a door marked F ENTRYWAY and through another door into a stairwell. Straightaway I could hear the muffled sounds of a party taking place high above us. Somewhere around the third floor we encountered a trio of freshman girls who were on their way out, bickering their way down the stairs. All three were dressed in makeshift togas fashioned from white bedsheets.

"This is so embarrassing."

"I said I'm sorry! He told me it was a toga party! What do want me to do?"

"You should have checked with someone else."

"Wait, where's Harriet?"

"We have to go. The shuttle's here."

"I think she wanted to stay."

"Are you sure?"

"Harriet isn't coming. Let's go."

"Love the togas," said Lucien as we passed them. "You girls look fantastic."

The music grew louder as we ascended the stairs. We reached the top floor and stepped out into a well-lit corridor strewn with debris. A trash can had been knocked over, spilling crushed beer cans and empty Solo cups everywhere. Someone had scrawled PFUCK PFORZHEIMER on the wall in orange highlighter.

Lucien knocked on the door. No one answered. He knocked again, louder. The door swung open, releasing a wave of heat and sound. A shirtless Goliath appeared. He had a receding hairline and broad shoulders with the kind of bulging neck muscles that only grow on football players. The Goliath crossed his arms and smirked.

"Who the fuck are you?" he demanded.

"I'm Lucien. Adler said we should come by."

"Are you on the list?"

"I believe so?"

"These chicks with you?"

"Yeah."

"Do you have any booze?"

"Were we supposed to bring some?"

Goliath shrugged. "We're running low."

"Can we come in?" Lucien asked.

"Maybe," he said. He disappeared and returned after a moment with a handful of beer-stained pages covered with names. "You said *Lucien*, right?"

Lucien nodded.

Goliath ran an enormous finger down the list and found Lucien's name at the bottom of the second sheet.

"Okay, you're good," he said. He stood aside and made way for us to enter. Lucien went in first, followed by Sara and then Emily. But when I attempted to enter, Goliath held up a hand and pressed it into my chest.

"You want to come in?"

"Yeah."

"Are you on the list?"

"I'm with them."

"That's not what I asked. Do you even know anyone here?"

"Uh, Adler. I know Adler."

"Oh really," he asked, smirking. "What's his last name?"

"Come on, man. You just let my friends in."

"How many push-ups can you do?"

I blinked. "What?"

"You heard me. Think you can do twenty?"

"I don't know. Maybe."

"How about this: if you do thirty push-ups in a row, I'll let you in."

"Right here?"

"Thirty push-ups," he said. "Let's go."

I looked past Goliath, hoping that Lucien would materialize and rescue me, but he didn't. I got down on the ground and stretched my legs back. The floor was sticky and smelled of stale beer. I lowered myself into a push-up. "One."

Goliath burst out laughing. "Holy hell. I was kidding," he said. "You can come in if you're that fucking desperate."

I stood up. "Thanks," I mumbled.

The room was hot and dark, the air dense with sound and the moisture of a hundred sweating, dripping bodies. Piano chords rang out in the darkness as Kid Cudi sang about memories, and a kick-drum bass line shook the floor with every beat.

Condensation formed on a window, crying out to be opened. A lonely strobe light flickered in the corner, lighting up faces in the crowd at random. Over by the beer pong table, duct-taped to the wall, a long, thin UV blacklight glowed a radioactive shade of violet.

I felt a squeeze on my shoulder. It was Lucien. He was with Sara and Emily. He tried to say something, but I couldn't hear him over the music.

"What?"

"I said we lost you! Where'd you go?"

"I was looking for the keg," I said.

"It's tapped."

"What?"

"The keg. It's out."

"Oh. It's really hot in here."

"Bloody hot, isn't it?" Lucien yelled back. "Someone should open that window."

"What?"

"The window! Someone should open it."

Sara placed a hand on Lucien's shoulder and brought her lips close to his ear. She whispered something to him. Lucien nodded. "We're gonna go dance!"

He took Sara by the hand and disappeared into the crowd, leaving me alone with Emily. I caught her eye and smiled. She looked away. I could tell she wasn't thrilled to be stuck with me. I tried to think of something to say.

"This party's pretty wild, huh?"

"What?"

I leaned in and put my mouth closer to her ear. "I said this party—it's pretty crazy. So many people."

"Yeah," she replied. She didn't look at me when she spoke.

"Do you want to dance?" I asked.

"What?"

"I said do you want to dance? It's okay. We don't have to."

"I'm going to go find a drink," she said. "But thank you. I think I just saw my friend."

"Should I come with you?"

"That's okay. You stay here. Enjoy the party." She dipped into the crowd and I lost sight of her.

I realized that everyone else was holding a drink. All of a sudden I felt very naked without one. I did a lap of the room and found what remained of the bar. They were out of mixers and almost all out of alcohol, too. I grasped a sticky bottle of vodka and dribbled what little was left into a cup.

I parked myself by the bar, leaning up against the wall with my arms folded, trying my best to look natural. But no one was looking at me. When people glanced in my direction, their eyes skipped right over me like I wasn't even there.

A figure in a white dress emerged from a dark mass of bodies and approached the bar. As she drew closer, I noticed that the dress was actually a toga. This must be the Harriet who the girls in the stairwell had been referring to. Even with everyone else at the party dressed in normal clothes, she hadn't been embarrassed into leaving with her friends. There was something kind of cool about that—something I respected.

Harriet floated over to the bar for a second, surveying the wreckage of empty bottles. It was difficult to see her face clearly in the darkness, but from what I could make out she had a slender, graceful figure. For a moment I considered going up to her and introducing myself. She was standing there alone. It would be easy to go over and strike up a conversation. That was what Lucien would do. But then I remembered how Emily's eyes had flitted around the room, searching for anyone else. What was the point? I watched her for a moment longer and then she pushed back into the crowd and vanished.

A burst of static ripped through the air as the audio cord was snatched out of the speakers.

"Party's over! Everyone out! That's your third noise complaint! Time to go home, people!"

The lights came on. The room was filled with startled, blinking faces.

"Atlas! You coming?" It was Lucien, his arm wrapped around Sara's waist.

"Where's Emily?" asked Sara. "She with you?"

"I think she went home."

"Let's head out," said Lucien.

We decided to walk back to the Yard, taking our time strolling through the warm night to the sounds of distant laughter. About halfway home we ran into a group of Sara's friends heading in the opposite direction and she left us momentarily to chat with them.

As we waited on the sidewalk for Sara to return, a mischievous look came over Lucien's face. "Want to see something?"

"Sure."

He reached into the pocket of his trousers and pulled out a small orange prescription bottle. "Look what I picked up," he said, shaking the pills like a box of Tic-Tacs. "Always check the medicine cabinets."

"What is that?"

"Xanax. Thirty bars." He held the bottle out like a trophy. "It was just sitting there."

"Wait, you took that from the party?" I blinked. "Why?"

Lucien shrugged. "Why not? You never know when these

things will come in handy. You'll be thanking me in a couple months when you're stressed out of your mind with finals."

I looked at Lucien, puzzled. I didn't know what to say.

"Besides," Lucien continued, "it's no big deal. He can just get a refill. Insurance pays for it anyway." The pills rattled together as he slipped the bottle back into his pocket, and just like that he moved on. "Come on," he said. "Let's get Sara."

We ended the night, the three of us, by jumping off Weeks Bridge, the old stone footbridge that intersects the Charles River between Leverett and the Business School. It was Lucien's idea.

Clouds covered the moon. Cast-iron streetlamps stood sentry in pairs at regular intervals along the bridge, giving off a soft orange light. We stripped to our underwear and climbed onto the stone parapet. I looked down at the black river beneath us, some thirty feet below with only the glimmer of the streetlamps' reflection rippling on the surface. Lucien took Sara's hand and they jumped together. She screamed. It felt like a long time before I finally heard the two splashes. Lucien surfaced and yelled at me to jump.

I've always had a great fear of heights, and had I been up on the bridge sober in the daytime, I never would have been able to bring myself to jump. But because I was drunk, and because I didn't want to disappoint Lucien, I took a deep breath and stepped off the bridge into the darkness.

CHAPTER 2

My parents were born in a country that no longer exists. They met as university students in Prague, finding each other amid the euphoria and chaos of the Velvet Revolution. They fell in love and within a few months they were engaged. By the time their country split in two, they had already left to pursue a new life in the United States, moving into the basement of my aunt's house in Baltimore—the same basement where I was born. When my parents arrived in America they spoke only a few words of English. My dad held an advanced degree in mechanical engineering from the Czech Technical University in Prague, but he soon discovered that academic credentials from Eastern Europe held little weight in his new country. He found a job at a movie theater, sweeping up popcorn and discarded cups and candy after the films were over. My mom first worked as a maid at a Super 8 Motel, but when her English improved, she got a job as a waitress at a Czech-owned coffeeshop in Ellicott City called The Bohemian Table. A few months after I was born, my parents moved to a little one-bedroom apartment down the street from my aunt.

My dad died from gastric cancer when I was two, so I don't really remember him. I guess I do have one memory of him, or at least a fragment of one. But it's nothing more than a snapshot of a bearded face looking down at me in a dark room. I've never known if it is a genuine memory or something I imagined so long ago that I've forgotten it was never real. The more I've thought about it, the more I've come to believe it is the latter: an image put together by my subconscious; a forgery drawn from a composite of old photographs and imagination.

I didn't realize we were poor because it was all I knew. Everyone around us was the same. I wore secondhand clothes and never had more than two pairs of shoes. It was only when my paintings started selling and I was brought along to events at houses resembling palaces that I found out not everyone lived the way we did.

My mom couldn't afford day care or after-school programs, so when I wasn't in school I was usually at the café. That was where I first started drawing, as a toddler with crayons on the backs of paper menus. It was my mom's way of keeping me entertained in the absence of friends or toys. But soon it was all I wanted to do. It was as if I had discovered a kind of paradise.

That's what I remember when I think of my childhood: all the time I spent drawing and painting. I had this one videotape called *The Mystery of Picasso*. It was a French documentary from the fifties showing Picasso live drawing in a studio. The filmmaker used stop-motion photography and a special type of lighting and translucent paper so that you could see the pen and brushstrokes appear on-screen as if by magic. I couldn't understand the words but I was mesmerized by the images on the screen. It helped that he drew animals and funny-looking faces and things that looked like monsters, but I think the main reason I liked it was the way those thick black lines seemed to draw themselves and the way the picture gradually revealed itself to the viewer. What began as a splash of color and a tangle of looping black lines would suddenly transform into a picture of a dove or a rooster. I must have watched that movie a thousand times. I would sit cross-legged in front of our television with my crayons and a pad of paper and copy what I saw on the screen—over and over and over again.

They say that practice is the root of genius, right? At least, that seems to be the theory: genius is the result of thousands of hours of repetition and practice. I don't agree with that. I've always believed that practice can make someone very, very good, but practice alone will never produce genius. True genius requires something more, something given. Encoded into DNA is an extraordinary talent that, if nurtured, presents an individual with the possibility of achieving the inconceivable. True genius occurs when a person with an extraordinary gift discovers what it is he or she was born to do.

By the time I was eight years old people were calling me a prodigy. At ten I won a citywide contest judged by a panel of faculty members from the Maryland Institute College of Art. My winning caused quite a stir. The contest was for high school students, but my mom had sent in an entry anyway because of the prize: $2,000 toward in-state college tuition. The committee voted to disqualify me once they learned of my age, but one of the judges, a Jamaican-born painter named Marcus Powell, got in touch with my mom to express his disappointment at the decision. He told her he wanted to meet me.

Marcus's studio was in the old Mount Royal train station, a granite-and-limestone building with terra-cotta roof tiles and a clock tower one hundred fifty feet tall. I remember thinking it looked like a castle. The college had bought the disused station from the B&O Railroad in the 1960s and converted the space into artists' studios. Marcus met us at reception and we walked to a restaurant around the corner.

After we ordered, Marcus gave me a tote bag stamped with the MICA logo. It was heavy. I took a peek inside. There were paintbrushes, a tin of coloring pencils, pastels, watercolors, sketch pads, and an MICA baseball hat. I looked up at Marcus, confused.

"For *me*?" I asked.

"If you win the contest, you deserve a prize," he said. "That's only fair."

"Oh, how kind you are," my mother said. "What do you say, Christopher?"

"Thank you!"

"Let's have a look," said Marcus. He reached across the table and into the bag and pulled out a sketchbook and the tin of coloring pencils. He stripped off the plastic wrapping and popped open the tin. "Why don't you crack on with these while I chat with your mum?"

I caught bits and pieces of their conversation as I played and experimented with my new tools. Marcus had a lot of questions: about where we lived, what school I was going to, and how I'd learned to draw. I heard him ask about my father. He said he'd lost his dad at a young age, too. He was raised by his mother and grandmother until she passed. They didn't have a lot, but his mother found a job at a private arts college in Kingston that had enabled him to attend for free. He looked at my mom and said she reminded him of his own mother.

And then I realized the questions had stopped, and neither of them were saying anything. I looked up and saw they were both watching me draw.

"Looks like someone's having a rollicking time," said Marcus. He pointed to a winged figure in my drawing. "Is that Icarus?"

"Who?"

"Icarus. You know Icarus, don't you?" he asked. I shook my head. "He flew too close to the sun and the wings melted off his back."

I screwed up my face into a frown. "But wings don't melt," I said. "Anyway, that's just an angel."

Marcus laughed. "Ah, an angel. Of course," he said. "Christopher, how would you like to take some art lessons with me? Not boring lessons. Fun ones. I was speaking with your mum and we agreed you could come here on the weekends. Would you like that?"

That was how it began. Every Sunday for the next five years my mom woke me at seven thirty and put me on the Route 12 bus. It was usually late and in the winter the mornings were cold and dark. Marcus would be at the Howard Street stop, waiting for me when I arrived. We'd walk the five blocks to the MICA campus and I'd spend the rest of the day in his studio. He taught me technical things: how to hatch and blend, about perspective and sources of light. And he taught me how to paint with watercolors and then with oils. He did all of this for free. My mom tried to pay him what we could manage, but he refused to take a cent.

I became somewhat well-known around MICA. I was a favorite of Marcus's MFA students, who were both impressed and amused by my frequent visits and my rapid progress. A few of them started jokingly referring to me as Doogie Howser, or Pablito—"little Pablo." Word got around that Marcus Powell had a young prodigy, and it wasn't long before I started getting attention from the media.

When I was twelve, the local CBS affiliate did a story on me for the evening news. An art dealer in D.C. saw the segment and called my mom to ask if I had representation. He told her all these nice, wonderful things about how talented I was and claimed he could position me as "the next Picasso." He said he had a lot of wealthy clients who would pay a fortune for my artwork. We said yes even though Marcus warned us that the guy didn't have a great reputation.

The next year was a blur of interviews and TV appearances. I didn't paint much that year, but I was featured in *The Washington Post* and then in a PBS special on child prodigies. The dealer promised *Oprah* would be next. That never happened, but he did bring me to fancy gatherings at his gallery in Georgetown, where he trotted me out in front of rich people and celebrities I was too young to know. I would later learn that Barbra Streisand bought a painting. So did Pierce Brosnan.

Had I been older, or had my mom been savvier, we might have suspected sooner that the dealer was ripping us off. It turned out that he was selling my paintings for far more than he told us while also charging us for all sorts of bogus expenses, inflated fees, and phantom taxes. It was often months before we saw any money at all, and when the checks finally arrived, the sums seemed impossibly small. He assured us this was all normal. By the time we realized he was lying to us, it was too late. The hype around my talent was dissipating. Each day that passed brought me closer to adolescence. Nobody wanted a painting by a *former* child prodigy.

When it came time for high school my choices were either the Baltimore School for the Arts or Centennial High School in Ellicott City. Centennial was my local school and also happened to be ranked the second-best high school in Maryland. They offered

AP classes and had a "gifted and talented" track. Marcus pushed me to attend Centennial over BSA. Having gone to an art school himself, he thought I would be better served by getting a broader, more general education. I could still work with him one-on-one after school. It was important, he said, not to be too narrow in my focus. He told me that to be a great artist one needed to understand history and philosophy and literature. Technique and skill alone would take me only so far. Great art, he said, required intellectual depth and an understanding of the past. That was what gave it meaning.

I didn't really fit in at Centennial. I was something of an outsider there—not because I wanted to be; that was just how it was. I had a few friends, but I didn't have a best friend or a girlfriend or really anyone I was that close to. I wanted those things desperately. I think everyone does.

Part of it was that the other kids didn't really know what to make of me. A lot of them had grown up together and gone to the same schools or played in the same sports leagues. And here I was, a transplant from the inner city with a different background and an unusual gift. I didn't fit into one of those clearly defined categories of high school identity. I wasn't a theater geek or a nerd, but I also wasn't a jock or a popular kid. I was just different. And different was lonely.

Painting gave me an escape. When I painted, it was like everything else was on mute. There was only the canvas in front of me. It was the way you feel when you're doing a puzzle and the only thing that matters to you in that moment is finding that one piece that fits in the top left-hand corner. All of a sudden you have a very clear purpose and life becomes incredibly simple. I didn't feel lonely when I was painting. That was how I got through high school.

I used to daydream a lot, too. I imagined a future filled with art shows and gallery openings, surrounded by brilliant people with interesting, sophisticated lives. I imagined living somewhere fancy like New York or Los Angeles, perhaps even Europe. I imagined coming back for my Centennial reunion and impressing all the popular kids, who would have grown up to have boring lives with boring jobs in boring places. I imagined escaping. I imagined being happy.

I didn't have a concrete plan for how I was going to make all of this happen. It was looser than that—more of a vague understanding that I was on a certain path and at the end of that path was a promised land. I trusted Marcus with the details. He knew what I had to do to get there. He was the one steering the ship. And that was fine, because I knew something good was waiting for me on the other side.

But all of that changed in the summer before my junior year when Marcus took me out for lunch and told me he was moving to Boston to take a job at Harvard. "You're doing what?" I asked, certain I must have misheard.

I cried when I got home. I still saw the world from the narrow-minded, self-centered perspective of a teenage boy. I couldn't understand how he could just leave and forget about me. What about our plans? What about *my* plan? I'd turned down a place at BSA on Marcus's advice. How was I going to improve without a teacher? What if I wasn't talented enough to make it? What would I do if art didn't work out? I'd never considered doing anything else.

Marcus assured me that his move was good for both of us.

He'd been offered a one-year contract as an instructor with the understanding that he would be promoted to a tenure-track assistant professorship. He said that as a professor on the faculty he'd be able to help me get into Harvard. He could lean on the admissions office and reach out to friends in the art world for recommendation letters. And in the meantime we could continue to work together remotely.

He told me that Harvard didn't want a class entirely made up of valedictorians. They also wanted students who'd achieved excellence in fields like athletics, music, and the arts. *That*, he said, was my route in. All we had to do was prove to the admissions office that I was one of the best artists in the country for my age.

Before Marcus left for Boston, he and I worked out a two-year curriculum centered on classical training in technique. The core idea was to learn through imitation. I was to work on copying and re-creating drawings and paintings by great masters. Over time I would internalize their techniques and methods, absorbing their mastery via osmosis. Marcus would provide guidance and direction, checking in every few weeks to see how I was getting on. The rest was up to me.

We began with the old masters of the Baroque period and worked our way up to the impressionists. Marcus loaned me art books and collected works filled with drawings and paintings by artists like Caravaggio, Rubens, and Velázquez. I began by tracing drawings from those books hundreds of times until I could feel the artist's hand atop mine guiding my pencil across the paper. I spent countless afternoons with van Goyen and van Dyck at the Baltimore Museum of Art, sitting with an open sketchbook in front of masterpieces like *Rinaldo and Armida*. As I became immersed in their work I began to feel as if I was getting to know the artists themselves—their personalities, their quirks. I could even imagine the sound of their voices.

I practiced painting impasto and limiting my palette to a handful of core colors, relying on the contrast effect to create the perception of different shades. I worked on paintings by Degas and Monet. And I branched out into splinter movements, trying my hand at pointillism, re-creating a full-size version of Seurat's *The Circus*. But my favorite were *les fauves*: Derain, Dufy, Matisse. I loved their bold use of color, the way they filled their paintings with bright blues and yellows and lavenders. Their paintings were full of energy and movement, and it was impossible not to feel a sense of freedom while copying them. Those were the most fun.

Marcus showed me little tricks and techniques to achieve certain effects. By the time I arrived at Harvard, I was good enough to paint pieces Marcus claimed could pass as originals to the untrained eye.

During those many hours I spent perfecting the art of imitation, I never once imagined using those skills for anything illegitimate or illegal. Of course, it never was my idea. As with most things we did, the idea belonged to Lucien.

CHAPTER 3

It was a Tuesday evening during our second week, and a thousand freshmen had descended on Annenberg Hall for dinner. I stood by the exit of the serving line, holding a tray, and searched for a friend—any friend—amid all the strangers that filled the hall. I found none. I recognized faces here and there, but I couldn't put names to them, and so I resigned myself to sitting alone at an empty table in the back.

I was terrified of Annenberg. Nowhere else on campus did I feel so desperately out of place. With its stained glass windows and Gothic spires, the structure resembled a cathedral. The central hall was immense with a ceiling eighty feet high held up by thick wooden beams engineered into a pattern of trusses and arches. A dozen chandeliers provided light. Portraits of college luminaries from centuries past hung on the wood-paneled walls. Without exception the portraits were of men—white men with white hair and stern, disapproving gazes and names like Nathaniel and Jedediah. The older the portrait, the sterner and more disapproving the gaze. As I sat alone near the back of the hall I could not escape the feeling that those gazes were being directed at me.

I had only been sitting a few minutes when Lucien entered with two friends in tow. The first was Will Gardner, a preppy New England guy everyone referred to simply as "Gardner." I'd met him a few times, but he never remembered my name. Every time I saw him, he was wearing the same uniform of khakis, a plaid button-down, and white New Balance sneakers. He was a multigeneration legacy from Connecticut and had gone to Groton. Lucien told me he had an older brother in the Fly Club and several cousins in the Owl. I envied the confidence he radiated as he strode around campus. He belonged at Harvard, and he knew it, too. He'd been preparing for this his entire life.

Lucien's other companion was a more mysterious figure. His name was Zola and he was rumored to be either the son or nephew of the longtime president of Equatorial Guinea. He dressed in expensive tailored clothes and spoke with a posh British accent because he'd been sent to boarding school in England at the age of seven. His Facebook page showed him posing for photos with Tony Blair and Jacques Chirac and attending various conferences around the world like the 2009 UN Youth Congress and the Rockefeller Foundation Next Gen Global Leadership Forum. One classmate I'd met during orientation said that he'd seen Zola arrive on campus in a chauffeured Rolls-Royce Phantom. A different acquaintance swore it was a Bugatti Veyron. There was another rumor that Zola's father had hired Rihanna to perform at his eighteenth birthday party in Paris. I wasn't sure quite what to believe.

Similar rumors circulated about Lucien, too. It was a well-accepted fact around campus that he was some form of European nobility. No one was certain of his exact title or even his specific country of origin, but it was broadly agreed that his father was either a lord or a count—or at least related to one. One rumor claimed Lucien had a pope among his ancestors, another that he was a direct descendant of Marshal Ney. Lucien was aware of this speculation and found it highly entertaining. He would play into it and encourage the rumors by feeding new and contradictory information to different people. Sometimes there was one pope in the family, other times it was a mere cardinal. There was either a château outside Bordeaux or a palazzo in Tuscany. Sometimes both. He saw it as a funny game and enjoyed seeing how far he could push the boundaries—how outrageous he could be without being called out. Occasionally he would tell an elaborate sob story about an ancestor who had lost his head following a revolution or about hereditary estates that had been lost as a result of Italian unification. It bothered me slightly to see the enjoyment he seemed to take in misleading people. But only slightly. I'd heard the true facts from him directly and, in fairness, they weren't all that different from the rumors. I brushed it off as a bit of harmless fun.

I stood and waved to Lucien and his friends. Lucien didn't seem to see me, but I caught Gardner's eye. I pointed at my table, motioning for them to come over. Gardner stared at me as if trying to place me. He gave me an awkward nod and then turned and followed Lucien and Zola toward another table. I sat back down, dejected.

As I ate my meal I glanced frequently over at their table, watching as the three bantered and laughed. Gardner was slouched with his arm dangling over the chair next to him. The other two were engaged in a back-and-forth. Zola punctuated his point by pounding the table with a closed fist. And when Lucien spoke, his hands entered a state of perpetual motion, dancing high and low, forward and back, fingers flashing open and closed. The way he moved his hands was somewhere between those of a conductor and those of an illusionist. The exchange came to an abrupt finish when something Lucien said caused Zola to tilt back in his chair and roar with laughter. The next time I glanced over, Zola was still laughing, wiping tears from his eyes.

I wondered if I should join them. Had too much time passed? Was there even a free seat available? Why hadn't I just gone over right when I saw them? Had Lucien seen me and ignored me? Or had he just not spotted me in the crowd?

Just then the guy sitting to Lucien's right got up and walked away. I took my chance and went over.

"Lucien! What's good, man?"

"Oh, hey, dude. Yeah, take a seat. You know these two fools, right?" Lucien asked, motioning to Zola and Gardner.

I nodded. "What's going on?"

"What up, boss? What's your name again?" asked Gardner.

"Atlas."

"Atlas, right."

"What's that blue shit on your hands?" asked Lucien. "It's on your shirt, too."

"Oh," I said, glancing down at my hands. "It's just paint. I came straight from the studio."

"Paint?" said Gardner.

"I'm taking painting."

"Painting! Did you know we could take painting?" Gardner asked Zola. "How the fuck do I get in on that? I need an easy class."

"I think you had to apply already."

"Damn," said Gardner.

"Atlas," said Lucien. "You're in Justice, right? Question for you. We were discussing this just before you came over. What were your thoughts on the cannibalism scenario?"

"Sorry, what? Did you say cannibalism?"

"Yeah, from the Justice reading."

"Oh, I'm not taking Justice."

"You're not?" Lucien frowned. "I could have sworn you were."

I shook my head. "Doesn't work with the rest of my schedule."

"Let's ask him anyway," said Lucien. "This is good, actually. We have in Atlas an unbiased third party—a blank canvas."

"Here's the scenario," said Zola. "You, Lucien, and Gardner are stranded in the middle of the Pacific Ocean. You're in a tiny lifeboat and have been lost at sea for twenty-three days. You have a dwindling supply of fresh water and no food at all. You haven't eaten anything for three weeks. You're all on the verge of starving to death."

"That doesn't sound very promising."

"Day twenty-four we wake up and realize that Gardner has died overnight," said Lucien, picking up the narrative.

"Hey," said Gardner. "Why am I the one that dies?"

Lucien ignored him and continued. "Gardner's dead. We're almost dead. We need to eat something ASAP or we're goners, too. *Capito?*"

"Got it."

"Is it fucked up for us to eat Gardner to save our own lives? Or, given the extreme extenuating circumstances, in this scenario would you consider cannibalism a morally acceptable act?"

"If we don't, then we'll for sure die?"

"Correct. We have maybe twenty-four hours left. We're barely hanging on."

"Hmm," I said, thinking. "Well, it would definitely still be fucked up to eat him, but . . ."

"But . . . ?"

An idea occurred to me. "Could we use him as fishing bait?"

"That was my answer!" exclaimed Zola. "That's why this is a stupid hypothetical. Cannibalism isn't the only option."

"No equipment," said Lucien.

"You could definitely make some kind of fishing line from your clothes," said Zola.

"No fucking way, bro," said Gardner. "You're gonna try to deep-sea fish with fucking shoelaces? Gimme a break, bro. Do you know how powerful those fish are? You'd need fifty-pound test, minimum. Your homemade shit wouldn't last ten seconds."

"Besides," said Lucien, "no hooks."

"Didn't primitive societies make hooks out of animal bones?"

"There's no fishing. We're too weak to fish. We only have two options. Option one: eat Gardner. Option two: we die. What do you do?" asked Lucien, directing the question to me.

I hesitated for a second. "I guess I'd eat him," I replied.

"You motherfucker," said Gardner. "I thought I could trust you."

"Good answer," said Lucien. "Okay, here's scenario two. This is where it gets tricky. Same situation: we're lost at sea, three weeks, no food, etc., etc. However, in this scenario Gardner gets sick but doesn't die. It's day twenty-four. We're all starving to death. Gardner is sleeping in the corner of the boat. He's weak, delirious. I come to you, and I say, *Hey let's kill Gardner and eat him.* What do you say?"

"No. Obviously."

"Why?"

"It's one thing if he's already dead," I said. "But if we have to kill him first . . . that's a conscious decision to end a life to better your own. And that's wrong."

"But if you do nothing, then everyone dies," said Zola. "No action equals three people dead."

"Yeah."

"But if you say yes, and you guys kill and eat Gardner—"

"Can we talk about something other than killing and eating me? Please? I'm trying to enjoy my dinner."

"—then only one person dies. The other two live," said Zola.

"You know Bentham, right? You know what he'd say about this."

"Who?" I asked.

"Jeremy Bentham."

"Oh yeah. I think so. The name definitely sounds familiar. He's in Greenough, right?"

My response was met with a half second of silence, and then the three boys all burst out laughing. I felt my face flush and my ears go warm as I realized I must have said something stupid.

"No," said Zola. "Jeremy Bentham is not in Greenough. He's pretty, pretty dead last time I checked."

"Famous philosopher," said Lucien.

"Oh. Oh right. Yeah, I thought you were talking about someone else."

"Guys, give him a break," said Lucien. "He's not in the class. Anyway, Bentham would argue you should take the action which results in the greatest overall utility. Utility is happiness minus suffering."

"In this case, the greatest number of lives saved," Zola added.

"It's actually a bit more complicated than that, but, sure, generally speaking, that's the utilitarian position," said Lucien. "Bentham would say you also have to look at the effects of the action on the happiness of externals such as family members, loved ones, etc. But for the purposes of this conversation, we can say that if you look at the situation pragmatically—rationally—your two choices are: one, do nothing and let three people die; or two, take action and save the lives of two people who would otherwise starve to death."

"This is so morbid," groaned Gardner.

"What do you do?" asked Lucien.

I was silent for a moment as I weighed up the moral calculus.

"You have to kill him," said Zola. "It's basic math. Either one person dies or three die. Screw your conscience."

"I don't think I could do it," I said.

"Are you sure?" asked Lucien.

"I mean, how do we know that we won't get rescued? For all we know, there could be a rescue ship just over the horizon. Maybe nobody has to die."

"Exactly. This is one of my issues with utilitarianism," said Lucien. "This whole idea of a moral doctrine reliant on calculations that require an inherently impossible knowledge of the future—it just doesn't make sense to me. Not only do we not know if we will be rescued; we also don't know the net utility of the rest of our lives were we to survive. It could be that we get rescued, go home, and dedicate our lives to feeding the homeless, solving child poverty, and curing terrible diseases. Or perhaps we survive but it turns out we're horribly traumatized from the experience and end up spending our remaining years inflicting misery on those around us. Maybe Gardner goes home, marries a nice girl, has a couple kids. But one of those kids grows up to be a school shooter. I mean, maybe my grandson turns out to be the next Stalin. It's impossible to know, right? You can't do a pure utilitarian calculus without a complete knowledge of everything that will ever happen."

"So, what would you do?" I asked, after a pause. "If you were in the boat."

"Oh, that's easy. I would kill Gardner. In a heartbeat," Lucien said.

"Why are we killing me and not Atlas?" asked Gardner.

"Or Atlas," admitted Lucien. "Either way, one of you is getting eaten."

"Really?"

"I don't go in for utilitarianism," said Lucien. "I'm more of a Thomas Hobbes, law-of-the-jungle kind of guy."

"Man's natural state is war," said Zola.

"Exactly," Lucien concurred. "It's you or me, baby. And it's sure as shit ain't going to be me."

Everyone was silent for a few moments. "But what about like . . . morality?" I asked.

"Well, morality is an inherently relative construct, right? It's not absolute. It doesn't exist in a vacuum. Our perception of what is moral or immoral is shaped by the context. Things like necessity. Circumstance. Intention. Desperation. Theft is an immoral act in the abstract, but when a homeless woman steals a loaf of bread to feed her child, is that immoral? I would argue it's worse to do nothing and let a child starve."

"I guess that's true."

"Look, the boat scenario is intentionally extreme. It's a thought experiment, right? What are your limits? Where is the boundary at which our societal norms begin to break down? Is morality—this abstract concept invented by humans to keep other humans from doing naughty things—important enough to you that you'd place it over your own survival? For me the answer is no. Maybe I'm just the only one willing to be honest about it, but I think survival trumps morality every day of the week. You gotta do what you gotta do to survive, no? Especially in an unjust society. That's what Camus argues, anyway."

"Camus?" asked Zola. "When did Camus ever get into this?"

"*The Myth of Sisyphus*," replied Lucien.

"*The Myth of Sisyphus*?" repeated Zola. "What on earth are you on about? That has to do with the absurdity of the human condition and man's duty to revolt."

"Well, obliquely, sure—"

"*Obliquely?*"

Lucien began to elaborate but I interrupted him.

"How do you guys know all this stuff?" I asked. "Is this all from that class or did you learn this stuff before?"

"What do you mean?"

"Like, all these authors and philosophers and stuff. Did they teach you this in school?"

"I dunno," said Lucien, shrugging. "I grew up with a lot of books, I guess. My parents didn't let me watch a lot of TV so I read a lot. And then my housemaster at Eton liked chatting about this kind of shit. He'd have us over for dinner and make us argue different positions."

"I took a philosophy course junior year," said Gardner. "Where'd you go again? Were you at Choate? Or am I making that up?"

"I just went to my local high school. I doubt you would know it."

"Where are you from?"

"Oh, um . . . near D.C."

"I thought you were from Baltimore," said Lucien.

"We moved around. It's all close."

"D.C. area, huh?" said Gardner. "You weren't at Sidwell, were you? Or Georgetown Prep? One of my good buddies went to Prep. Henry Brillembourg? The Brillmeister? You ever come across him? Lax guy. Goes to Trinity."

I shook my head. "I went to a place called Centennial."

"Huh," said Gardner. "Don't know it."

"It's a good school."

"Were you guys ISL? It's ISL, right? Or MAC? I'm pretty sure that's what Sidwell competes in."

"What's that?"

"Which conference were you guys in? For sports."

"I wasn't a big athlete. I think we just played against the other public schools in the area."

"Ohhh, it's a public school," said Gardner. "Okay, yeah. I wouldn't know it."

"He means a state school, right?" asked Zola. "Like a comprehensive?"

"Yeah," said Lucien.

"Do you really have to go through metal detectors in America?" asked Zola. "Or is that just in the movies?"

"We didn't have metal detectors," I said.

"So that's not real?"

"Some schools have them."

"*Really?*" asked Zola, wide-eyed. "Can you imagine? That's mad."

Lucien clapped his hands together. "Okay, change of subject. The plan for tonight: What are we doing?"

"The same thing we do every night, Pinky," said Zola.

"Which is?"

"Try to take over the world."

"Helpful, Zola. Extremely helpful," said Lucien.

Over the next twenty minutes, Lucien and his friends developed their plan of attack for the evening with a martial-like efficiency and a rigor that would have impressed even the most industrious field commander. Options were assessed, contingencies developed. Gardner took on the role of quartermaster, tasked with sourcing the evening's supplies. Zola acted as the intel officer, calling and texting a disparate network of sources, pumping them for information. Lucien oversaw general strategy and had the final word on any decisions that were made. My role in the chain of command was clear: I was the grunt. I was there to follow, not to ask questions or give an opinion. Which was fine because I didn't have much of an opinion to give. I couldn't quite believe they planned to drink on a Tuesday night. Lucien assured me this was a very normal thing to do.

The plan began to take shape. After dinner, Gardner (who had a fake ID) and I would go to C'est Bon liquor store in the Square to pick up beer. We would meet the other two in Zola's room in Thayer, where we would drink for an hour before stopping by another friend's room in Weld. At nine thirty we would meet up with a group of girls in Straus and go to the Dunster House happy hour before trying to get into Uno for karaoke night. If Uno failed, the fallback plan was to try a frat party at MIT that Zola swore would be fun. (No one believed him.)

Just as Zola was having some success in convincing Lucien that an MIT frat party was not in fact the lamest thing in the world, the strategy session was interrupted by Xander Rozhkov.

"Yooo, Lucien!"

Xander was olive-skinned and dressed the way I imagined nightclub owners dressed: in black jeans with a black V-neck a size too small, sunglasses, and a gold chain. As he drew closer his physical presence was preempted by the strong stench of weed.

"What's good, legend?" Xander slapped Lucien's hand. "Zola, how we doing? OH MY GOD! Is that William Mayflower Gardner the *Twelfth*?! *THE KING OF THE WASPS!* Your Royal Highness, what an honor!" Xander cackled wildly at his own joke. Then he noticed me. "Who the fuck are you?"

"Xander, this is Atlas. My roommate."

"Oooh, this is *the roommate*," he said, laughing. His laugh was a wild, high-pitched cackle. "The infamous roommate. The *virgin*."

"What?" I felt my face flush.

"It's cool, bro." Another cackle. And then in a dramatic whisper loud enough for everyone to hear, Xander added, "Don't worry. *Your secret's safe with me.*"

"Don't be a dick, Xander."

"Sure, bro. I'm joking. Whatever. I bet you get tons of chicks." Xander rolled his eyes. His attention shifted to Lucien. "Bro, I'm so high right now. Look at my eyes, dude. Why do you think I'm wearing these fucking shades? Pietro got this dank-ass weed sent in from California. Bro, you have to come try it. You're gonna die. It's fucking epic."

"Maybe this weekend," Lucien said.

"Nah, I'll be in the city this weekend. That reminds me, bro, come kick it with me in the city sometime. You should come this weekend! We'll go clubbing. Have you been to Boom Boom Room? Dude, come this weekend. I know the hottest chicks. They're all models. Not like the fucking gargoyles and sea monsters they have here! Jk, jk—I know you're into that, Gardner. I've seen the mountain trolls you bring home. *William Gardner . . . the troll hunter!*"

"Are you getting a table?"

"Bro, are you kidding? Of course we're getting a table. What do you think we are, a bunch of fucking peasants? Gardner, Zola, you guys should come, too. We'll stay at my house. But not you, virgin boy!" This last part he practically yelled. He slapped my back and shrieked with laughter. "I'm just fucking with you, bro. Not really. But kind of."

So this was what they really thought of me? How stupid I had been to think otherwise, and it was only a preview of what was to come. If I went with them that evening, I would be the butt of their jokes, a source of fun. I noticed the tables around us had gone very quiet. In my peripheral vision I saw turned heads and bodies swiveling in their chairs. I wanted to disappear.

"All right, bro, I gotta bounce," said Xander. "Later, noobs. Yo, Pietro! Wait up!"

"Lucien, do you like that guy?" Zola asked after he was gone.

"Xander? Yeah, he's jokes."

"He's a fucking hurricane," Gardner said. "I've never heard anyone talk so fast in my life."

"What do you think he eats for breakfast?" asked Zola. "Just a big bowl of cocaine, right?"

"Frosted Flakes."

"Cap'n Coke."

"*Honey Nut Coke-ios*," said Gardner.

Everyone went silent. Zola turned to Gardner. "*Honey Nut Coke-ios*? Really? That's the best you could do?"

"Screw you," said Gardner. "Seriously, though, how the hell did that guy get into Harvard?"

"You'll never believe this, but apparently he's a savant," Lucien said.

"*A savant?* At what?"

"Math."

"No fucking way," Zola said.

"Dead serious. I heard he's in Math 55."

"Bullshit. That kid has to be a Z-lister."

"He's all right once you get to know him," said Lucien. "We should definitely go out with him in New York sometime."

"That guy's an asshole," I said, getting up to leave.

"You still coming to pick up booze?" Gardner asked.

I shook my head. "I can't, guys. I've got some things to take care of at the studio."

We cleared our trays and stepped outside into the twilit evening. Lucien and his comrades bounded off toward Harvard Square, while I slunk away to the Carpenter Center feeling entirely worthless.

I found it deserted. I swiped my key card to enter my studio and, without turning on the lights, sank down to the floor with my back against the wall. I closed my eyes and inhaled the sickly, intoxicating scent of chemicals and paint. It was the smell of solitude.

I began to reach into my pocket for my phone, tempted by a sudden urge to call home just to hear my mother's voice. But in the next moment I felt sad and pathetic for wanting to do so. I wasn't a kid anymore. I was eighteen. An adult. What would the other guys think if they knew I had run off to call my mom?

The door opened and the lights flickered on. It was Marcus.

"All right, big man? Everything cool down there?"

I nodded.

"Budge up," he said. I shifted over to make room and he sat down on the floor next to me. "So, tell me, what's going on, then? Feeling a touch of homesickness?"

"It's nothing," I said. "Just tired."

"On a day like this? A beautiful day, on a beautiful campus? You ought to be out there exploring and such. Having some fun, meeting some girls. Not sitting here all lonesome."

"I think this was a mistake," I said.

"What?"

"Coming here. These kids are all so next level. They all went to these fancy private schools and they're always talking about politics or some writer I've never heard of, or how their dad runs this company or that company. What am I supposed to say to that? Half the time I don't even know what they're talking about. I don't belong here, Marcus. I know it. They know it."

"Don't worry about all that nonsense. That's all it is—nonsense. Nonsense and posturing. Trust me. I see it every year. Freshmen showing up, thinking they got to be impressing everyone all the time. Showing off how smart they are, how they're the best and the brightest. Chris, I'll let you in on a secret. You know why they act like that?"

I shook my head.

"Because they're scared. Just like you. Scared they don't belong. They're all thinking the same things as you."

"No they're not."

"I've been teaching a long time," he said. "And listen, Chris, you're miles ahead of where I was when I was your age. I told you when I got to the Academy in New York, all the instructors were, like, *Oh, he's just an illustrator. He can only render but he can't paint.* They meant it like a put-down. And since I was coming from Jamaica, they were, like, *This guy is useless. What kind of schools they have there?* I got told, *Go back to year one because you cannot draw.* And you know what? It hurt, but they were right. I took it again and I improved." Marcus paused. "You're not in that position. How long have I known you, Chris? You're just as smart as any of the kids here. Maybe you're not as polished as the kids coming from the top, top schools, but so the hell what? Who cares about that?"

"I think they care."

Marcus shook his head. "Don't get down on yourself like that. It's not where you're coming from that matters. It's where you're going."

I felt my phone vibrate. I glanced down at the screen and was surprised to see a text from Lucien.

> In Gardner's room. Strauss 304. Lots of booze. Cute girls. Come join when ure done. Gonna be a fun night

I read the text again and felt my spirits lift. Lucien had my back.

CHAPTER 4

Two helicopters drew circles in the sky. I approached the wrought-iron gate and peered through the grillwork at the collage of flashing lights and neon vests. Long trails of yellow police tape spilled outward from Memorial Church and crept through the Yard like shoots of an invasive neon vine. A cop yelled at me to back away. The Yard was closed until further notice.

With nowhere else to go, I returned to Greenough and found Lucien hanging out with Gardner.

"Yo, boss, did you hear what happened?" Gardner asked. "Some guy killed himself in the middle of the fucking Yard."

"What?"

"Yeah, bro. He blew his brains out on the steps of Mem Church," said Gardner. "With a gun!" he added unnecessarily.

"Was it a student?" I asked.

Gardner shook his head. "I don't think so. I heard it was some rando townie. Pretty brutal, though, right? Thank God he didn't pull a Virginia Tech."

"Atlas," Lucien said, "do you mind if Gardner chills here until they let people back into the Yard?"

"Sure. Stay as long as you want."

"It's fucking annoying," said Gardner. "I have a paper due tomorrow and I left my laptop in Weld. Like, why the fuck did he have to do it in the Yard?"

"You can check out a laptop at the library," I said.

"Ya, I know, but that's not the point, is it?"

"What *is* the point, then?" snapped Lucien. "Because you've been bitching about this for the last hour."

"It's just inconsiderate. There's no reason this dude couldn't have done it at his house instead of in the middle of a fucking college campus. This guy was just like the assholes who throw themselves in front of trains during rush hour."

"I'm sorry this man's death has been so inconvenient for you, Gardner," said Lucien. "If only he'd known about your paper, I'm sure he would have been open to rescheduling."

"Laugh it up, Lucien."

But Lucien wasn't laughing. "It's not funny," he said. "Happened to a guy I went to school with."

"He killed himself?"

"He was in the year below. John Blair. Nice kid. A little odd. Didn't have a ton of friends, but he was a nice kid all the same."

"Jesus," said Gardner. "Well, that's heavy."

"Yeah," said Lucien, shrugging. "I mean, it's just one of those things, right? It's a part of life. A shitty part of life. But it happens."

"No one saw it coming?" I asked.

Lucien considered the question.

"I didn't," he said. "He seemed okay, you know? Like, yeah, I knew he had to be lonely. But he wasn't the only one. And no one realized it was *that* serious. I certainly didn't. I guess he was just good at hiding it." Lucien pushed his hair back. "Or maybe we just didn't know what to look for."

"How'd he do it?" asked Gardner.

"Does it matter?"

Over the next few days more details emerged about the man who had taken his life in the Yard. As far as anyone could tell, he had no direct connection to Harvard. He just happened to live close by in Somerville and had grown up in the shadow of the university. According to the *Crimson*, he'd lost his job and his house during the financial crisis and had been struggling with depression ever since. Before he killed himself, he wrote a thirty-five-page suicide note that he posted online. The *Crimson* included a link to the suicide note in their article. I didn't read it, but I found a printout on Lucien's desk.

It was around that time that I woke one morning and found a letter jammed into the crack beneath our door. It was addressed to Lucien and sealed with wax. The envelope was embossed with an esoteric coat of arms. Two crocodiles stood on either side of a hexagon, within which was a cooking pot resting atop a fire. Above the hexagon sat a small sphinx with the date *1795*. At the bottom was a Latin phrase, *Concordia discors*.

I was about to hold it up to the light to try and see what the envelope contained, but Lucien burst through the door into our suite.

"So it's you, then!" he said excitedly.

"I'm sorry?"

"It's you! You're *the artist*!" Lucien said. "I can't believe it's you. We've been trying to figure this out for ages."

"What artist?"

"The prodigy. The one that everyone's been talking about. Why didn't you tell me?" Lucien said.

I shrugged and offered him the envelope. "By the way, this came for you."

"Oh, sick," Lucien said. He ripped it open and took out an invitation printed on heavy cardstock. He scanned it quickly and tossed it on his bed.

"What is it?" I asked.

"I'll tell you as soon as you tell me all about your art."

"What did you mean when you said *the one everyone's been talking about*?"

"There's a rumor flying around that there's a guy in our year who's supposed to be the next Picasso. It's you, isn't it? Someone said it might be you. We looked you up and found all this stuff online. That's so cool, mate! I don't know why you've been keeping it a secret."

"I wasn't keeping it secret. I just didn't think you would care."

"You have a studio, right? Can I see it?"

"Sure," I said. "Anytime." He looked at me expectantly. "Now?" I asked.

"Yes, Atlas, now!"

A few days earlier I'd finished working on a copy of Monet's *La Grenouillère*. I also had a piece of my own close to completion, titled *Trinity*. It was an abstract representation of the Garden of Eden, the culmination of a six-month project centered on the theme of the nature of evil. The Tree of Knowledge dominated the center, in dense black set against a golden backdrop. The tree grew up from the dark earth, long branches twisted and swirled like trails of black smoke across the canvas, the leaves tiny specks of illumination. Adam and Eve beneath the tree, their pale, twisted bodies intertwined with the serpent in a tangle of knots.

Lucien stood in front of the painting with folded arms. He cocked his head at an angle and leaned in close so that his eyes were only inches away, as if he were checking the canvas for fingerprints.

"It's not finished yet," I explained.

"Mate, this is gorgeous," he said. "Absolutely gorgeous. Your style . . . it reminds me of Ernst. You must get that a lot."

"You know Ernst?"

"Of course I know Ernst. I almost went to Oxford for this, remember?" He traced the long, winding outline of the serpent with his index finger. "Have you ever read any Milton?"

"No," I admitted.

"You probably should," he said. "I read *Paradise Lost* this summer. Well, the first half, anyway. It wasn't as hard to get through as everyone says. I think you'd like it . . . especially"—he pointed to the painting—"if you're into all this."

"It's just one of those books . . ."

"I know what you mean," he said. "Everyone likes *the idea* of reading it but no one ever does. It's quite good, though. Not what I expected. Satan comes across much better than you'd expect. He's actually quite likable."

"Really?"

"Yeah. He's got this sort of rebellious underdog appeal. And God is portrayed as this real hardo who forces the angels to worship him and treats them like slaves. You're like, *Hang on—who am I supposed to be rooting for again?* Anyway, I'd recommend it." Lucien motioned to the other work I had pinned to the walls. "Do you mind if I take a look round?"

"Oh. That stuff isn't really ready yet."

Lucien ignored me. He strolled around the room scanning my studies and half-finished drawings. He came to a stack of sketchbooks and lifted a small black notebook off the top of the pile.

"I'd rather you didn't," I said. "That one isn't really meant for other people." I reached out to take it back. Lucien stared at me and opened the book to the first page.

"Why?" he asked.

It was the pocket sketchbook I carried around campus. It was a kind of pictorial diary of doodles and illustrations, random notes, reminders and ideas written in a personal shorthand of abbreviated words and fragmented sentences.

"That one's filled with random ideas and sketches. It's stream-of-consciousness stuff. It wouldn't make sense to you."

Lucien shrugged and placed the notebook back on the table. I breathed a sigh of relief as he turned his attention to a copy of a Monet painting I'd finished the previous week.

"Is this a Monet?" asked Lucien. "It is, right? I've seen it before. I had to memorize it for A-levels. What's it called again? *La Granville*? No . . . Monet, 1869, *La . . . Gran* something."

"*Grenouillère*," I said. "*La Grenouillère*."

"That's right," Lucien said. He reached out and touched the canvas. "It's still wet. Did you paint this?"

"It's just a copy," I said. I pointed to a high-resolution image of the original I had taped up on the wall. "I've been doing a lot of those recently. Marcus says it's the best way to develop technique."

"Ever do any old masters?"

"Sometimes."

"Want to paint me a Rembrandt?"

I laughed. "I could paint you a shitty Rembrandt."

Lucien's eyes flickered back and forth between my copy and the high-res image. "This is absurd. They're identical."

"I'm getting better at Monet. He's easier than you'd think."

"*Getting better*? Mate, this is unbelievable. Who else can you do?"

For the next half hour Lucien put me through what can only be described as an interrogation. When did I begin painting? Where did I get my ideas from? Did I have a special routine? Had I ever tried painting high? Wasted? What about on acid? What did I think of Basquiat? How about Dalí? Had I ever tried copying either of them? Would that be difficult?

He asked what I planned to do with the Monet copy. "Could I have it?" he asked.

"Sure," I said, after a pause. "But why?"

"Oh, you know . . . I'll hang it up in my room and we can tell girls it's an original from my family's collection." He winked. "Joking," he said. "But have you ever thought about trying to sell one? Do people ever do that?"

"You mean, like, a forgery?" I laughed and shook my head. "No, I haven't."

"Do you think you could pull it off? Hypothetically," said Lucien. "Could be a laugh. Monet is too famous—obviously. But maybe someone random. Someone like . . ." His tone was light and playful, and so I didn't take him seriously. I decided to play along.

"Da Vinci?"

"I was going to suggest Michelangelo," said Lucien. "But fine. Leonardo it is."

"Should we head back?"

"Lead the way, *kemosabe*."

The day had grown cooler, and a brisk, fall wind swept through the city. As we turned onto Prescott, I remembered the letter addressed to Lucien marked with the strange symbol.

"It's a punch invite," said Lucien.

"Punch? I thought that happened sophomore year."

"This is for the Pudding. It's a club that freshmen can join. Think of it as a JV final club. The first round is next Thursday. Adler was telling me all about it. He's a member."

"The Pudding?"

"The Hasty Pudding Club. It's a weird name, I know. It's one of these old WASP things that's been around forever."

"And they throw parties and stuff?"

"Yeah, mate. It's supposed to be a riot. I've heard the parties are absolutely mental. Adler said they've got one called Leather and Lace where all the girls wear lingerie. Wait—did you not get an invitation?"

"I don't think so. I only saw yours."

"Must be a mistake." Lucien frowned. "Do you want one? I might be able to help."

"Yeah," I said. "Definitely. Is that all right?"

"Of course. I just didn't think you were into this sort of thing," he said.

"Oh. Sure I am."

"Everyone thinks you're very aloof. You're always off doing your own thing."

"Do I come across like that? I don't mean to."

"You know, I can help you if you want."

"With the Pudding?"

"With that, sure. I meant more generally, though. Girls, parties, meeting people—that sort of thing. I can help with all of that. But only if you want, of course."

"I'd like that."

We were only a few steps from Greenough when a strong gust of wind barreled down the street, bending the branches of trees and scattering carefully gathered piles of leaves into a more natural state of chaos. A discarded copy of the *Crimson* was caught up by the wind and cartwheeled toward us. Lucien stopped it with his foot and picked it up, pausing to look at the front page. I reached the front door and held it open for him.

"You coming?" I called out.

Lucien didn't seem to notice. He stood unmoving, his eyes fixed on the newspaper, his face twisted into the vexed expression of someone stumped by a math problem. His eyes lifted and settled on a point far away in the distance. I called his name and he snapped out of his trance.

"He was wearing a tuxedo," Lucien said, glancing down at the paper again.

I let the door swing shut and walked back to Lucien. "Who?"

"Matt Peterson. The guy who shot himself. It says here he was wearing a full white tuxedo."

"Weird."

"Who even owns a white tux? That seems like something you would rent. Do you think he rented it? He must have, right?"

"I don't know." I hesitated, confused. The wind picked up again. "Let's go, man. I'm getting cold."

"Sorry, mate," he said. "Coming."

As we walked inside, he seemed tired, no longer interested in talking. I asked him what was wrong.

"I can't get over the tux."

"What about it?"

"It's sad." He was quiet and when he spoke again his words were soft and low. "He got all dressed up."

I couldn't think of anything to say in response. It was strange seeing Lucien this way. I left him alone and went into my room to finish the Edward Said reading assigned for my Expos class.

CHAPTER 5

The invitation from the Hasty Pudding Club requested "cocktail attire." Lucien told me that meant "wear something smart." No jeans. A tie. A suit if I owned one.

I didn't.

For a brief, frivolous moment I pretended I could afford to buy one just for the occasion, going so far as to spend an hour on the J.Crew website browsing options. But then I remembered my unpaid cell phone bill, the money I owed Lucien for alcohol, and the books I'd have to buy next semester.

I did own a tie. It was striped, red and blue, and patterned with the Harvard crest. I added it to the outfit I'd worn for my admissions interview: a pair of light khakis and a red button-down shirt. It was a simple outfit but it made me look neat and presentable. Professional, even.

Lucien had a different opinion.

"Um . . . Atlas?"

"Yeah."

"Would you like to explain to me what the hell you are wearing?" He lobbed the question from across the room like a lazily tossed dart. It arced through the air, tracing a parabola, slow at first before picking up speed. When it struck me in the chest, it landed with a great thump.

"Please tell me you're joking," he said. "Is that a Harvard tie? Christ, Atlas. Are you trying to look like the world's biggest square? I mean, talk about *nerd alert*," he said, shuddering for effect.

Thump. Another dart.

"You told me to wear a tie," I said.

"Not that one."

"It's my only tie."

"And where in God's name did you find that shirt? It's horrible."

Thump.

"JCPenney."

"I'm not even going to ask what that is."

"What's wrong with my shirt?"

"Well, it's shiny, it's a size too big, and it makes you look like a valet driver. Apart from that? Nothing, it's wonderful."

Thump. Thump. Thump.

I could feel my face turning red. "This is all I have." I felt like an idiot. "Look, this was a mistake. Let's just forget the whole thing. You should go without me."

"Don't be absurd," he said. "You're coming and that's final. Let me shower real quick and we'll figure this out. You can borrow some of my clothes. Stay here; I'll be back in two." Lucien snatched his toiletry kit and towel on his way out.

As the door swung shut, I caught a passing glimpse of myself in the mirror. I stood up and wandered over for a closer look.

I never would have drawn a face like the one in the mirror. It was clumsy and amateurish, with soft, poorly defined features and a general lack of symmetry. The nose was too large and the lips were too thin. There were dark charcoal half-moons beneath the eyes. An absence of color in the cheeks suggested a sickliness. It was not an attractive face. It was not the face of someone who would sail into the Hasty Pudding Club.

I opened a beer and sat down in Lucien's desk chair. Doubts and dread swirled inside me, feeding off one another. Lucien wasn't going to let me back out. Why had I asked him to get me an invite? I didn't belong at an event like this. And they would know it, too. I was going to make a fool of myself. What if I never lived this down?

Lucien returned from the shower and stood in front of the mirror, working a comb through his long blond hair. I caught his eye in the reflection.

"No second thoughts, Atlas," he said. "You're not dropping out now."

"But—"

He cut me off before I could say another word. "Don't be a fucking baby," he snapped, squinting with annoyance. "It wasn't exactly easy to get you on the list. I had to pull strings. How is it going to make me look if you can't be bothered to show up?"

He immediately seemed surprised—even embarrassed—by the harshness of his own tone. He gave me a smile. "Come on, mate," he said. "It'll be fine. Just stick with me. Talk about your art. They'll love that."

I nodded, resigned to my fate, and watched Lucien get ready. He rubbed pomade on his hands and ran his fingers through his hair, slicking it back. I'd seen him complete this particular ritual on a number of occasions and was always impressed by the economy of motion—the efficiency and tidiness—with which he styled his hair. It was one of those things I had never quite learned how to do. Whenever I tried using a hair product, I never seemed to use the right amount. I had spent the better part of half an hour that evening combing and recombing my hair, pressing down loose strands, trying to manipulate it into a presentable shape.

Lucien took a gray suit from his closet and laid it out carefully on his bed. Then he went back to his closet and took out a light-blue shirt and a navy tie. All of his clothes were perfectly pressed, with crisp, clean lines. He eased himself into the shirt, buttoned it up, and selected a pair of cuff links from a box on his dresser. He slipped on the pants, then his socks, and finally the tie. It only took him one attempt to tie it the perfect length. Next, Lucien retrieved a dark green shoebox. Inside was a maroon velvet bag containing a pair of brown leather shoes with pointed toes. He stepped into the shoes and then checked his reflection in the mirror. Satisfied, he turned his attention to me.

"I've got a suit you can borrow," he said. "Don't lose the jacket, though."

"Are you sure?" I asked.

"Yeah. Just don't lose it. It's fucking expensive. It cost three grand. My mum will kill me if you lose it."

"Three thousand dollars for a jacket? Are you kidding me?"

"Yeah, so don't lose it. Seriously." He turned to his closet and took out a navy suit and a white shirt.

"I can't take that, man. Do you have one that isn't so expensive? What if someone spills a drink on me?"

"It's fine. Just be careful. Try on the shirt. It might be a bit big on you but I think we can make it work. Lemme find you a tie."

The suit was soft and light and lined with silk. As I stepped into the pants and felt the silk lining cool against my skin, it occurred to me that I had never worn anything as comfortable in my entire life. Lucien selected a thin orange tie. This, too, was silk, and patterned with small blue dolphins. I draped the near-frictionless fabric around my neck and with hardly any effort at all it flowed into the shape of a tie. I turned it over. The label said Hermès.

"Thank you."

"Don't lose the tie, either," Lucien said.

"Lucien . . . you do realize I don't walk around losing my things all the time, right?"

He laughed. "Just don't fucking lose it."

The jacket was made from the same impossibly soft material as the pants. As I slipped it on I closed my eyes and imagined myself in the kind of tailor shops I had only seen in films. When I opened my eyes and looked at my reflection in the mirror, a near stranger stared back. I looked older, more mature. The suit was sleek and seemed to elongate my body, stretching it into a shape more commensurate with a man than a boy. I felt transformed.

"Much better, right? It's a tad big but overall not bad." Lucien glanced at his watch. "Let's get a little tipsy before we go."

Half an hour later we left Greenough and cut through the Yard on our way to the clubhouse on Garden Street. Lucien was quiet as we walked, which was unusual. I didn't mind. The evening air was cool, and once inside the gates of the Yard the sounds of the city became muted and then fell away until there was just the brisk clicking rhythm of our shoes on the cement path.

We came into the area of the Yard called Tercentenary Theatre, a large rectangle of grass bordered on one end by Widener Library and at the other by Memorial Church. Other than the yellow points of light provided by streetlamps, Tercentenary was cast in darkness. We passed by the great façade of Widener, with its stone steps we'd gathered on to take our entering class photo and the thick columns that looked as though they could have been stolen from a palace of Rome. A muted light came through the library's main glass door, and at the base of the furthest column to the right, two students huddled over a laptop and shared a joint. All around us, oaks and elms stretched their limbs up into night, forming a dense canopy that blocked out the light of even the most earnest of the stars.

We continued down the path and walked past Weld into the Old Yard. A string of redbrick dormitories ran around the perimeter. We joined the long procession of freshmen—the guys in blazers, the girls in heels and dresses—heading in the direction of Garden Street.

"Look how many people there are," I said.

"I heard something like five hundred people go to the first round."

"Five hundred?"

Lucien nodded.

"How many end up getting in?"

"I heard thirty-five. But I think the real number is less because legacies are automatic."

"So we're fucked."

"Completely," Lucien said. "But why not give it a go?"

I'd expected a grand clubhouse—something to rival the final club mansions on Mount Auburn Street—but instead we were met by a shabby clapboard structure with peeling white paint. It looked more *Animal House* than Monticello. The building was three stories tall, with a sloping, tiled roof. A piece of cardboard was duct-taped over a broken window on the second floor. Outside, a few hundred freshmen waited in a large, nervous mass.

The door opened and a tall figure with blond hair and red trousers appeared on the steps of the building and invited everyone in.

We shuffled up the steps and into the packed main room. The

walls were painted merlot and decorated with framed playbills from decades past.

"Look at that big fucker," Lucien said, pointing at the wall behind us. A gigantic stuffed alligator, perhaps nine feet in length, was mounted on the wall. It was missing an eye and the hide was cracked in places.

"I heard TR shot that," said a kid behind us.

"Who?"

"Teddy Roosevelt. I heard he shot it back in the day."

"Hello! Everyone! Your attention, please!" It was the tall guy with floppy hair. He was standing on a table in the center of the room. A hush fell over the gathering. "Can you all hear me? My name is Crosby, and I'm the president of the Hasty Pudding Club. I want to welcome everyone and thank you all for coming. We're thrilled to see so many of you here tonight. The purpose of this evening is for you to get a feel for what our club is about and for us to get a feel for what you guys are about. It's a little bit like a first date," he said, smiling. Nervous laughter rippled through the crowd.

"We have a lot of our members here tonight. They're here to get to know you, and I encourage you to try to meet as many of them as you can. Look for people wearing laminated name tags. Those are the members. Oh, and whatever you do, make sure you say hello to our wonderful punchmasters, Paige and Fernando. Where are you, guys? Come up here."

A stocky guy with dark hair clambered up on the table and introduced himself as Fernando. He was joined by an African American girl dressed in navy corduroys and a pink cardigan. She wore hoop earrings and had dimples when she smiled. She said a few words and then they both climbed down off the table.

"Paige and Fernando run the whole show," said Crosby. "If you talk to anyone tonight, talk to them. I'll let the rest of our board introduce themselves in a moment. Make sure you meet as many board members as possible. Oh, and if you have the misfortune to meet those two clowns over there in the corner in Hawaiian shirts—"

I stood on my tiptoes and saw two guys wearing Ray-Bans and matching Hawaiian shirts. Both were sipping from cans of Bud Light. One had a mustache, the other a trucker hat embroidered with the letters c.e.o.

"—ignore them," Crosby continued. "They're idiots. They don't matter."

"Hey! Fuck you! Since when do we not matter?" one of them yelled out. He turned to the people around him. "Trust me, we matter."

"A lot," added the second, nodding. "We're very important people."

As Crosby wrapped up the introductions, I noticed the atmosphere in the room began to change. There was a rising tension in the air, a primal restlessness that spread through the crowd like a fast-moving virus. Kids around me were beginning to jockey for position, edging closer and closer to the center of the room, eyeing one another with suspicion like passengers at the boarding gate of a full flight who expected to fight to secure overhead storage space.

The instant Crosby finished speaking, the event turned into a free-for-all. Anyone with a laminated name tag was instantly swarmed by freshmen, all jostling for attention. The room became a blur of heat and noise and bodies jammed together. I started to sweat in Lucien's jacket. I introduced myself to a couple board members and joined a few conversations but mostly I stood listening to other kids recite their résumés and talk about which prep school they had attended. It was hard to get a word in, and I could tell the evening wasn't going well for me. I was overcome with a desire to be anywhere other than this hot, sticky room.

Lucien, on the other hand, was firmly in his element. He floated around the room from conversation to conversation without the slightest hint of effort. One moment he had Crosby in stitches, the next he was exchanging phone numbers with the club's treasurer. A few minutes later he was deep in conversation with Paige. There were eight other people standing with them, but they might as well have been standing on a different planet, because the conversation was solely between Lucien and Paige. Lucien saw me looking over at them from across the room. He waved at me to come over and I bumped and edged my way there.

"Here he is!" Lucien said.

"Is this the one?" Paige asked.

"Atlas, this is Paige, obviously. And, Paige, I give you the one and only Atlas."

"Nice to meet you," I said.

"Atlas," she repeated. "I love that name."

"It suits him, doesn't it?"

"So you're the famous artist? Lucien has been telling me all about you."

"Oh, I'm not famous."

"He's being modest. Stop being modest, you fuck! Tell her who you sold your last painting to. Go on."

"It wasn't the last one," I said.

"Who?" asked Paige.

"Pierce Brosnan."

"The actor?"

"James muthafucking Bond," Lucien said. "How cool is that?"

"Amazing! Did you get to meet him?"

"No, I mean, it wasn't him; I mean, he didn't buy it himself," I said. "His person . . . he's got a guy who buys his art for him. He goes to all the auctions and bids on stuff for him. It's pretty common. A lot of rich people do that."

"His art advisor," Lucien clarified.

"Art advisor, yeah," I said. "But it's not like that kind of thing happens all the time. And I don't even know if that guy really works for Pierce Brosnan. He could have been lying."

"You're still being modest, Atlas. Stop being so fucking modest. Goddamn Thomas Crown has your painting up on his walls." Lucien pointed to the eight dejected freshmen who were still standing there, hanging on to the conversation, hoping for a turn to speak. "None of these noodles can say that, can they?"

Paige burst out laughing and then caught herself. "Lucien!" she chided.

"I was a National Merit Scholar in high school," chimed one.

"I passed eighteen AP exams. That's the state record in California."

"I won the Carnegie Mellon bagpipe scholarship for the best high school bagpipe player in the country."

"I interned at McKinsey last summer."

"You see?" Lucien said. "Fucking bagpipe champions. Do you know how many people in the world play bagpipes? Like, seven in the whole fucking world."

"There's actually hundreds of us," the bagpiper began. "And it's one of the fastest-growing wind instrument communities in the . . ."

"Be proud of what you do, man," Lucien said to me.

"You should be proud," said Paige.

I *was* proud of what I did. But I also hated being the center of attention. I made a shitty Thomas Crown joke and then Lucien changed the subject. A guy who knew Paige from Andover edged his body in front of mine, relegating me to the circle's outer orbit. I lingered on the fringes of the conversation awhile longer, not saying much, and then I decided to leave.

I didn't want to be there. What was the point, anyway? I wasn't going to get in. I slipped away and made in the direction of the front door, stepping outside, expecting an empty street and a clear night.

Instead, I found the two guys in Hawaiian shirts standing on the front steps, smoking.

"So I thought I was just crazy hungover," said the mustachioed one to the other. "But, I mean, this was like the worst fucking hangover of all time. And then I realized I was suffering from withdrawal."

"Like alcohol withdrawal?" asked the guy in the C.E.O. hat.

"Yeah."

"Christ. That's heavy duty, man," C.E.O. said. At that point they both turned and looked at me, registering my presence for the first time.

"Smoke?" Mustache asked me.

"Thanks. I'm good," I said.

"No, I meant do you have any smokes? This is my last."

"No, I don't. Sorry."

"Fuck." He turned to his friend. "We'll have to hit up C'est Bon. I'm not going back in. It's a fucking sweatbox."

"You peacing out?" C.E.O. asked me. "You know it's only eight thirty, right?"

"I'm getting some air," I lied. I sat down next to them on the steps. "You guys had the right idea out here."

"I gotta say, I'm severely disappointed with the turnout so far. Every kid I've met so far has been a fucking tuna."

"Or a lampshade," said C.E.O.

"You're goddamn right. The whole place is filled to the brim with tunas and lampshades. It's like one big tuna fucking salad in there."

"What's a tuna?" I asked.

"Christ, kid. If you have to ask . . ."

"It's like this. Imagine if you were sitting down at dinner with your buddies. You're having a great time, but then, out of nowhere, a guy shows up and dumps a massive tuna on the middle of the table. And I mean like a proper four-hundred-pound monster bluefin tuna. You were having a great time but all of a sudden there's this massive fish sitting there, and everyone's like, *What the fuck is this fish doing here?* No one can get past it."

"It smells bad, it doesn't look nice, it wants to be the center of attention but just kills the conversation. Ruins the vibe."

"Completely ruins the vibe!"

"And everyone is like, *Can someone please get rid of this fucking tuna so we can go back to having a good time?*"

"That's a tuna."

"Got it?"

"Yeah, for sure," I said. I had no clue what they were talking about. "And a lampshade?"

"A lampshade is the human equivalent of elevator music. They're like wallpaper. They blend into the background."

"They're at all the parties, sure. But they never do or say anything worth remembering and so no one ever remembers a single thing about them. Just like a lampshade. No one ever leaves a party and remembers what kind of lampshades they had."

I nodded. And then I realized he could have been describing me.

"What he's trying to say is lampshades are what you might call *fucking boring*."

"They bring nothing to the table."

"Talking to a lampshade is only slightly better than talking to a real lampshade."

"So, what's worse? A tuna or a lampshade?" I asked.

"Are you kidding?"

"He's gotta be kidding."

"I don't think he is kidding," said the C.E.O. "You don't get it, do you?"

"A tuna is worse. Way worse."

"Like, a million times worse. They're aggressive. They get in your face."

"A lampshade knows its place. You stick a lampshade in the corner and they stay out of the way. Tunas like to be front and center. They're diabolical."

"Switching topics: How's the talent level in your class? I've seen like three cute girls all night. That's not elite."

"Not elite at all," his friend added.

"So, who are the hot freshman chicks? Throw me some names."

I thought for a second and then reeled off four or five names.

"Interesting. This is good intel, kid. That last one—is she the lax chick I've been hearing about?"

"Annie? Oh, yeah, I think she plays lax."

"I've heard there's a lax smokeshow flying around. She sounds pretty elite."

"That's probably Annie. I heard she has a boyfriend, though," I said.

"Boyfriends are out."

"So out."

"Hey, kid, what's your name?"

"Everyone calls me Atlas."

"*Calls you?*"

"It's a nickname."

"That's a stupid fucking nickname. What's your real name?"

"Chris."

"That sucks, too. Stick with *Atlas*. I'm Dante," Mustache announced. He waved his cigarette at his buddy. "This is Steinway."

"Like the pianos," Steinway added.

"No relation," said Dante.

Steinway threw Dante an annoyed glance. "You always say that. Why do you always say that? Do you really have to blow up my spot like that? Every goddamn time."

"Well, it's true, no? There's no relation."

"When did I ever say there was?"

"It's implied."

"*It's implied?* What the fuck does that mean?"

"You know what it means."

"Are you accusing me of pretending to be the heir to a fucking piano fortune? I say *like the pianos* because it's easy to remember.

But then you say *no relation* and it makes me look like a fucking asshole."

Dante put his hand across his chest and bowed his head. *"Je suis très désolé."*

"Whatever," said Steinway, shaking his head. "So, kid, what's your deal?"

"Sorry?"

"What do you do? Where do you live? Who do you know? Et cetera, et cetera."

"Well, I'm in Greenough. I'm thinking about major—"

"Getting bored . . . getting bored . . ."

"I'm also an artist," I said. "I paint."

"That's more interesting," said Steinway. "At least you didn't say you're *really into investing*."

"Christ," growled Dante. "If we get another class of fucking wannabe hedge fund managers, I'm actually going to murder Crosby."

"We make films," said Steinway. "Short ones. I write them. This idiot is okay with a camera."

"I used to paint," said Dante.

"Did you?"

"Houses. One summer in the Hamptons. It was . . ." Dante paused to take a long drag on his cigarette. ". . . fucking awful."

"Hey—I've always wondered this," Steinway said. "How come housepainters wear white? They always get paint and shit on their clothes. You'd think they would wear black or something so you couldn't see the paint."

Dante shrugged. "How the fuck should I know?"

"You were a painter, weren't you?"

"It was more of an honorary position. This was a summer in high school. I quit after a week."

"I mean, doctors wear white coats because that's supposed to show that they're clean and hygienic, but with painters it's like the opposite. Their clothes always look filthy. Do you know, kid?"

I shook my head. "No idea. Most houses are white, I guess. Maybe that's the color they use the most."

Steinway snapped his fingers and turned to Dante. "That's a smart answer. I ask everyone that question, and no one ever knows. I like this kid."

"Hey, kid."

"Yeah?"

"You sure you don't have any smokes? Don't fuck with me."

"Sorry, man."

"No worries. *Váminos, muchacho.* Time to hit up C'est Bon." Dante put out his cigarette. Steinway threw me a casual salute and the two wandered off into the night.

CHAPTER 6

I left that evening certain my run with the Hasty Pudding Club was over. But a few days later, when the invites for the second round were sent out, we received not one but two invitations. To my astonishment, I hadn't been cut.

Lucien was just as surprised. He hadn't been able to understand why I'd left so early. I tried explaining it to him. I told him how I'd felt awkward and self-conscious and how I wasn't any good in those situations.

"You know what your problem is? You need to be more confident," said Lucien. "You're a funny guy when you want to be. I've seen it. Loads of times. Like the other day at dinner: you had everyone in stitches. You just need to have more confidence. Just be yourself."

I nodded. "I mean, I get that. But it's not that easy. You can't just decide to become confident."

"Sure you can," said Lucien. "I used to have the same issue."

"Yeah, right."

"No, I'm serious. I know it's maybe hard to believe now, but I used to be worse than you. I was really shy. I hated meeting new people. All of that. It was terrible. The worst was moving and having to start again at a new school. I'd get so nervous I would throw up."

Lucien was right: it was hard to believe. I studied his face, searching for traces of deception. Was he just telling me this to make me feel better? It sounded so unbelievable. But his tone was earnest, and he didn't look like he was making it up.

"I promise you," he said.

"What happened?"

"I decided to change." Lucien scratched his ear. "I'm trying to think of the best way to explain this."

I waited for him to go on.

"I heard this story about Richard Nixon once from my dad," he said. "He was in an elevator with Nixon on the way up to a party. This was a few years after Watergate. And Nixon looked terrible. He was hunched over. He looked tired and frail and old. But then the elevator doors opened, and the cameras came out, and Nixon became a completely different person. My dad said it was like someone flipped a switch. His eyes lit up. He stood up straight. He had this huge smile on his face and all this energy. My dad told me it was like watching a puppet come to life."

"I don't get it," I said.

"It's all an act," said Lucien. "That's all it is. Confidence is an act. If you act like you're confident, you can trick people into thinking you *are* confident, even if you're not. And if you do it for long enough, you can even trick yourself. Once you do that, you're golden."

"But how did you do it?"

"I had this trick that worked for me."

"Yeah?"

"I would pretend that I was like an actor playing a character who was really outgoing and charismatic," said Lucien. "I could kind of get outside myself and stop thinking of me as me. It was like whatever was going on was only happening to the character and not actually to me. If the character said something stupid or made a fool of himself, it didn't matter. That helped me stop worrying so much. You should try it. See if it helps."

I looked at him, doubtful. It sounded too simple. Lucien shrugged. "Just try it. What do you have to lose?"

At the next punch event I followed his advice. My character was named Atlas, and I gave him all the traits I longed to possess. He was self-assured and comfortable in his own skin. He wasn't timid or afraid to make eye contact with girls when he spoke to them. He was funny and disarming—cocky even. I borrowed bits and pieces of this new personality from others: from Lucien, from Zola, from characters in films, from the lax bros and lady killers I'd known in high school. They were hardly alike, but they all shared a certain reckless quality. It was a fearlessness, a lack of vulnerability, a swagger.

We had just arrived at the second punch event when Lucien and I spotted Paige, the punchmaster, and went over to start chatting with her. She was holding a clipboard with a long list of names.

I pointed to the clipboard. "Are you grading us?"

She laughed. "Just marking down attendance."

"I'll take a 10," said Lucien. "And you can put a 10 down for Atlas, too."

"No problem," said Paige. "It's out of a hundred."

"Ha ha, very funny. But seriously," said Lucien, "what are you giving us? A? A+? I deserve at least an A+."

"*At least . . .* wow," said Paige. "A+ for humility."

With attention focused on Lucien, I took the opportunity to lift the clipboard and pen out of her hands. "I'll take that. Thank you!"

"Hey, I need that," she protested, laughing.

"Excellent work, Atlas. So, what did she give us?"

I ran my finger down the list. "Lucien . . . Lucien . . . Here you are. Lucien Orsini-Conti. Oh. Oh boy," I said, my face furrowing into a frown.

"What is it?"

"Not good, Lucien. Not good at all." I cleared my throat and pretended to read from the page. *"Lucien Orsini-Conti: small, strange little fellow. Seems a bit slow in the head. Said he still needs help tying his shoes. Enjoys playing with model trains. 3/10. Unlikely to advance."*

Paige laughed aloud.

"Is that all it says?"

"And then someone else has just written *weird smells* at the end here."

"Outrageous. Slander," said Lucien. "What does it say for Gardner?"

"1/10. Absolutely not."

"At least he's not getting in, either."

"Okay, okay, very funny. I do need that back, though," said Paige. "I have a job to do, remember?"

Just then another punch came up to us and greeted Paige. "Hey, David!" she replied. "So nice to see you again. Do you know Lucien and Atlas?"

I turned to him, brandishing the clipboard. "David . . . last name, please?"

"It's Ampleforth. Dave Ampleforth."

"Ampleforth, excellent," I said, pretending to take notes. "And you are from?"

"Florida."

"*Florida.* Very good," I said. "Favorite color?"
"Green?"

I grimaced. "*Green . . .* ," I repeated aloud, scrawling it on the paper. "Interesting . . . And final question: If you could have dinner with one figure from history, who would you choose and why are they important to you?"

"Huh. I need to think about that for a second . . . Maybe Nikola Tesla? I'm an engin—"

"*Tesla. Hmm . . .* ," I said. I stared at the clipboard as if deep in thought and then took the pen and drew a large X across the page. Out of the corner of my eye I saw Paige stifle a laugh. "I'm afraid that's not the answer we were looking for." I handed the clipboard back to Paige and patted him on the back. "Good luck with the rest of the process."

To my amazement, Lucien's advice seemed to be working. I walked away feeling kind of embarrassed at acting so obnoxiously but also impressed with myself that I'd managed to pull it off. I'd hung around Lucien long enough to realize part of his charm—part of the reason why so many people liked him—was because he didn't take anything too seriously and he wasn't afraid to do these slightly outrageous, brazen things. My nature was to be the opposite. I would pile self-imposed pressure on inconsequential situations and become hyper self-aware of every action to the point of paralysis. But by imagining myself as a character with other traits I was finding a way to slip the bonds of anxiety and self-consciousness that had always held me back and free myself from the mirror of my own mind.

It wasn't quite as easy as Lucien made it sound. It took effort. I found it draining playing the character—pretending to be someone else. There were moments when I felt certain I would be exposed as an imposter. But I wasn't. And it worked. I made it through to the third round, and then the fourth, and then to the fifth and final round, watching as the number of prospective candidates dwindled from over four hundred to a few dozen.

The final event was a brunch held at the clubhouse. Only fifty punches were invited. And of those only thirty-five would make it into the club. Naturally Lucien was included in the fifty. Zola was, too. As was their friend Kane, a rower from Sydney, Australia. Gardner didn't make it. To everyone's surprise, including his, Gardner was cut after the fourth round. The rumor was that he'd been blackballed because he'd bullied a board member's younger brother at Groton. Gardner said that was bullshit and he didn't even know the kid.

He wasn't the only notable absence at the final event. Xander, the notorious kid from New York City, had been cut. As had the contingent of lacrosse players from Manhasset who went everywhere in a pack. Gone, too, were the swimmers from Deerfield and Hotchkiss, the popular golfer from Choate and the Intel science champion from California. All these well-known, well-liked kids were missing from the final event. And yet somehow I was there.

I am certain I would have been cut had it not been for Lucien. Not only did he guide me through the whole process, telling me what to wear and what to say and who to say it to, but he also took other measures to ensure my progress. Shortly after the second event he began a casual fling with Paige. He would never admit to it, but I suspect he asked her to push me through as far as she could.

They came for Lucien at twelve thirty a.m. on the Monday before Halloween. We'd heard rumors it was going to happen that night and so we had stayed up late, waiting for the knock on the door.

It was a nervous evening. Neither of us was able to concentrate on work. Several times we heard phantom knocks and opened our door to an empty hallway. To pass the time, Lucien put on an old Steve McQueen film about an escape from Devil's Island. He claimed it was one of his favorites. I sat and watched it with him, but my mind wasn't on the film. Around midnight I got ready to go to bed. I had an early class the next morning and was about to brush my teeth when Lucien received a text message from Adler. He showed it to me.

> Congrats. Get ready for the freight train. It's gonna be a rough ride.

"I think this means I got in, right?" asked Lucien.

I read the text and then glanced at my own phone. I felt a knot form in my throat when I saw that I hadn't received a similar text.

"Hell yeah. That's awesome," I said, trying to be enthusiastic for Lucien. "Congrats, man."

"What do you think the freight train is?"

"Hazing?" I suggested.

"Shit, did you get one?" Lucien asked. "A text?"

"No," I said.

"Oh. I don't think it means anything. Adler's a moron. He probably jumped the gun."

"At least one of us got in," I said.

"Don't read into it, mate. You never know."

Just then there was a knock on the door.

"That's probably for you," I said.

Lucien went to the door and opened it.

"Get a jacket and a blindfold," I heard a voice say to him.

"What about Atlas? Should I get him, too?" Lucien asked.

"Shut the fuck up. No fucking talking."

Lucien went to his closet and took out a winter coat and a tie to use as a blindfold. He threw me a pained look and shrugged, helpless. "Sorry, man," he mouthed. And then he disappeared out the door.

I sat down on his bed and fell backwards, letting my head hit the mattress. I heard footsteps in the hallway growing fainter and fainter until they were no more, and there was just a silence that overwhelmed everything, even my own thoughts. I blinked and felt the warm trace of a tear slide down my cheek. And then there was another knock at the door.

I didn't get up right away. Lucien must have forgotten something. More knocking. I wandered over and twisted the knob. On the other side was Steinway dressed in a dark suit. Behind him stood Dante, a cigarette tucked behind one ear.

"Get a jacket. Something warm. Now," said Steinway.

For a moment I didn't move. I stood there with a blank look on my face, trying to comprehend what this meant.

"Now, dipshit! Move it!" Dante said. "What's wrong with these kids?"

I grabbed my winter coat and a scarf. They tied the scarf around my head, covering my eyes, and then guided me through the hallway, down the stairs, and out into the cold. Even though the scarf was tied so tight that it hurt, I couldn't help but smile. I'd made it. Out of five hundred kids, close to a third of our class, I was one of the few who'd gotten in.

The rest of the night is a blur. I was led around the Yard blindfolded and handed off to various people who ordered me to do things like take shots or do push-ups or sing embarrassing songs. There was a lot of standing around and waiting. There was a lot of drinking and at one point I thought I might throw up. But throughout the whole ordeal I was so consumed by giddiness that I really didn't care what they were making me do.

After what must have been an hour, I was led up the steps of Widener and told to remove my blindfold. When I took off the scarf, my vision was blurred and I wasn't able to recognize the two people standing in front of me in the dim light. But I heard them tell me I'd gotten in and would receive more details the following morning.

Lucien was pacing the room when I got back.

"Atlas! Did you make it? You did, didn't you?"

I nodded, beaming.

"Fuck yes!" he said. "God, that's a relief." Lucien bounded over and embraced me. "We fucking did it, man."

I hugged him back, feeling happier and more grateful than I had for as long as I could remember. I knew what this meant. It was the start of a new life—the life I'd always wanted. And I owed it all to him. "Thank you," I said.

I slept through my morning classes, waking up in a daze at ten o'clock. I remembered the events of the previous night and bounced out of bed, excited to share the news with my mom.

"Oh, *miláčku*, that makes me so happy! I'm so proud of you! Didn't you tell me only twenty students get accepted? Oh, wait until I tell your aunt Hana. She will be so proud."

"Thirty-five," I said.

"Still, only thirty-five. And out of how many?"

"Five hundred, I think."

"*Pět set?* Oh my goodness. Tell me again about this club."

"It's sort of an arts and theater club. JFK was a member."

"President Kennedy?"

"And Teddy Roosevelt. And FDR. And two more presidents that I forget. I think John Adams."

"My goodness. Chris, this is such wonderful news. I will have to call Hana straightaway. I wish your father was here to see how well you've done," she said. "His son at Harvard. And walking in the same shoe steps as President John Kennedy. He would be so proud of you."

"Mom, you're not crying, are you?"

"No, no. *Samozřejmě že ne*," she said. But I could tell she was.

"By the way, Marcus told me to give you his best," I said.

"Oh, Marcus! How is Marcus? *Děláš to, co ti říká, ano?*"

"Yes, Mom. Of course. Always."

"*Dobrá*," she said. She repeated the word a second time. There was a brief pause. I was about to say goodbye when she cut in. "Chris," she said, hesitating. "There is something else."

I could tell from her tone that it was bad news. My heart sank. I knew what this was about. Months ago my mom had been served with a summons informing her that she was being sued for $4,112.17 by Orcus Property Management LLC. We assumed it was a mistake. The summons was meant for someone else. Neither of us had ever heard of this company before. How could they be suing us?

But it wasn't a mistake. We learned that Orcus Property Management was the new owner of a housing development we'd lived in before moving to our current address. They were suing us for unpaid rent, saying we'd broken our lease four months early. It was bullshit. We had broken the lease, but our contract gave us the right to break it provided we gave the landlord two months' notice—which we had done. None of that seemed to matter. According to Orcus we hadn't given proper notice, and there appeared to be nothing we could do to prove otherwise. There wasn't even anyone we could speak to. Orcus had no website. No listed phone number. Their address was a P.O. box in Delaware. Our adversary was a faceless LLC that only communicated through servers and summonses. Each month a new summons arrived demanding an even larger amount than thirty days before. They wanted us to pay their legal fees, too. In just a few short months, the sum we supposedly owed Orcus had grown to well over $5,000. It was always in the back of my mind, a maleficent, looming presence.

"I spoke with the lawyer," she said. "The one Hana suggested. He says we have to pay."

I felt a knot form in my stomach—a great, twisted ball of stress. "The whole amount? There's nothing we can do?"

"He says it is better to just pay. Otherwise they won't stop. It will keep going and going. He said this is what they do. They do this to everyone. He said they won't leave us alone until we pay."

"But this is insane. We don't owe them anything. They weren't even our landlord when we lived there."

"I know, I know. I told all of this to Hana's lawyer and he says 'Mary, just pay them.' He told me they won't stop."

"Can't we take them to court?"

"Yes, of course. But how much is the lawyer? And what if we lose?"

"It's not supposed to be this way, Mom. This isn't fair."

"I know," she said. "It's not fair, but so what? What would you have me do?"

"I don't know," I said. "It's just not right."

My mother switched into Czech and reminded me of how my grandparents had lost their house, built brick by brick by my grandfather, and were expelled from the Communist Party after their neighbors denounced them as "enemy informants" guilty of "anti-communist activities." The neighbors, the story went, had been jealous of my grandparents' larger house and wanted it for themselves. So they wrote a letter filled with lies and put it in the hands of a local apparatchik with connections to the Interior Ministry. And that was all it took. Within a few weeks the house was theirs. I knew the story by heart.

"Okay," I said. "So we pay them. How much should I send?"

"Only what you can. You have some savings, yes? From the summer? I'm sorry it has to be like this. If your father was still here . . . Thank you, *miláčku. Miluji tě.*"

I assured her I had plenty saved over from my summer jobs, even though the truth was I'd already gone through most of it trying to keep up with Lucien and his friends. They'd already grown tired of dining hall fare and preferred to eat out: sandwiches for lunch from Cardullo's and Darwin's, Saturday brunch at Zoe's, burgers from Mr. Bartley's and B.good, late-night takeout from the Kong. One night Xander had gotten a craving for fast food and had a taxi take him to the McDonald's drive-through in Central Square, where he ordered a hundred dollars' worth of chicken nuggets, fries, and milkshakes and held a subsequent feast in Weld 204. They went out a lot, too, not just at Harvard but to parties at other schools in Boston, which meant we spent a lot of money on alcohol and taxis. In a few short weeks I'd raced through the majority of my savings, and the income from my student job did little to slow my drawdown. I knew it wasn't sustainable. I knew I couldn't afford to do the things Lucien and his friends were doing—at least, not all the time. But they didn't know that, and I didn't want them to know.

There was one resource I hadn't yet tapped. Harvard offered loans of up to $2,000 a year to students on scholarship. The loans were interest-free until you graduated and carried nominal interest after that. I saw the option as a kind of reserve parachute. Entering the school year, I'd been determined to avoid taking on any debt, but it was comforting all the same knowing the option was there if needed. This felt like the time to use it. I didn't see another option. After saying goodbye to my mom, I walked over to the office of financial aid and filled out a loan request form for all of the $2,000. I felt strangely grown-up as I handed the form to the financial aid officer. She told me it would take a few days to process the request, but I could expect to receive a check by the end of the week.

I was just about to leave when Kane, the Aussie rower, came bounding up the front steps. "Are you here about the Pudding?" he asked.

"What do you mean?"

"The dues, mate. It's heaps more than I thought. Are you here about a loan?"

"How much are the dues?"

"You didn't see the email? It's like a grand per term," said Kane. "Plus another grand for the initiation fee."

I stared at Kane, not fully believing him. This was the first I'd learned about dues. No one had said anything about it during the entire punch process. Surely they didn't expect everyone to afford $3,000 per year in dues. It was a preposterous amount. "That can't be right."

Kane opened the email on his phone. "Yeah? See here. It says, 'All new members are required to pay a onetime initiation fee of $950, in addition to biannual dues of $1,125 per semester.'"

The numbers stung. I didn't need to do the math to know it was too much. I felt hollow and fought the urge to laugh. After everything, it all came down to money. Why couldn't they have told me that at the start?

"Yeah, mate," Kane said. "I was gonna have a yarn with Crosby later and explain I'm on a full ride. Come along if you want. I'm sure we can suss something out."

"They couldn't have told us this a month ago?"

"I know, mate. It's bloody irritating. I'm hoping they'll give us a discount or let us by on reduced dues."

"Okay," I said in a low voice. "Well, let me know if you find anything out."

When I got back to my room I read the full email from Crosby. In addition to details about dues and club rules, there was an invitation to the initiation dinner on Saturday evening and a list of newly elected members.

I ran my eyes over the list, unconsciously sorting the names into two categories: those who came from wealth and those who did not. I sighed. The former dwarfed the latter. It wasn't even close. There was a Cabot on the list, as well as a Winthrop and two members of the Weld family. There was Rachel Foster, the daughter of a private equity billionaire, and Abigail Zhao, whose parents had recently given Harvard $75 million to build the Robert and Lily Zhao Student Center. Mark Johnson's dad ran BET for Viacom and sat on the board of General Motors, while Evan Wilkins was the heir to the third-largest supermarket chain in the United States. Victoria Roth's father was a former governor of New Jersey, and Henry Frank's parents were part owners of the Red Sox. So that's why no one had thought to mention the dues before. For most of the kids in my class, it simply wasn't relevant information. Three thousand dollars was nothing but a phone call home. Not for me. For me it was the end of the road.

The rest of the morning flowed by like a time-lapse video of another person's life. I drifted through three hours of lectures without absorbing a single thing my professors said.

That evening I explained my situation to Lucien.

"You can't be serious," Lucien said. "What about your paintings? I thought you made loads of money from those?"

I shook my head. "It's much less than you think. After the dealer takes his cut and you pay all the fees and taxes, there isn't a whole lot left over."

"Don't you have new ones you could sell?"

"Just *Trinity*, the one I showed you. I stopped working on new stuff when I got here because Marcus wanted me to focus on technique."

"But surely if you sold that, you'd have enough, right?"

"I could. But even if I went to a dealer tomorrow, it could be months before he found a buyer."

Lucien was stumped. We sat in melancholy.

"Atlas," Lucien said, "I may have an idea. Just go with me on this one. You know the Monet painting you did? How long did that take you?"

"A few weeks," I said. "Why?"

"Well, I was thinking . . ."

"I hope you have a better idea than trying to pass it off as a real Monet. The original is on display at the Met."

"Don't be absurd." He paused. "Well, I guess I have two ideas. The first idea is you could sell those paintings to people as replicas. You know: like, people would be aware they're buying a copy, but they do it anyway because it's nicer than a poster."

"And charge what? Fifty bucks?"

"Well, I would have paid three hundred for the Monet. Easily. But I take your point. I like idea number two better anyway."

"What is it?"

"You said it takes a few weeks to paint one of those?"

"A Monet?"

"No, a replica in general. You do other artists, too, right? How long does it take you to do an average replica?"

"It depends," I said. "On size . . . who the artist is . . . how familiar I am with his techniques . . . a lot of things. Where are you going with this?"

"Let me ask this a different way. What is the quickest you could get one done?"

I thought it over. "For Henri Martin . . . a couple weeks. Pisarro or Camoin, maybe less. I'm good at Camoin."

"Camoin could work. How much do his paintings go for?"

"I have no idea. Why?"

Lucien ignored my question and grabbed his laptop. After a minute or two, he turned the laptop around to face me and pointed at the screen. His browser was open to the Sotheby's website. I looked closer and saw dozens of listings for Camoins.

"You see? Most are selling for around twenty grand. And his

work hasn't been properly catalogued. He's perfect. You said you could finish one in a week or two?" He spoke with a manic energy—never blinking, never breaking eye contact. "Here's the idea," he continued. "If you walk into Sotheby's and try to sell them a five-million-dollar Monet, they'll take one look at it and either throw you out or call the police. Most likely the latter."

"They would call the cops," I said.

"Right. But let's say you go to a small Boston art gallery or a pawnshop and offer them a random painting done by an artist who was never particularly famous. Let's say a painting worth around ten or fifteen thousand dollars. If it's the right kind of place, the kind of place where they don't ask a lot of questions . . . I think you could easily walk out of there with a few g's in cash."

"Are you kidding?"

"I've heard stories about this from my aunt. She owns a gallery in Stockholm. Apparently it happens all the time. You just have to go to the right kind of place."

"Why do you keep saying *the right kind of place*? What does that even mean? What the hell is *the right kind of place* for selling fake art?"

"Atlas, chill."

"A pawnshop owned by the mob?"

"Plenty of galleries buy this stuff."

"You're out of your mind."

"No, listen. The other day my art history professor was telling us that over fifty percent of art on the market is fake. Even the experts can't tell a good fake from a genuine piece. Look, you paint and I'll handle everything else. We'll split the proceeds down the middle."

"Do you realize how illegal that would be?"

"Of course. It's forgery. That's, like, the second most illegal thing you can do with art, after stealing it."

"Well, why don't we just do that? Let's hit up the Gardner Museum and grab a couple Rembrandts!" I heard my voice growing louder and angrier. "Three hundred million should hold us over for a little while. Or fuck it . . . there's a 7-Eleven down the street. We could rob that right now!"

"Atlas . . ."

I stood up, furious. "Oh, and don't worry," I snapped. "I've already figured out how we sell the paintings. If the billionaire Russian oligarch falls through, we can sell them to your buddies at the local Boston pawnshop, who apparently—in addition to buying shitty jewelry—are in the habit of collecting fine art. Fuck, Lucien! This isn't a fucking game, man. *This is my life.*" My outburst finished, I collapsed into a chair and dropped my head in my hands.

Lucien was quiet. I glanced up and saw the look in his eyes and I knew he was serious. He put his arm around my shoulder.

"We can do this," he said. "Trust me. There's no way we would get caught. We would be smart about it. You need the money, right?"

"No, man. This is insane."

"How's this: I'll loan you the cash now so you can pay the initiation fee and the dues for this semester. You'll pay me back in a few weeks with a Camoin. I want a world-class forgery, though. I'm talking about something I could go hang in the Louvre."

"No chance. I'm not risking getting kicked out of Harvard and going to prison over a stupid club."

"I'm trying to help you. Just do the painting. I'll handle everything else. I'll be the one taking all the risk. Even if I get caught, how the hell will they find out where I got the painting from? I can say I bought it at a yard sale. There's no way the police would ever find out you painted it."

"Why are you offering to do this?" I asked.

"I want to help."

"But what's in it for you?"

"It isn't fair that you can't join because you don't have the money. I want to help. That's all."

"And?"

"And . . . it would make for a great story one day. This will be a real adventure, Atlas."

"I need to think about it," I said.

"Sleep on it. Let's talk tomorrow."

He went into his room and closed the door. I had a response paper for Expos 20 due the next day, but I wasn't able to focus. I sat at my laptop for an hour and did little more than stare at the white expanse of an open Word doc—the blinking cursor marking the passage of time. All I could think about was how jealous I was of Lucien and Zola. They didn't know what it was like to think about money all the time—to have to check the price of textbooks before enrolling in a class or choose between joining a social club and supporting a parent in need.

That night I lay in bed staring at the ceiling, trying to think of another solution. But it was hard to think past Lucien's idea. It was lodged in the back of my mind, impossible to forget and impossible to ignore. It was like finding an envelope marked "Answer guide: Do not open" the night before a final exam. I knew I shouldn't look. It was wrong even to consider it. But there it was, lying on my desk, begging to be opened. What if I just looked at the first page? Only to see if I was prepared, of course. That wasn't cheating, was it?

Lucien was right about one thing: it was doable. I'd heard stories about all the fake art on the market and about dealers who didn't care if a painting was fake as long as they could sell it. I was confident in my own ability. If someone else could pull it off, I was sure I could as well. And I wouldn't be the first artist to do it, either. A lot of famous painters had done it in their youth to support themselves before achieving success and recognition. Marcus had once told me that Michelangelo had launched his career by forging sculptures he sold to the cardinal who eventually became his chief patron.

All it would take was one painting. No one would notice one painting. No one would find out. One painting and my problems were solved.

When I woke up the next morning I found an envelope on my desk containing $2,000 in cash. There was no note. No explanation. But I suppose none was needed. I knew what the money was for and what it meant to take it. And I took it anyway.

CHAPTER 7

Candles fluttered in the darkness. Dozens of tiny yellow teardrops danced over pools of wax. They were small tea lights—ineffective in the vast room.

The girl seated to my left was preparing to tell a joke of her own. Her name was Claire and she was dressed up as one of the Blues Brothers. For the past fifteen minutes she'd been bent over her BlackBerry, composing a limerick about a fellow Pudding member. I'd seen several drafts and had helped her out with one of the rhymes.

"Okay," she said. "I think I'm ready."

"Good luck."

Claire pushed her chair back, placed her hand on my shoulder, and vaulted herself up onto the chair. For a second it seemed she might lose her balance, but then she steadied herself. She waved her other arm to get everyone's attention. Someone let out a loud cheer. The sound of spoons clinking against wineglasses brought the room to a hush. Claire lifted her BlackBerry and cleared her throat.

"This is for Garrett," she announced to the room. A group of boys at the table next to us started whooping and banging their fists on the table in a steady drumbeat.

"Get some, Garrett!" a voice yelled out.

"Yo! Shut up!" came another.

Claire squinted at her phone and began to read from the screen:

> There once was a boy named Garrett Brown,
> Whose smile turned down into a frown,
> The day he was told,
> That lo and behold,
> The Brooks Brothers store had closed down.

The room broke out into applause and cheers. Claire sat down. She was flushed. "Did you like it?" she asked. Before I had a chance to answer, a senior at our table raised his glass and called for a down in one. For what must have been the fifth time that evening, our whole table got to their feet and began singing:

> *Down in one, down in one, down in one,*
> *Down in one, down in one, down in one-un,*
> *Down in one, down in one, down in one,*
> *Down in one,*
> *DOWN. IN. ONE! Down in one!*

At the song's conclusion, everyone at the table drained their wineglass in one go. We'd barely finished when the next table began their own down in one. The song dominoed around the room.

Claire wasn't the only one in costume. At our table alone there was Spider-Man, Britney Spears, a penguin, an elf, and Magnum, P.I. It was our initiation dinner, but it was also Halloween night, and about half the older members had come dressed for the costume party that would follow the dinner. The rest of us were wearing either black tie or some hybrid of the two themes.

I was wearing a white dinner jacket that Lucien had picked out for me. He'd insisted on accompanying me to the tux store in Central Square. "I'm going with you," he said. "I've seen those shows on MTV. I know the horrible things you Americans wear to your proms. I'm not lending you cash so you can buy some tacky polyester number with a clip-on bow tie and a fedora. Not happening, mate."

At the store, Lucien had requested a shawl collar and a cummerbund instead of a vest. He convinced me to go with a white jacket. I didn't love it at first—I had it in my mind that tuxedo jackets were supposed to be black—but then he showed me some pictures of famous actors wearing white jackets and I came around. He helped me with my bow tie as well. And by that I mean he tied it for me, having first refused to allow me to purchase a pre-tied option.

Lucien already owned a tuxedo he said had been made bespoke for him by a tailor in London. He also had a pair of low-cut velvet slippers embroidered with his family's crest. I thought they were women's shoes, but when we arrived at the Pudding and I heard other guys being complimented on *their* velvet slippers, I realized the slippers were the mark of a veteran, an insider. I wondered where I could get a pair.

After a final down in one, Crosby stood on his chair and declared dinner over. He asked everyone to go upstairs so the staff could clear away the tables before guests started arriving for the Halloween party. I wandered over to the bar, where I found Dante. He offered to give me a tour of the house and took me up the narrow winding staircase to the second floor. It was decorated much like the first floor, with old posters and club photographs. There was a TV room with a couple of big leather sofas and a game room containing a chess set and a poker table around which a number of members were huddled, snorting lines of cocaine. I was somewhat taken aback by the sight of people doing it so openly.

"Do you want some?" asked Dante.

"Thanks, I'm good."

"Suit yourself," he said. I lingered by the door as he went over to do a line. He returned sniffling.

"To the Krok Room!"

I followed him around the corner into a room with cobalt-green walls. There was another stuffed crocodile, this one larger than the one downstairs. Dante pointed to it. "Teddy Roosevelt shot that," he said.

"I thought he shot the one downstairs."

Dante stared at me as if deciding whether or not this was true. He shrugged. "Yeah, maybe. Who the fuck knows?"

Halfway down the stairs, I paused and took stock of the scene developing below. The tables had been cleared away. A bouncer stood guard at the front door holding a list of names. Behind him a drunk couple, victims of the down in ones, clutched at one another, oblivious of their surroundings. Guests poured into the main room and collected in a puddle by the bar. Board members scurried about like frantic worker bees, setting some things up, putting other things away, searching for power cables and aux cords and strobe lights. Even though I'd been a member for only a few hours, I felt easy and settled like I'd been there my whole life. I looked down at the gathered crowd and saw the smiling faces of new friends and acquaintances clustered in groups of twos and threes, ordering the chaos like familiar constellations in the night sky.

My eyes kept returning to one face in particular, a pale, pretty one framed by dark, shoulder-length hair. It was Harriet Anderson, the toga-wearing girl I'd seen at the party on the first night of school. She was wearing a red dress and talking with another girl in the corner of the room. As I watched her she turned her head and our eyes met. I looked away quickly so she didn't think I had been staring at her. A moment later I glanced over again and saw she was still looking at me. It was her turn to look away.

On the handful of occasions we'd crossed paths, I'd never had the right opportunity to introduce myself. I always had a reason not to do it or a reason to wait. Maybe she was talking to someone else. Or just looked too beautiful. Maybe I was too sober and too afraid. But that night my excuses evaporated and I couldn't think of a single reason not to go over and talk to her.

She was studying a picture on the wall, her back to me. I cleared my throat, but she didn't turn around. I decided to do something I had seen Lucien do with girls and patted her lightly on the head. She turned around, a confused look on her face.

"Hello," I said.

"Do you always do that?"

"Do what?"

"Go up to girls you've never met and pat them on the head? I'm not a dog, you know."

My cheeks flushed. I tried to think of a witty reply. "Do you not? I thought that was how everyone said hello . . ."

"No, they don't. That was a very weird thing to do." She glared at me, eyes filled with disdain. "Who do you think you are?"

"I'm sorry," I said. An awkward pause followed, and I could feel my cheeks turning redder and redder. Just as I was about to turn tail and run, she burst out laughing.

"I'm joking," she said. "I'm sorry. I couldn't resist."

"Oh, thank God," I said, smiling weakly.

"I'm Harriet, by the way."

"Atlas," I said.

She extended a hand covered by a red wool mitten. I shook it and saw she was wearing a matching mitten on the other hand. She held her wineglass the way a child might, her mittened hand wrapped tightly around the glass stem. Paired with her evening dress, the mittens made her look faintly absurd. I liked that she didn't seem to care. "Atlas . . . ," she said. "As in a book of maps?"

"I think it's meant to be more like the guy from Greek mythology."

"You think?"

"I know."

"So you're Greek, then?"

"Not exactly."

"No?"

"I'm Czech. Well, I'm American. I was born here. But my parents came from Czechoslovakia."

"Oh." She paused. "So, in other words . . . you're not Greek at all."

"That's right."

"How does a Czech end up with a Greek name?"

"You ask a lot of questions."

"I'm curious," she said.

"My roommate gave it to me."

"Your roommate?" She gave me a quizzical look. "Care to explain?"

"He thought my real name was boring."

"So he gave you a new name?"

"Yes," I said.

"Atlas."

"Right."

"So, if I have this correct, your roommate thought your name was boring, so you let him rename you after a character from Greek mythology?"

"It sounds kind of ridiculous when you put it like that," I said.

"How else would you put it?"

"That's a fair point," I said.

"What's your real name?" she asked.

"Christopher."

"That's a nice name."

"I always thought so."

"Like Christopher Marlowe," she said.

I nodded.

"The playwright," she clarified.

"I know who that is."

"Are you sure?"

"Of course. The sixteenth-century polymath who wrote *Cats: The Musical*."

She laughed. "That was Shakespeare."

"Right."

"Marlowe is better known for his masterpiece, *Doctor Fünke*."

"An *Arrested Development* reference. Very nice," I said.

"Thank you."

"*Doctor Fünke* . . . that's the one about the disgraced doctor turned struggling actor who makes a deal with the devil to land his dream role as an understudy in the Blue Man Group?"

"It's my favorite."

"*Death of a Timeshare Salesman* is also very good."

"Excellent," she agreed. "But violent."

"Extremely violent. Blood everywhere. Whoever would have thought one could do so much damage armed only with a stack of glossy brochures and a complimentary cheese platter," I said. "Okay, my turn to ask you a question."

"Ask away."

"What's your costume supposed to be?" I asked.

"It's a long story."

"I've got time."

"Fern Arable."

"Who?"

"The girl from *Charlotte's Web*. I had a stuffed pig and everything."

"*Had*—past tense?"

"Correct."

"Where is it now—the pig?" I asked.

"Wilbur?"

"Yes."

"I may have temporarily misplaced him."

"You lost Wilbur?"

"A drunk guy ran off with him about ten minutes ago. It's only partly my fault."

"Wait. Isn't the girl called Charlotte?"

"No. Charlotte is the spider. Hence the web. The girl's name is Fern."

"Right," I said, nodding. "That makes sense. Spiders weave webs. Teenage girls do not." I paused. "Unless of course you take the view that the web is something of a metaphor."

"A metaphor for?"

"I don't know . . . a tangle of emotion, teenage angst, and paranoid delusion that has led a young girl, forced to confront death for the first time, to believe that she can talk to animals?"

"It's an excellent theory," she admitted. "But then the title of the book would have to be *Fern's Web*."

"Sure. Or *The Psychotic Girl and the Farm*. Feels like we're splitting hairs here, though."

"That would also work. Shades of Hemingway," she said. She thought for a moment and then laughed to herself. "Okay, I've got one."

"Go on."

"It's dark."

"Let's hear it."

"*Tender Is the Piglet*."

"That's fucked-up," I said, shaking my head. I pointed to her hands. "What's up with the mittens, though?"

"The mittens keep my hands warm," she said.

"So nothing to do with your costume?"

"They're actually not even mine."

"Oh God. You traded Wilbur for the mittens, didn't you?"

"Well . . ."

"How could you? Protecting Wilbur is Fern's one job."

"It's so cold, though! And that's technically Charlotte's job. You really need to reread the book."

Just then our attention was diverted by the sound of cheering. We looked over in the direction of the noise and saw Lucien atop a chair with a full pitcher of beer in one hand and a large group gathering around him. He waved his free hand, calling for attention.

"Hello!" Lucien shouted above the din. "Oi! *Attenzione! Ragazzi! Un po di silenzio, per favore!*"

The DJ killed the music and the room was quieted by a series of synchronized shushes. All eyes were on Lucien.

"Thank you, thank you," said Lucien. "Apologies for interrupting tonight's festivities but I'd like to make a quick toast." There were some light cheers as Lucien paused and cleared his throat. "As some of you may know, I was born in a little country by the name of Sweden: a land of Vikings, tall, beautiful blondes, and affordable, easy-to-assemble furniture."

"Fuck yeah, Ikea!" someone yelled from the back.

Lucien continued. "In Sweden, instead of *cheers*, we say *skål*. Everyone!" He raised the pitcher of beer high above his head and everyone shouted "*Skål!*" in unison.

"We also have a song in Sweden similar to the one sung by the members of this club," he said. "The name of this song is 'Helan går,' which roughly translates to . . ." Lucien paused, and cleared his throat. ". . . 'DOWN IN ONE'!"

The whole room cheered.

"If it is all right with all of you, I'd quite like to sing it."

Naturally this was met with large whoops of approval. And Lucien began to sing:

Helan går
Sjung hopp faderallan lallan lej
Helan går
Sjung hopp faderallan lej
Och den som inte helan tar
Han heller inte halvan får
Helan går!
Sjung hopp faderallan lej!

Lucien took the pitcher of beer in both hands and drank it all. The music started up again, and Lucien was carried away on the shoulders of a pair of classmates, holding the empty pitcher above his head like a trophy.

I turned to Harriet. "That was impressive."

She rolled her eyes. "That's one word for it."

"What word would you choose?"

"For Lucien? Or for the performance?"

"Do both," I said.

"The performance . . . obnoxious?"

"Hmm."

"Cocky?"

"Confident," I countered.

"Attention seeking?"

"That's two words."

"True."

"And for Lucien?"

Harriet pursed her lips. "One word?"

"Only one."

"Shady."

I couldn't hide my surprise. "Did you say *shady*?" I asked. "That's your word for Lucien?"

"Never mind. I shouldn't have said that."

"Wait, why *shady*?"

"Forget I said that. Honestly. I don't know him very well. He just did something kind of weird to my friend that gave me a bad vibe."

"What happened?"

"I don't like spreading gossip," she said.

"I won't tell anyone," I said.

She sighed. "Do you know Chloe Campbell?"

I shook my head.

"She's a close friend of mine. They're in Justice together, in the same section."

"Chloe and Lucien?"

"Yeah. And she used to really like him. She thought they were good friends. They would hang out after class sometimes and work on assignments together."

"Okay."

"I guess a couple weeks ago they had to come into section and present their ideas for their midterm papers to the TF and the rest of the class. And Lucien and Chloe had been talking about paper ideas the weekend before and Chloe had this really cool, creative idea basically imagining a private space colony on Mars and using that to compare and contrast how the laws and the governance would function under different philosophical traditions. It's a little out there, but, yeah, creative and sounds like a fun paper. Anyway, she tells Lucien this idea. He loves it—says he thinks it's really smart. But then the day comes to present in class and when the TF asks who wants to go first, Lucien puts up his hand and recites her idea word for word."

"Really?"

"She was super upset about it. The worst thing was she didn't have a backup. So, it looked like she wasn't prepared and it's going to hurt her grade."

"Are you sure that's what happened? Maybe there was a misunderstanding?"

"That's how Lucien tried to play it off. She confronted him

afterwards and he was like, *I thought we were just brainstorming ideas. I didn't know you planned to use that one.* But she's like, *No, I told you that was the one I was going to present.* I saw her that afternoon and she was so upset. She was crying really hard."

"Huh. I mean, I know him pretty well and I really don't think he would have done that on purpose. I get that he can definitely split opinions. I know some people think he's arrogant or whatever. But I don't think he would do something like steal someone else's idea. He's supersmart. And also the arrogant thing is sort of an act. He's not like that all the time. He plays it up. For girls, you know? Girls like cocky guys."

"Do they?" she asked.

"They seem to like *him*." I shrugged.

"Well, he's very good-looking," she said. I felt a pang of jealousy at the words. "But not my type," she added quickly. She paused and gave me a look. "Not everyone finds arrogance attractive."

"Luckily for you, I'm extremely modest."

"I could tell."

"And handsome and charming and funny, of course."

"Of course," she said. "Are you guys close?"

"Me and Lucien?"

"Yeah."

"Yeah," I said. "I mean, we're roommates. He's one of my better friends."

Her mouth dropped open in shock. "Oh my God. I had no idea. I'm so sorry. I didn't mean to speak badly of your friend."

"Oh, don't worry. Like you said, you don't know him well."

"Ugh. I shouldn't have called him shady. I don't know why I said that. I'm a little drunk. You won't tell him, will you?"

"Oh, I'm telling him the second this conversation finishes."

"Please don't!"

I laughed. "Relax. My lips are sealed."

"Is Lucien the one who came up with *Atlas*?"

"Yeah."

"Do you mind if I call you Christopher instead?" she asked.

"Sure," I said. The question implied a level of familiarity and intimacy that took me slightly by surprise. I smiled. "I'd like that."

"Okay, good. I think it suits you better. Atlas wasn't very intelligent, you know? He was always getting tricked and taken advantage of. You seem smarter than that."

"Thank you—I guess?"

"So, Christopher, what's your special talent? Everyone here has one. Wait. Let me guess. You're on the squash team."

I laughed. "No. Definitely not. Not even close. I don't think I've ever been within a hundred yards of a squash court."

"Tennis? Track?"

I shook my head.

"Not sports, then," she said. "Are you some sort of science genius? National Spelling Bee champion?"

I laughed. "Is that the vibe I'm giving off? King of the nerds? Yikes."

"That's not what I meant!"

"It sounds like that's exactly what you meant."

"I'm sorry," she said. "You just don't strike me as the football player type. That's a compliment, by the way."

"Well, it's a big jump from 'not a football player' to National Spelling Bee champion."

"Okay, what do you actually do?"

"I'm an artist," I said.

"Tortured or starving?"

"Tortured."

"The best kind," she said.

"What about you?"

"Neither tortured nor starving."

"I meant what are you good at?"

"You're not going to guess?"

I thought for a moment. Clearly, she must have some kind of specialty because she'd thought to ask me that question herself. I was fairly certain she wasn't an athlete because they tended to hang out together and travel in packs. I supposed she could be on a random team like sailing or track, but all the times I'd seen her around campus, she was never once wearing DHA sweats or any kind of team gear. Maybe she was a musician—a violinist or a pianist? I remembered that I'd seen her a couple times walking out of the Barker Center, which was next to my dorm and was home to the English department.

"I think you're some sort of writer," I said.

She cocked her head to the side and looked at me, her eyes brimming with curiosity. "Wait—how'd you know?"

"I have my ways," I said.

"Someone told you."

I shook my head. "When I told you my name, your first thought was Christopher Marlowe—a playwright. The only people with favorite playwrights are actors or writers," I said.

"Are you implying I'm not attractive enough to be an actress?"

"Your words, not mine," I said. The second the words came out of my mouth, I regretted them. She gasped and put her hand over her mouth.

"Oh God," I said. "That was a joke. I'm so sorry."

"That was extremely rude."

"I'm so sorry. I was completely joking. It sounded funnier in my head. Dammit. And I was doing so well," I said.

"Were you?"

"I thought so."

"Your words, not mine," she said.

"What I meant to say was . . ."

"Yes?"

". . . an actress would have dressed up as a character from a film, not a book."

"Good recovery."

"So what kind of writer are you?"

"A poet."

"I didn't realize they still had poets."

"They do."

"I thought it was one of those professions which had gone extinct, like philosophers. Or explorers."

"I think they still have those, too," she said.

"Are you sure?"

"Fairly sure."

"If you say so."

Just then the girl Harriet had been with earlier called out her name from across the room. "It appears I'm being summoned," said Harriet.

"I guess you better go, then."

"It was nice meeting you," she said. "If you happen to find Wilbur . . . please let me know."

"That sounds like something I'd need your number for."

"I suppose you're right," she said, removing a mitten to type her details into my phone.

"Harriet!" her friend called. "We're going."

"I must run," said Harriet, pressing the phone back into my hands. "Until next time."

CHAPTER 8

"Rise and shine, sweetheart."

My eyes cracked open and Lucien's figure swam into focus.

"It's noon," he said.

I groaned and rolled away from the light. My brain felt too big for my skull.

"Drink this. It will help." Something heavy struck me on the back.

I sat up and rubbed my eyes and discovered I was still wearing my tuxedo. A blue Gatorade nestled up to my left hip. I looked out the window and found a wet, gray autumn day.

"I feel terrible."

"You *look* terrible. Want some Advil?"

"I'll be all right."

"Good. Here, check this out. I found it in Widener this morning." Lucien tossed me a thin paperback. I collapsed back onto the bed. "It's too early for books."

"It's already noon. Look at the book."

"*The Forger's Apprentice: Life with the World's Most Notorious Artist.*" I looked up at Lucien.

"How cool is that? I've got more." Lucien handed me another book with the title *The Art Forger's Handbook*. I opened it to a random page and began to read:

Your ground laid, or better still uncovered, you will now be keen to prepare your paints, consider your medium and your oils and varnishes, select your brushes, all according to the methods employed by the Old Masters you aim to follow . . .

"I looked up the author of that book," said Lucien. "Eric Hebborn. He's dead now, but he was, like, a legend of the art world. Made millions forging van Dyck and Rubens. Look at this thing." He took the book from my hands and began flipping through it, pausing on certain pages to show me sections containing diagrams and what looked like recipes from a cookbook. "See? This thing reads like an instruction manual."

"You got this from Widener?" I asked.

"All of them. They had more, too. I thought these would be enough to get us started. We can divide them up. Get through them twice as fast." Lucien picked up another book and held it out to me. "Here, start with this one. Read it and tell me what you think. That's all I'm asking. Humor me. If it turns out that I'm crazy and this is a lot riskier than I think it is, we forget all about it. Cool? Come on, Atlas. Don't be a square."

I took the book and turned it over in my hands. I felt a familiar pressure to go along with him. I trusted him and I wanted him to like me as much as I liked him. My life had changed immeasurably ever since we'd become friends, but it still felt fragile, like it could be taken away at any point. I didn't want him to think I was a loser. And he had never led me astray before. "Cool," I said. "I'll begin this tonight."

That evening, after I'd finished working through an econ problem set, I left Lamont and returned to my room and started the first of the forgery books. I didn't dare read it in the library. I imagined hidden security cameras and nosy librarians raising eyebrows at the titles as they searched my backpack on my way out. Perhaps they would wave over the off-duty HUPD officer grabbing a coffee in the Lamont Café. Worse yet, maybe I would run into Marcus, book in hand, and have to explain to him why I was reading *The Art Forger's Handbook*. Fueled by this paranoia, I kept the books in a shoebox under my bed and only read them late at night with my door closed and the blinds drawn.

Over the next few weeks I went through half a dozen of Lucien's books. Some I skimmed. Others I read from cover to cover. What I hadn't anticipated was that I would find them fascinating. There were stories of self-taught painters whose forgeries ended up on the walls of famous museums, of billionaires who wasted entire fortunes on collections of fake art, of grifters and con men who tricked the world, and of experts made to look like fools.

The memoirs of convicted forgers were my favorite. They read like a strange hybrid of thriller and how-to manual. Most contained detailed descriptions of each forger's process and included practical things like lists of supplies and directions on how to acquire them. Much of it was common sense: Don't paint an exact replica of a well-known painting. (Instead, create a new painting in a certain artist's style.) Make sure you use period-appropriate pigments. Choose an artist who was both prolific and disorganized when it came to keeping records. Don't use a new canvas.

There were other, more technical elements to the process: steps taken to ensure the painting would pass a detailed forensic examination. For example, one has to ensure that varnish looks as it is supposed to when viewed under a black light. Older varnish appears a different shade of green from new varnish. There is no way to artificially age varnish, but one forger came up a solution that involved using a solvent to evaporate the varnish off of cheap old paintings and into paper towels. The paper towels, once wrung out, released the old varnish in liquid form, ready to be applied to the surface of his newly painted forgery.

One of the hardest things to figure out had to do with the length of time it takes oil paint to dry. Unlike acrylic paint, which dries in a matter of hours, oil paint takes far longer—months or even years—to dry and harden all the way through. As a result, an oil painting that is fifty years old looks very different from one painted a week ago.

I found the solution to this problem in a book about Han van Meegeren, a Dutch forger of Johannes Vermeer. Van Meegeren had figured out that if he mixed oils with a type of polymer glue, he could create oil paintings that dried completely within a few days. After a week the glue-paint mixture hardened to the point that the paintings could have been a century old. Evidently van Meegeren's solution had worked rather well because one of his forgeries, *The Supper at Emmaus* (1937), was so convincing that the world's leading expert on Vermeer had declared it Vermeer's greatest masterpiece.

Inspired by van Meegeren, I began experimenting with different glue-paint mixtures. The first few glues I tried were too powerful. They dried too fast and made the oil too viscous to paint with. I found a wood glue that worked well except that the glue's flaxen coloring gave my pigments a yellowish tint. Of all the different additives I tried, it was a bottle of clear Elmer's paste that worked the best. Within hours the combined glue-paint mixture was dry to the touch, and yet the glue was weak enough that it didn't feel as though I was painting with honey.

It was hard not to feel a sense of exhilaration while reading this stuff. Perhaps it was the thrill of discovering forbidden knowledge or the feeling of being let in on a secret. It was intellectually thrilling, too, a game of wits. The more I read, the more I was drawn in.

Lucien felt the same way. While I was interested in the technical and artistic ingenuity of the forgers themselves, Lucien was more taken with the layers of complexity and planning that went into the broader con. And in one another we found a natural partner to share and discuss the things we read about. In the way that some young men bond over their shared obsession with comic books or football, we began to develop a close friendship through our interest in the underworld of art crime. It wasn't long before we were texting each other throughout the day with thoughts and ideas—interesting things we had read about. In the evenings we would talk through hypothetical plans, identifying the strengths and weaknesses of differing strategies.

Lucien was particularly taken with the story of a man who had fabricated provenance for his forgeries by inserting fake documents into the archive of the Tate. He had realized that museum security was only concerned with items being stolen *out* of the archive and paid no attention to what people brought in with them. By adding his own documents to the files, he corrupted the very system of records used to verify provenance and hijacked the reputation of one of Britain's foremost institutions in order to lend credibility to his fakes. Lucien thought this was genius.

Our discussions had the feel of one of those after-dinner conversations when people try to plan the perfect crime. We were talking about forgeries, but we may as well have been discussing a plan to rob a bank or get away with a murder. It was all hypothetical. At least, to me it was. It was an intellectual exercise—a game.

It was also a chance for me to spend time with Lucien—or, rather, a reason for him to want to spend time with me. It was *our* project. And I didn't want it to end.

I reminded myself that Lucien had said we could drop the plan the second it seemed too risky. I was sure he would get cold feet in the end. Or that we would discover an obstacle so insurmountable the only choice was to give up. But as the days went by, I realized that he had been right all along. The plan wasn't crazy. It wasn't impossible. It began to dawn on me that we might actually go through with it.

In my research, what had surprised me more than anything was how even the most careless and incompetent forgers were able to enjoy years of success before they were caught. A few were highly skilled artists with formal technical training. But others were self-taught amateurs who'd figured it out on their own. One guy relied on custom stencils of birds to forge Audubon paintings, using what was effectively a paint-by-numbers system. Another spent years using regular house paint to create fakes he sold as oil paintings by Chagall and Giacometti. Both of these men produced hundreds of forgeries that sold for millions of dollars. They weren't careful. There was nothing about their approach that could be described as sophisticated or thoughtful. They didn't spread their risk geographically. Instead, they saturated their local market with a sudden influx of works by the same artist. They didn't use fake identities or numbered bank accounts. They relied on erratic accomplices with criminal records and drug problems. They made sloppy mistake after sloppy mistake. And yet both escaped detection for more than a decade.

Lucien noticed this as well. "If these idiots got away with it for so long, we'll be golden," he said. "Also, listen to this: this one chap in Germany sold fourteen forgeries for a combined forty-five million euros . . . and he got three years! Three years for selling fifty mil of fake Légers and van Dongens! Mate, you get a longer sentence for selling weed! The powers that be clearly do not give a shit about art forgery."

"I know," I said. "Why does it feel like no one is even looking for these guys?"

"Because they're not. Think about it. How would you even go about policing it if you wanted to? The market is so opaque that no one even knows who they're dealing with half the time. How can a central authority have a clear picture of what is going on in a market when half the transactions are private, off-the-books deals between billionaires and shell corporations? You can't see patterns if you don't have the whole picture. And besides, cops have more important shit to worry about, collectors don't have a clue what they're doing, and the middlemen—the auction houses, the art advisors, what have you—they're making money off transactions. They don't care if the art is real as long as the money is." He exhaled and took in a long, deep breath. "By the way," he said, "I've thought of the perfect cover story for when we sell the paintings. I was thinking I could pretend to be from a wealthy Boston family. One of those über-WASP clans. Like a Lowell or a Lodge. I'll tell them the painting is a family heirloom I've just inherited."

The idea felt more elaborate than it needed to be.

"Why a Boston family? You don't sound like you're from here."

"Oh, come on. I can pull off the accent."

"What if it doesn't sound right?"

"I can handle it."

"But why not say you're British? Or European or something?" I asked.

"Use your brain, mate. Why would someone from London fly all the way to Boston to sell his dead grandmother's painting? Doesn't make any sense. Trust me, I can do the accent. I'll borrow a bunch of clothes from Gardner. All these preppy New Englanders wear the same shit."

As Lucien practiced passing himself off as a Bostonian, I refined my ability to imitate Camoin. I started with a copy of a well-known piece that was a fine example of his style. Marcus found me working on it one afternoon and expressed his concern that I seemed to be treading water.

"There are steps forwards and steps backwards. And then there's staying in the same place. That's the most dangerous one," he said. "No matter what, you have to keep moving, trying new things, experimenting. You can't get caught standing still. That leads to stagnation. And stagnation leads to depression. And then you're fucked. I can tell you that from experience."

"How so?"

"You get stuck in the mud feeling like you're not making any progress, so you lose your motivation and you start to feel worthless 'cause you don't even want to paint anymore. And it's a spiral down. So keep moving! Finish this up, and on to the next."

"Okay. I just like Camoin's effect with water," I said, "the way it seems to move on the canvas. He makes it look alive. I have this idea for a new piece and I want to work that in."

"Good. Great. Excellent. Just remember what I told you," said

Marcus. He started to walk away but then snapped his fingers and turned around. "Hey, Chris, one more thing."

"Yeah?"

"December twenty-ninth. You have plans?"

"I don't think so."

"They asked me to give a talk at the Morgan Library down in Manhattan. They're putting on an exhibit of Afro-Caribbean art and want me to speak at the opening. You should come. I'm sure they'll have some big, fancy dinner with all the art world fat cats—you know, the good and the great, and so on."

"Awesome. I'd love to go. How's your speech?"

"Nonexistent," said Marcus. "Time to go change that."

Lucien had chosen well with his suggestion of Charles Camoin. His works sold for enough to make the risk worthwhile but not enough to attract undue attention. Another plus was his productivity. Camoin was supposed to have painted more than three thousand works of art during his lifetime, and the fate of most of those paintings was unknown. Camoin had destroyed a large number himself during severe episodes of depression that visited him periodically throughout his life. The rest were simply unaccounted for. No one had ever bothered to commission a catalogue raisonné detailing all the known works of Charles Camoin. This meant no one knew for certain everything Camoin had produced. There were likely hundreds of works that had sat in private collections for decades, hidden from public view. That a few would begin turning up for sale decades after his death was nothing short of a certainty.

The final aspect of my preparation was to read up on Camoin's life and select the period of his career I wished to draw from. I came across a biography in the Fine Arts Library containing translated passages from his diaries and letters. Every night before I went to sleep, I read a few entries in order to understand the way his mind worked. His diary entries veered from morose and self-pitying to exuberant and prideful. One day he would appear to be on top of the world, and the next he would retreat into apathy that verged on nihilism. I picked up on notes of envy in his correspondence with his close friend, Matisse, and noticed that the only artists he ever praised were those that died long ago. As for artists of his own generation, Camoin tended to qualify their success in a manner that suggested he took it as a personal slight.

His most stable period seemed to come in the last decade of his life. Following the end of the Second World War, Camoin rented a studio overlooking the harbor in Saint-Tropez. He must have been fond of the view from his window, because during his stay he produced dozens of paintings of the harbor. The Saint-Tropez paintings were all quite similar to one another. Many featured the same boats in identical settings at different times of day. I went to the Sotheby's website and discovered that a few in that genre had sold for around $30,000 at auction. It was the kind of number Lucien and I had kicked around as a reasonable goal during our late-night walks to discuss the plan.

Out of the entire Saint-Tropez canon, my favorite painting was a scene of the harbor at sunset. Three boats, no more than hazy specters with masts, stood in the foreground, melting into the emerald ocean while the sun sank beneath the dark blue ridge of the horizon, bleeding yellow, then orange across a periwinkle sky. I decided to paint a piece in a similar vein.

The next day I told Lucien I was ready to start.

"Great. Do you need anything?"

"A couple of canvases from the '40s or '50s. Also frames."

"Where do I get those?" Lucien asked.

"Antique shops, secondhand stores, yard sales," I replied. "They shouldn't be too hard to find. We just need to find some shitty old paintings. I'm going to strip the paint off, so as long as it's old, I can make it work."

Lucien discovered a junk store in Porter Square with a large stock of old, kitschy paintings. The owner sold him four for a grand total of $75. It was money well spent. The old canvases were crucial because of craquelure. *Craquelure* is a term used to describe the network of cracks that develop in a canvas's surface over a period of many years. It happens because canvases expand and contract with changes in temperature and humidity. The only way to replicate craquelure in a convincing manner is to paint over an older canvas already displaying the effects of it. Craquelure was evident on all of the paintings Lucien bought, and, thanks to my books, I knew the pattern existed not only in the top layer of paint, but also in the underlying layer of gesso. As long as I carefully cleaned away the original paint layer while leaving the gesso undisturbed, I would be left with several "brand-new" sixty-year-old canvases. The unique pattern of cracks would still be present in the gesso and would telegraph through to the new layers of paint I added on top. As the oil dried, the cracks would form just as they had in the original.

Once I had the old canvases in my possession, I began the task of removing the original artwork. This was trickier than I'd expected. After half a century, oil paint hardens to the point where it becomes impervious to alcohol and turpentine. The problem was that any solvent strong enough to remove fifty-year-old oil paint would also remove the gesso underneath. Without the gesso there would be no craquelure, presenting me with a tricky problem. I got around it by following a technique I found in *The Art Forger's Handbook*. I took two canvases and covered them with paper towels soaked in acetone. Acetone isn't a particularly strong solvent and is usually only good for removing a painting's varnish. But the paper towels prevented the acetone from evaporating, and after about six hours the paint underneath had totally dissolved, leaving me with two blank canvases and their original layers of gesso.

It took me a little over two weeks to finish the painting. I worked on it every evening in my studio and didn't go out to parties at all. The timing wasn't great. I wanted to see Harriet again and hoped to run into her on a night out, but Lucien made me promise I wouldn't go out until the painting was done. To give me more time to paint, he even offered to do most of my homework for me. He summarized all the readings for my freshman seminar and even wrote an eight-page essay for my Expos class analyzing Dostoevsky's exploration of morality and redemption in *Crime and Punishment*. I was torn between delight and exasperation when the paper was returned with an A and a comment from my teacher saying it was the best piece of work I'd turned in all year.

One night Marcus stopped by my studio unannounced. I was working on the Camoin and had my easel set up facing away from the door, so I didn't see him come in.

"What's this?"

"Jesus, Marcus. You almost gave me a heart attack."

"Sorry. I should have knocked." He came closer and peered at the canvas over my shoulder. I felt a sudden shot of panic as I realized he might figure out what I was up to.

"Hey, can I show you something?" I asked, trying to draw his attention away.

"Is this one of yours?" Marcus asked, still staring at the painting.

"Oh, that's nothing. I was just messing around."

"Chris, this is a straight imitation. The composition, the aesthetic, the perspective—it's all classic Camoin."

"You think so?"

"No. I know so."

"I guess I was trying to do a fresh take on his style."

"It's too close. I wouldn't even call this derivative. This is a straight copy. There's no originality here." Marcus stared at the canvas and frowned. He dabbed the wet paint with his index finger and rubbed his finger against his thumb. Then he lifted his hand to his nose and sniffed the paint. I felt my chest tighten and I held my breath. "What paints you been using?" He asked.

"Oh, just the usual—Gamblin," I said. "I did try mixing my own oils as like an experiment, but I sort of gave up with that. It didn't come out well."

"Huh," said Marcus. "You know what? Let's scrap this," he said, pointing to the Camoin. "You've been doing too much copying lately. Let's get you back working on some original pieces."

"Okay, if you think that makes sense."

"Right now you ought to be trying to figure yourself out. You've got this vast possibility of what you can be, and this time should be about tapping into that and finding your voice. What we've been doing before—that was just to work on your technical skills. Once it starts bleeding over to the creative side, that's when it's time to move on."

Once he was gone, I breathed a sigh of relief. He hadn't guessed at the truth. But I couldn't risk him finding me working on it again. I told Lucien what had happened.

"How much do you have left to do?"

"Not much. I'm finding it tough to do an hour here, an hour there. I'd work much faster if I had a big block of time to work uninterrupted."

Lucien snapped his fingers. "Thanksgiving," he said. "Why don't you stay here over Thanksgiving and do it then? Campus will be a total ghost town."

"I'm supposed to go home for Thanksgiving."

"So? Call your mum and make up some reason you have to stay on campus. I'll stay with you. We'll make a time of it."

"I don't know. I kind of have this tradition with my mom. We don't do the normal turkey thing. We always go to this diner by my house and get chocolate chip pancakes. We've been doing it for as long as I can remember. It was always this big treat when I was a kid. She'll be crushed if I'm not there. Besides, aren't you supposed to fly back to Europe for Thanksgiving?"

Lucien waved a hand dismissively. "I'll change my flights. It's fine. I'm going home for the Christmas holidays anyway. And my parents are away this week." He could see my reluctance and he continued to press. "Come on," he said. "We'll do our own Thanksgiving. We'll get a turkey, a case of champagne. Kane will be here. I bet we can wrangle up some girls. It'll be a laugh, mate."

"Maybe. I don't know. It'll be a big deal if I miss this. My mom will be torn up."

"It's going to be *fine*, Atlas. Jesus. It's just one Thanksgiving. Who cares? Tell your mum you have to study for finals. Just make some shit up. She'll understand."

I gave in and I agreed to tell my mom later. But evening came, and I couldn't bring myself to call her. She would try to hide her disappointment, which would make it even worse. I put it off for a day and then two. Finally, on the day before we were supposed to leave for Thanksgiving, I called. After I told her, there was a long silence.

"Chris, I don't understand. What do you mean you're not coming home?"

"We have finals coming up. I wish I could come home, but I need to stay here and study."

"Is everything okay? Why don't you bring your books home? You can study in your bedroom like before."

"Mom, I'm sorry but I can't."

"Maybe then I will come to Boston and we can have dinner together. I will bring you some things from home—whatever you need."

"How would you even get here?"

"I will take the bus," she said.

"Mom, don't do that. I'll be home in a few weeks. It's almost the end of the semester. I just have to get through finals and then I'll be home for a month."

"*Miláčku*, what is going on? Why are you being like this? You were never like this before."

"I'm sorry. We have a lot of work here and everyone's so smart. It's a lot of pressure. I just want to do well."

"Me—I am also sorry," she said. "I am sorry that my son doesn't tell me these things."

For all his talk about how fun it would be to spend Thanksgiving on campus, in the end, Lucien didn't stick around. He got a last-minute invite to stay with a friend in New York City. He claimed it was an invitation he couldn't turn down. On Wednesday afternoon he waved goodbye and climbed in a cab headed for the train station.

That night I wasn't able to sleep. I kept imagining my mom sitting alone on Thanksgiving. Around one in the morning I gave up trying to sleep, dressed, and walked to the Carpenter Center and painted until dawn. I finished as the sun was coming up. Exhausted and delirious, I applied a light coat of varnish and brought the painting back to my room, where I left it to dry under the small heat lamp Lucien had bought to speed up the process. Then I packed a bag and caught the T to South Station and boarded a bus to Baltimore. I slept most of the eight-hour journey, but I made it home in time to catch my mom as she was leaving for the diner.

CHAPTER 9

The man in the leather jacket was watching us. I was sure of it. I could see him over Lucien's shoulder, eyeing us from his table by the window. He couldn't hear our conversation, could he?

It was a cold day in the second week of December and there was a foot of snow on the ground. We were sitting at the Starbucks on Newbury Street, across from the Winslow Gallery.

"Let's run through the plan one more time." Lucien spoke with an accent that wasn't his. It was a version of Gardner's, borrowed for the occasion. He was dressed like Gardner, too, in khakis and boots from L.L.Bean with a Groton sweatshirt beneath a dark green Barbour. A pair of horn-rimmed tortoiseshell glasses completed the look.

"Dude," I said, hushing him, "not so loud." I reached a hand down and felt the duffel bag at my feet. It was still there, the painting inside.

Lucien rolled his eyes. "Relax."

"There's a guy behind you. He keeps looking at us."

"So what?"

"What if he's watching us?"

"Can you be serious, please?"

"I *am* being serious."

"No one's watching us."

"Lucien, I can see him. He's doing it right now."

"Which guy?"

"Don't look," I said. "He's sitting right behind you. The guy with the leather jacket."

Lucien pretended to stretch, twisting his spine one way and then the other, stealing a glance behind.

He turned back around, exasperated. "That's a random fucking tourist, Atlas."

"You don't know that," I said.

"Look at him. He's wearing a shirt that says WICKED SMAAHT on it. Who do you think he works for? The CIA? FBI? Why would anyone be watching us? We haven't even done anything yet." Lucien combed his fingers through his hair, pushing it back and to the side. "Now, tell me the plan."

"We don't have to go through the plan again. I know it."

"Great. I want to hear it."

"What if he works at the gallery?"

"Are we still talking about this? He's a fucking tourist, Atlas," said Lucien. "Just chill. Take a goddamn breath. And that's enough coffee. You're too wired. Gimme that."

As Lucien went to toss out the remainder of my coffee, I reached again for the bag, tracing the edges of the painting's frame with my fingers, making certain it was still there.

"I'm fucking nervous, man," I said when Lucien sat back down.

He took off his glasses and gave me a cold look. "I told you that you didn't have to come," he said. His words were measured and clipped. "I said I would handle it, and it was fine for you to stay behind. But you insisted on coming."

"We're in this together, I wasn't gonna—"

Lucien held up a finger and silenced me.

"I want to be clear about this," he said. "If you're going to freak out in there, then you need to go home. Right now. If you think you can handle this like a grown-up, then shut the fuck up and do what we discussed. It's your decision."

Lucien put his glasses back on and leaned back in his chair, arms crossed. He stared at me without saying anything. His jaw was clenched, his lips pressed tightly together. He cleared his throat.

"In thirty seconds I'm going to walk across the street to that gallery. You can either come with me or you can go home. It's up to you."

Lucien slid his chair back, pulled the bag out from under the table, and made for the door. I followed him. I wasn't any less afraid, but I didn't want him to know that.

The Winslow Gallery was a Boston institution. Founded in the 1790s, it was the oldest art gallery in Massachusetts, and the only one in Boston to have any true national standing. But according to an article in *The Boston Globe*, Winslow had been struggling badly since an ill-fated attempt to expand internationally had collided with the financial crisis.

That was one of the reasons Lucien selected it. I'd suggested the smaller and newer Rothmere Gallery. I suspected their dealers wouldn't be as familiar with impressionist works and thus might be easier to trick than the more experienced handlers at Winslow. Lucien dismissed the suggestion out of hand.

"That's exactly why we should avoid Rothmere and target a place like Winslow. Rothmere does contemporary. Those guys know fuck all about impressionist art. They've probably never even heard of Camoin. There's no chance they're going to buy a painting they don't know how to value."

"Fair enough. But can't we find somewhere less legit than Winslow? These guys are the best in Boston."

"No. This is the plan and we're sticking to it. Two reasons. Number one, they're on the verge of closing down. They need cash. Badly. If we dangle a bargain in front of their faces, something they can flip for easy money, they'll snap it up. They'll be thinking about the money, not the painting."

"What's the second reason?"

"Impressionism is their wheelhouse. They're experts, right?"

"Isn't that the issue?"

"No. That's the beauty of it. First of all, they're not experts. They're salesmen—salesmen who consider themselves experts. And that means they'll be overconfident. They'll trust their eye. They'll put too much stock in their own snap judgment, and they won't bother calling someone in for a second opinion."

"But—"

"It's all about vanity," Lucien said. "That's the secret. You have to play to their vanity. Let them believe they're the smartest person in the room. They already suspect that about themselves. So encourage it. When people start believing they're the shit, that's when they let their guard down. Hubris. Arrogance. Whatever you want to call it. That's why rich people get conned so often. Look at Madoff. Rich people think they're too smart to be conned. All you have to do is pump up their ego until they let their guard down. And the second they do, you make your move. Before they've even realized it, the wax has melted off their wings and they're crashing back down to earth."

A chime sounded as we entered the gallery. On the walls hung portraits and seascapes dating from the time when Massachusetts was a colony. There was a fireplace on one wall. A large round wooden table dominated the center of the room.

A dour, balding version of Mister Rogers emerged from a door in the back. He was thin and wore a maroon cardigan with dress pants. A pair of reading glasses dangled from a strap around his neck, and a frown was fixed on his face.

"Yes?" It was clear from the man's voice that he really meant: *What do you want?*

"Hi there. Good afternoon, sir," Lucien said in a perfect imitation of Gardner's voice.

"If you're looking for a bathroom, I suggest you try the Starbucks across the street."

"Oh no. That's not why we're here. I've got a painting I was hoping to ask you about."

"Did you make an appointment?"

"I don't think so, I mean—"

"Did you make appointment or not? It's a simple question."

"I didn't realize I needed one. I'm sorry, sir. My grandmother just passed away." Lucien unzipped the bag and produced the painting. "She left me this. I was wondering if you might take a look."

The man looked at the painting and frowned again. He took it from Lucien and peered closely at the frame. Then he flipped it over and examined the back of the painting. He pulled out a magnifying glass and began working his way over the entire thing.

I meandered around the room, texting and pretending to check out the paintings on the wall, playing the role of the bored best friend.

The man turned back to Lucien. "Where did you say you got this?"

"My grandmother left it to me."

"Did it come with any documents?"

"Documents?"

"Provenance documents. Receipts, bills of sale, certificates of authenticity, and so on."

"Oh, there was this." Lucien took a plastic folder out of the duffel bag and withdrew a browned and crinkled sheet of paper.

At the same antique store where he'd picked up the frames, Lucien had also bought an old typewriter that he used to draft a record of sale.

Le Port de Saint-Tropez, à l'aube, et le Port de Saint-Tropez, au crépuscule, from M. Camoin to Capt. H. Lyman, witnessed by Mme. Camoin.

He wrote a signature above each of the three names (including a perfect forgery of Camoin's signature) and dated it 24 June, 1947. I'd followed him down to the kitchen in the Greenough basement and watched as he poured tea on the paper and then placed it on a baking tray in the oven. After about ten minutes he took it out and tore one of the corners and then folded it up and put it in his pocket.

"My granddad bought it for her in France. After the war. He was an infantry officer."

"Do you mind if I take this all to the back for a moment?" the man said. "I want to have a colleague take a look."

"Dude, we have to go. Our train leaves in thirty minutes. Can't you do this in New York?" I interrupted. Lucien had told me to start making a fuss if this happened.

"How long do you think it will take?" asked Lucien.

"Fifteen minutes," said the man.

"We can't miss this train," I said. "Everything else was sold out until, like, nine."

"Maybe I'll take it down to New York," Lucien said to me. He looked at his watch. "We're already cutting it close . . . I'm sure we could find a place down there to do this. Doesn't Alison work at a gallery?"

"Yeah, take it to her."

"Sorry, sir. I don't think we have time. Thanks for taking a look, though."

"Hold on, hold on," the man said. His eyes scanned the painting, checking it for imperfections. "How much were you planning to ask?"

Lucien shrugged. "Whatever you think is fair. A friend of mine is an art history major and she thought it might be worth fifteen thousand dollars."

The man looked to the ceiling and pretended to run numbers in his head. He sucked his teeth loudly. "I can't do fifteen," he said. "What about twelve?"

"Okay," Lucien said. "I think I'm going to take it to New York and see if I can get a better offer."

I stared at Lucien, horrified he had just turned down $12,000.

"Hold on, now," the man said. "I'll tell you what. I'll give you thirteen thousand. Will you take a check?"

"Thirteen?" Lucien asked.

The man nodded.

"I'll take thirteen if it's cash."

"Cash is fine. I'll just need a few moments to retrieve it from the safe."

I tried to make eye contact with Lucien, but he ignored me. I sat down on an antique chair in the corner, took out my phone, and stared at the screen, pretending everything was normal. A minute later the man returned, clutching a clipboard and a manila envelope. He handed the envelope to Lucien.

"That's it?" Lucien asked.

"Thirteen thousand. You can count it if you want. I need you to print your name here, sign here, initial there, and then sign and date the bottom." Lucien passed me the envelope as he filled out the form under the name *Stuart Lyman*. I looked inside the unsealed envelope.

The man smiled and stuck out his hand. "Have fun in New York, boys. Here's my card. If you have any other paintings, you know where to come."

As we turned for the exit, Lucien shot me a look that said lock it up. He skipped down the gallery's steps, hailed a cab, and told him to take us to Harvard Square.

"Holy shit," I said, punching him in the arm. "Holy shit. Thirteen grand? Are you kidding me?"

Lucien let loose a whoop that almost gave our taxi driver a heart attack. "I told you we could do it!"

"We did it. We fucking did it. That was unreal!"

Lucien grinned. "How was my accent? Pretty solid, right?"

"You nailed it."

"Thirteen grand . . . Okay, let's split ten up the middle. So five each. I'll take two more for the money I lent you. That leaves us a thousand to cover future expenses."

"Future expenses?" I asked.

"Yeah, for the next time."

"What next time?"

"The next painting, of course," Lucien said.

"But we're done."

"Oh, come on, Atlas. You saw how easy that was."

"We're quitting while we're ahead. I'm good with five grand. This is enough. It's *more* than enough."

"You've got to be joking. This is, like, free money. He practically begged us to take it."

I noticed the cabdriver had turned down the radio and appeared to be listening to our conversation.

"Let's talk about it later," I said. "Not here."

As we rolled to a stop at a red light, an idea popped into Lucien's head.

"Hey, what are you doing on the twenty-ninth?" he asked.

Why did that date sound familiar? I couldn't remember. "I don't know," I said. "Nothing, I guess."

"It's Grace's deb ball that night. She's given me a couple invites. Do you want to come? It's in New York at the Waldorf."

Grace was Lucien's new girlfriend. He'd met her during a trip to New York City with Xander earlier in the fall. She was a freshman at Columbia and the daughter of a finance billionaire. I had yet to meet her, but I had heard plenty about her from others. Most of them described her as a socialite. Lucien had once shown me an article about her on the *Vanity Fair* website.

"What's a deb ball?" I asked.

"Debutante ball. You know—it's like where girls get presented to society or whatever."

I had no idea what Lucien was talking about.

"It's a party, all right? Black tie. New York City. It's going to be epic," said Lucien. "Zola's coming. I was going invite Gardner, too. But why don't you come instead?"

The way he asked the question caught me off guard. Even

though Lucien and I had grown closer over the last two months, I still considered myself something of a lesser friend. Zola and Gardner were his two best friends; everyone knew that. But here he was inviting me to something over Gardner. I felt a warming, selfish sense of pride. And then I remembered that the twenty-ninth was the date of Marcus's talk at the Morgan Library.

"That sounds awesome," I heard myself saying. What would I tell Marcus? I guess I could figure that out later.

"Good man!" Lucien said. "It'll be an enormous night."

"What about Gardner?"

"Oh, it's fine. I didn't invite him yet."

"You sure?"

"Hundred percent. Gardner said he always goes to Palm Beach for New Year's, anyway." Lucien grinned and held up the envelope of cash. "In the meantime . . . we need to celebrate." He rapped on the plexiglass window separating us from the cabdriver. "Hey, buddy? Slight change of plans. We'd like to go to South Station."

The cabdriver grunted in response and pulled into the turning lane.

"Why are we going to South Station?" I asked, suddenly concerned.

"Because that's where they keep the trains. We're going to New York, baby."

"No, no, no. Lucien, I can't go to New York. I've got a final on Monday."

"Relax, mate. So do I. We'll be fine. Let's go out with Grace and her friends in the city tonight. We'll grab the first train back tomorrow morning and you'll be in Lamont by lunchtime. You remember Grace's friend, Daniella?" Lucien asked. "The one I showed you on Facebook. Apparently, she has a thing for you."

"She does? How does she even know who I am?"

Lucien winked. "Let's just say someone put in a good word. You're welcome."

An hour later I was sitting next to Lucien in the first-class cabin of the Acela Express to Penn Station. Outside the window, a fine mist of snow and ice kicked up from the tracks.

CHAPTER 10

"I'm confused." Marcus's voice crackled on the line. The connection was poor. I didn't catch what he said next.

"Sorry, Marcus, you cut out. Can you hear me?"

"I can hear you just fine, Chris," he said, the line now clear and crisp. "So, what's the problem? I put this on your radar more than six weeks ago, well before Thanksgiving. You said you were all good. I sent you the invite, the guest list. Not a peep. And now you call me the day before and tell me you cannot make it anymore? I mean . . . Chris, man. Come on, now. You serious?"

"I know, I know. I messed up. I'm sorry. I thought it was next week. I had the date wrong."

"Next week? You mean in January? When I never said anything but December? Be real with me, Chris. What's the problem? Is this a money thing? I coulda found someone to put you up."

"It's not that."

"Then what? I had to ask a big favor to get you an invite. Have you seen the guest list? Adam Weinberg, Glenn Lowry, David Zwirner, the director of the New York Academy. I even asked Erick and April to meet us for a drink beforehand so I could introduce you. Jesus, boy. What are you thinking?"

Knowing Marcus would react this way, I'd put off the phone call for weeks. It wasn't a mature way to handle it. But every day for two weeks I'd woken up and decided to kick the can down the road a little further. And then, finally, I had run out of time.

"I'm really sorry. I don't know what to tell you. I put it in my calendar wrong and then something else came up and I only realized today that there was a conflict."

"Don't give me that nonsense. I can tell when you're not being straight with me. What's the conflict? What could possibly be more important?"

"Well, the thing is—" I began, but he cut me off.

"That was a rhetorical question, Christopher," he snapped. "Look, if you don't want to go, fine. Don't give me this primary school bullshit of dropping out the day before with a totally make-believe excuse. What am I supposed to tell Erick and April? Back home we had a saying: 'You can tell the tree by the fruit.' Well, you're doing the tree a real disservice. Your mum raised you better than this." With that, Marcus stopped abruptly. I realized he expected me to fill the resulting silence. "Well?" he asked.

"Marcus, I mean . . . ," I said, trailing off as I tried to think of what to say next. "I don't know. Look, I'm sorry. I fucked up, okay?"

"Not good enough. I'll talk to you later."

I heard a click as the line went dead. I hung up the phone feeling ashamed and guilty but also relieved that it was over. I knew he was right. But part of me didn't care. I'd spent my whole life doing the smart thing, the responsible thing, the thing I was supposed to do. And I was tired of it. I wanted to have some fun. Was that really so awful?

A short burst of shrill squawks cut through the air, rattling my eardrums. I groaned. The parakeets had woken up. They were my mom's new pets, and they seemed to resent my presence. There were two of them, yellow Australian parakeets, that she kept in a cage in the kitchen. One was named Kiki, the other Ludo. I couldn't tell them apart. I'd been surprised to find the birds on my return home from school. We'd never owned any pets. Like most kids, I'd wanted a dog when I was younger, but my mom always vetoed the idea. She didn't have time to look after a dog or the money to pay for one. When I asked her about the birds, she told me she'd bought them because she hated how quiet the apartment had become since I left. She'd thought having the birds would cheer her up and make the apartment feel a little more alive. But now she said she regretted buying them. It made her sad to see them cooped up, trapped without enough room to fly. She wanted to set them free, but she knew if she did, they would die because they'd spent their whole lives in captivity. She had no choice but to keep them in their small cage on the kitchen counter.

I could tell she was happy to have me home, and she seemed more relaxed than when I'd left for school. Back then she'd been on edge. The situation with Orcus Property Management had hung over us—a constant point of stress. She didn't even like checking the mail because she was afraid of discovering a new summons.

She took a whole week off from work so that we could spend time together. One afternoon we went to a skating rink. Another we spent at the aquarium. It was a bit strange because we hadn't really done that sort of stuff when I was younger. She worked on the weekends. And when she got home from work she was tired and her feet hurt and she went to bed early. It made me kind of sad to think about all the things we could have done if she hadn't had to work all the time or if my dad had been around to help out.

The day after Christmas we saw the Moscow Ballet perform *The Nutcracker* at the Hippodrome. The tickets were my Christmas gift to her. She cried when she saw them. She'd studied ballet in her youth at the State Conservatory in Prague, even landing a small role in the Czech National Ballet's production of *The Nutcracker* at the Smetana Theatre. But at thirteen she was dismissed from the school due to concerns over her height and weight. She had never lost her love of dancing, though, and she had often remarked to me how much she wished she could take me to see the ballet at the Hippodrome. But the tickets had always been too expensive and money too tight to justify the expense.

At first, she tried to reject the gift. She pushed the tickets back into my hands and told me to return them. She scolded me for spending so much on her. Where had I gotten the money? Didn't I need it for books? To pay my cell phone bill? What about for a winter jacket? Wasn't mine getting old? We could go to Modell's and a pick out a nice, warm Carhartt.

I didn't need a new jacket, I told her. And besides, I couldn't return the tickets anyway. I followed this lie with another, making up a story about how arts students could get discounted tickets to plays and shows through Harvard's Office of Student Services. She was quiet as she considered this new information. And then she nodded and smiled. I wasn't sure that she believed me. But she didn't ask any more questions, either.

She did have questions about the debutante ball.

"It's like prom but for people who live in New York City," I told her.

"Who is this girl? How do you know her?"

"She's Lucien's girlfriend. They've been dating for a few months."

"But New York is so far. Where will you stay?"

"Lucien said I could stay with him."

"His parents, they live there?"

"He has a hotel room."

"So not with his parents?"

"I don't think so."

"And what would you wear? Do you have clothes for this? It sounds very fancy."

"Lucien has an extra tuxedo. He said I could borrow it for the night."

"Lucien, Lucien, Lucien. I hear so much about this boy."

I showed her an article about the ball I'd found in *The New York Times*. She was taken aback by what she read. The article mentioned Kennedys and Rockefellers. One debutante was the granddaughter of a sitting U.S. senator; another was the daughter of the former ambassador to France. These were names and titles that meant something to my mom. All of a sudden she became quite proud that I'd been invited. She asked me to take photos and had me print a copy of the article to show my aunt.

The day of the party I took a bus up to New York City. I tried to sleep but the man behind me spent the first hour chatting to a friend on speakerphone. When we hit traffic, we lurched forward with sudden, violent jerks that made me feel sick. I closed my eyes and imagined myself somewhere else.

When I opened my eyes again, we were in New York City. I figured the bus would drop us off at Penn Station or some other major terminal, but instead we came to a sudden halt outside a foot massage parlor. There was no announcement, no official proclamation that we'd arrived at our final destination. The driver simply parked, opened the door, and got off. I emerged from the bus eager to escape, feeling half-drugged by the captive, stale air. I hailed a yellow cab and asked the driver to take me to the Waldorf.

It was late afternoon and the day was slipping into darkness. I rode with the window down, drinking in the chilly winter air, letting it whip over my face like a cold, cleansing stream. As we traveled through Manhattan, I watched the cityscape transition from squat tenements crowded together to wide avenues and soaring towers of concrete, steel, and glass.

I spotted the Waldorf from several blocks away. It was all done up for Christmas with tinseled garlands and strings of white lights. Giant gold wreaths, six feet in diameter, were fixed to the tall windows on the second floor. At the base of the hotel a warm orange glow emanated from an overhanging canopy, and doormen welcomed guests as they shuttled in through revolving doors.

I entered the hotel and went up a marble staircase to the lobby. I called Lucien and told him I'd arrived. He gave a room number on the twenty-seventh floor and said to come up.

"This is absurd," I said, looking around the suite. "Check out the bathroom! How much do you think this room cost?"

Lucien shrugged. "Grace's parents are paying for it. I told you tonight was going to be good fun."

"Where's Grace?"

"Down the hall, getting ready. She's in Marilyn Monroe's old suite," Lucien said. I must have looked incredulous. He laughed. "Room 2728. Look it up. Zola's here, by the way. He's just next door."

"Oh, sick. Let's see if he wants to grab a drink."

"There's a bar in the lobby. Get Zola. I'll be right down."

From our table at the bar I had a good view of the comings and goings in the hotel's busy lobby. I'd always thought of a lobby as a place that people passed through on their way to somewhere else, a segue between the hotel and the outside world. But here I noticed that very few people walked straight through the lobby without stopping at least once. Some ran into friends and became drawn into conversations. Others stopped to sit down and rest. People entered and then seemed to linger, hovering around the room like bees around a hive.

I saw a lot of kids our age. I noticed how similar many of them looked. They all had fresh tans and perfectly styled hair and wore neat, pressed clothing in the same hues and shades. They all seemed to know each other, too. They greeted each other with whoops and yells, high fives and hugs. It was as if they all belonged to a secret club.

"Earth to Atlas . . ." I heard Lucien's voice and turned and saw both Lucien and Zola staring at me. "Hey, space cadet."

"You all right, buddy?" Zola asked.

"What? Sorry, I zoned out."

"I said what are you doing this summer?"

"Oh, I'm not sure yet. Hopefully painting. I applied for a fellowship."

"What about you, Lucien?" Zola asked.

"I don't know. Maybe something in Hollywood? Do you guys know Greg Glover? He's a senior in the Pudding," said Lucien. "He's going to work at Disney next year. He made it sound pretty elite. I've been considering looking into it."

"Yeah," I said, nodding. "You would make a great Donald Duck."

Zola laughed. "It's true! You have the height."

"Hilarious," said Lucien, unimpressed. "Trouble is I don't really know anyone in LA. So I'm kinda stuck. It sounds like everyone is going into finance. That sounds so rut, though. I kinda want to do a start-up."

"Like Zuckerberg?"

"Yeah. But, you know, not lame and backstabby. I need an idea, though. A good one. You don't have any, do you?"

"What about a Groupon for college students?"

"How would that work?"

"I dunno. Maybe, like, discounts for bars or textbooks or something."

"I bet Groupon already does that. What about you, Zola? Any ideas?"

Zola smiled. "It's funny you should ask. As it happ—"

"Oh God," said Lucien, cutting him off. "Not the puppy rental thing again."

"It's a good idea!"

"No it's not!"

"Think how amazing it would be to press a button on your phone and have someone bring you a puppy for half an hour. That would be incredible. I'd use it all the time."

"That's bloody animal cruelty. Tell me, Zola, what are you going to do with your fleet of five million puppies when they're not puppies anymore?"

"I don't know. Set them free."

"What does that even mean? Set them free where? *The wild*?"

"Or people can adopt them."

"I'm not having this conversation again," said Lucien. He shook his head. "You guys are useless. I don't know why I bother keeping you around. Finance it is."

"I've heard banking hours are brutal," I said. "Eighteen-, twenty-hour days. Weekends, too."

"I know . . . ," groaned Lucien.

"It's a grind, that's for sure," Zola said.

"Oh, don't you dare pretend to know what life is like for us peasants with our menial banking jobs," said Lucien. "We all know what you'll be doing this summer."

"Yeah? What's that?" Zola asked.

"You're going back home, right? To run the country. That is the plan, isn't it?" Lucien asked. He loved winding Zola up. "What's your summer job? Minister of education? Secretary of defense? Generalissimo?"

"Yeah, yeah. Fuck off," said Zola.

"You should take me with you," said Lucien. "I'll be your advisor. We'll scale the ranks of power together. It'll be like that film. What's it called again . . . um . . ."

"If you say *Blood Diamond*, our friendship is over."

"Jesus, Zola! Come on. No. I'm talking about the other one."

"Ah, yeah," said Zola with heavy sarcasm. "That *one* other movie about Africa."

Lucien stared at the ceiling and clicked his fingers, trying to remember. "Fuck. What's it called. It's got Forest Whitaker in it . . ."

"*Last King of Scotland*," I said.

"Wow," said Zola.

Lucien banged his fist on the table. "That's it. That's the one. *Last King of Scotland*! It'll be just like that. I'll be your chief aide and confidant as you gradually transform from beloved man of the people into a paranoid, eccentric despot who has lost all touch with reality. Think how fun *that* would be."

"Well, thank you for comparing me to Idi Amin, you racist fuck," said Zola. "You do realize that Uganda is a completely different country to Equatorial Guinea, right? It's on the other side of Africa. Three thousand miles. That's like me telling you to run for president so you could be just like that guy . . . hmm . . . what was his name again? Oh yeah. Hitler."

"It's completely different. Number one: I'm not even eligible to be president. I wasn't born here," said Lucien. "And number two: the U.S. Constitution, with its system of strong checks and balances, is fundamentally at odds with the concept of the *Führerprinzip*, making it almost impossible for any one individual to centralize power to the extent Hitler did in Germany."

"I hate you. You know that? We have a constitution, too. We're a fucking democracy."

"Kind of," said Lucien.

"What do you mean, *kind of*?"

"I mean your uncle has been president since, like, 1963."

"That's not true."

"Okay, since when?"

"He's not my uncle. He's my half uncle. And since '79."

"There you go."

"What's your point?" asked Zola.

"My point is he's been president since Chairman Mao. That doesn't exactly scream democracy."

"Oh my God," said Zola. He closed his eyes and exhaled loudly. "You're such a dick."

"You know you love me," Lucien said, blowing Zola a kiss.

Lucien tipped back his chair and yawned. He stretched out his arms behind him, arching his spine and pushing out his stomach. And then he collapsed into a slump.

"Ugh," he said. "I need an espresso." He yawned again and cast a lazy gaze over the lobby. "Oh, look," he said. "There's Zoe. And Daniella."

I followed his line of sight and saw the two girls over by the concierge desk. I didn't know Zoe but I'd met Daniella once before when we'd come down to New York before winter break. She was one of Grace's friends from Columbia. Not the city. I didn't quite understand the significance of this distinction, but I'd heard both Lucien and Grace say it more than once. From what I remembered, Daniella was from Florida, somewhere near Miami. Her parents were doctors. Lucien told me that. He'd tried to set me up with her last time we were in New York, but it hadn't happened. Apparently, it had been my fault for failing to make a move.

"Who are they?" asked Zola. "The girls."

"Daniella and Zoe. You've met them before, haven't you? Grace's friends."

"I don't think so," said Zola.

"Huh. I thought you had. I'll get them over." Lucien waved a long arm in an attempt to catch the girls' attention. That didn't work, so he got to his feet and waved both his arms over his head as if signaling a distant ship. But still they didn't see him. "All right. Fuck it," Lucien said. He climbed up onto his chair and cupped his hands to his mouth. "ZOE! DANIELLA! HEY! OVER HERE!"

The room went silent. Everyone stopped and turned their heads to look at Lucien. But only for a moment. Just as swiftly, the silence ended and they went back to their conversations as if nothing had happened. The girls were doubled over laughing. Lucien broke into a confident smile and waved them over.

"Lucien! You're so ridiculous!"

"I can't believe you just did that. You're insane," said Daniella.

"You were far away. And I was tired. It was the only option," said Lucien. "How are you both? Good holidays? Join us for a drink. I'll get some more chairs."

I stood up to say hello to Daniella. I had decided earlier that when I saw her I would give her a kiss on the cheek. That was how Lucien and Zola greeted girls. I thought it made them look mature and sophisticated. But now, in the moment, I felt horribly unsure as to which cheek I was supposed to kiss. Was it the right or left? One cheek or both? I panicked, went the wrong way, and narrowly avoided kissing her on the mouth.

"Oh, okay . . . hey," she said, laughing.

"Sorry," I said. "That was awkward."

I pulled back and saw Zola staring at me, eyes wide.

"Did you just go in for a make-out?" he asked. "Bold!"

Both girls were laughing now. Daniella swept a hand through her light brown hair and then brought it to rest on my shoulder. Two gold bracelets circled her thin wrist, clinking together with the motion of her arm. "Happens all the time."

"Hey, I don't think we've met. I'm Zoe."

"Atlas," I said. "Maybe better if we just do a handshake."

She laughed and we shook hands.

"Seamless," she said.

Lucien pulled up two extra chairs and the girls sat down.

"We were just talking about ideas for a start-up," said Lucien.

"My cousin has a start-up," said Zoe. "She founded this company called Gilded."

"Wait. I didn't know that," said Daniella. "I love Gilded!"

"She's honestly my hero," said Zoe. "She just got named to the Forbes 30 Under 30. That's literally my dream."

"What is Gilded?" I asked.

"It's like flash sales of luxury clothing and jewelry. But it's all really nice. You can find amazing stuff on there for really cheap," said Daniella. "I use it all the time."

"I've been thinking someone should do a website like that for art," said Zoe.

"How would you do flash sales of art?"

"Not so much flash sales," said Zoe. "I was thinking of an e-commerce site that makes collecting art accessible to, like, college students and young people. Nothing crazy expensive. Like a site where people can buy prints and editions. I guess it would be more like an eBay for art."

"That's a good idea," said Lucien.

"Hey! Don't steal it!"

"No promises," he said. He held up his hands. "I'm joking. I'm joking. I wouldn't dream of it."

"Zoe! It's five fifteen!" said Daniella, suddenly panicked. "Grace is going to kill us."

We had to get ready as well, so we paid the bill and went up to our room to change. Zola and I dressed in regular tuxedos. Lucien was Grace's escort, so he wore a special tailcoat with a white vest and gloves.

At seven thirty Zola and I went downstairs to the ballroom. We stepped out of the elevator and into a long, mirrored hallway lit by crystal chandeliers with a black-and-white chessboard floor. At the end the twelve debutantes stood in a receiving line, greeting each of the guests as they entered. Like figures plucked from the top of a cake, they were dressed identically in long white gowns, with white silken gloves that came up past their elbows and fixed, rigid smiles. Grace was the tallest and most radiant, the light bouncing off her gleaming shoulders, her shining hair, the string of pearls glittering around her neck. As I came to her in the line, she greeted me with the same unchanging smile she'd given everyone else, and I couldn't help but feel a touch of disappointment.

At the end of the receiving line was a tall arbor covered in flowers and lights. Two attendants stood by, holding trays with flutes of champagne. A low hum of voices floated in the air. I took a glass and walked through the arbor.

A sudden bright flash of light blinded me as I entered the huge room. A photographer apologized for catching me off guard and asked for a second photo. Feeling somewhat dazed, I smiled for the photo. And then I lifted my head and took in a full view of the scene before me.

A horde of partygoers churned in the two-tiered ballroom. In the center of the room was a large hardwood dance floor and, beyond that, a stage on which a white-blazered orchestra appeared ready to perform. Circular dinner tables, perhaps fifty of them, were set up around the perimeter. Pink, yellow, and white flowers sprouted from the center of each table amid a twist of greenery. Even the walls were decorated, covered by looping chains of tinseled garlands speckled with red-and-silver baubles that glinted in the light.

"Not bad, eh?" said Zola, who'd followed me in.

"Is this real?" I asked, not meaning to say it aloud.

"What?"

"Nothing. Let's go find our table."

Dinner was three courses, served with plenty of wine. I spent most of it talking to Daniella. She was easy to talk to because she was happy to carry the conversation. For the most part it was gossip. This girl had just gotten out of rehab. That guy was dating so-and-so, but Daniella was sure he was gay. It was simple, banal conversation. Entertaining but ultimately rooted in others' misfortune.

The wine loosened everyone up, and by the time dessert was served, a small crowd had already gathered on the dance floor. The orchestra played a mixture of current pop hits and old-time swing. Everyone knew how to dance. Even the uncoordinated-looking guys whipped their dates around, dipping and spinning and twirling them.

"Let's dance," said Daniella.

"Go on without me. I'll join you in a bit."

"Liar," she said. "Why are you being so lame?"

"I can't do that," I said, pointing to the dance floor. "The spins and stuff. I never learned how."

"It's easy. Come on, I'll teach you. Have this and you'll be fine." She reached for an abandoned glass of wine and tipped the contents into mine, filling it to the brim.

"Are you trying to get me drunk?"

"You're already drunk," she said. "I'm trying to get you *more drunk*."

I laughed and accepted the glass. She watched me down the wine and then she pulled me to the dance floor.

I woke up the next morning in Lucien's hotel room with Daniella's body next to mine. The last thing I remembered was walking into a tiki bar–themed nightclub with Lucien and Grace. I remembered sparklers and a big bottle of Grey Goose. But not much else.

I do remember the morning. I remember lying there with Daniella still asleep and looking around the room at the $100 bottle of champagne swimming upside down in an ice bucket and the dress that must have cost thousands crumpled on the floor. How did I end up here? It was as if I'd walked through a door and stumbled into a different world.

CHAPTER 11

The letter from Harvard's Office for the Arts fellowship committee arrived in early January. My mom handed it to me when I came down for breakfast. I was still half asleep as I unfolded the neat, white sheet of paper and squinted at the thin, black lines of ink.

"Congratulations," it began. I felt a wave of relief. I'd been banking on winning this fellowship. My plan for the summer was contingent on the grant money.

I read on.

My application had been chosen. I was one of twelve students selected for that year's summer arts fellowship. After reviewing my list of estimated costs and expenses, the committee had decided to award me the sum of $1,400.

I blinked. *Fourteen hundred bucks? That must be a mistake.* I'd applied for five grand—the maximum amount. How was I supposed to live in Boston for three months on $1,400? That wouldn't even cover rent.

I spent the afternoon on the phone with a woman from the Office for the Arts. A mistake had been made. They hadn't realized I was on a full scholarship even though I'd marked the correct box on my application. Administrative error, she explained. She was very apologetic and promised to speak with the director to rectify the situation. An hour later she called me back. She apologized again. The program's funds were fully allocated. They had a tight budget. The recession, she said. She was sorry she couldn't do more to help.

Over the next few days I toyed with the idea of doing something completely different with summer. What if I tried banking? Or consulting? I had friends doing both. They said you could make $25,000 in a single summer. Twenty-five thousand! The thought was tempting. I imagined myself in a suit, walking through the lobby of a huge glass skyscraper and stepping into an elevator filled with familiar faces. One or two would nod at me and another would smile, but no one would pay me any particular attention. No one would ask me what I was working on or when my next show would be.

When I told Lucien I was considering Wall Street internships, he reacted like I'd just told him I was leaving Harvard to be a contestant on *Top Chef*.

"Are you insane? Why in God's name would you do that?"

"What other choice do I have?"

"You really want to be an Excel jockey at Morgan Stanley? You'll be bored out of your mind. Trust me. You're way too good at what you do. Let's just sell a couple more paintings. We'll pay for your whole summer."

He told me I owed it to myself to pursue my gift. If that meant I had to sell a few forgeries in order to give myself the chance to succeed . . . well, so what? Hadn't Michelangelo done the same thing? All we were doing was leveling the playing field. Who cared if some rich idiot with too much money bought a fake painting? As far as they were concerned, the painting was real. It would give them as much enjoyment as if it were the genuine article. It was a victimless crime, he said. The real criminals were the dealers and middlemen who ripped off both artists and clients by flipping art at double the price. We were tricksters, proving a point by getting one over on a corrupt and elitist establishment. By the time he was done, he had almost convinced me our fraud was a noble deed.

There was another reason I wanted to continue: I enjoyed the money. It was the first time in my life I'd had some to spend on myself. After we sold the Camoin, I was able to buy things I wanted rather than having to scrimp and save to pay for the things I needed. The money gave me a freedom I'd never experienced before. I didn't have to think about how much everything cost. And so, when Lucien pushed me to paint another forgery, I didn't put up much resistance.

We decided to make a few changes going forward. From now on, Lucien would go alone to make the sale. A single individual was less memorable and less likely to arouse suspicion than a pair of young men. And besides, Lucien looked older and more grown-up than I did. We also agreed we shouldn't sell any more in Boston. The gallery world was small, and Lucien made the point that it wasn't smart to be doing this in our own backyard. He would go to New York or D.C. to sell the next painting. By spreading the geographical dispersion of the forgeries, we diminished the chances anyone would notice a pattern.

He asked me to choose an artist with a higher profile for our next painting. Could I do Chagall? Manet? He wanted a bigger score. I pushed back. We compromised and I spent the remains of January working on a rather dull Vlaminck landscape.

It was the second week of term, just before course registration forms were due, and winter was in high gear. The roads were lined with banks of snow piled five feet high, and the pavements were sprinkled blue with rock salt. I was in Sever Hall, planning to check out a sociology course that fulfilled a core requirement, and had just ascended the stairs to the second floor when a familiar voice called out. It was Harriet. She was sitting by herself on a hallway bench, an open book on her lap.

"What are you reading?"

She dog-eared her page and held out the book.

"*Ulysses*. Enjoying it?"

"Trying to," she said.

"Slow going?"

"It's not so much that," she said, trailing off. She broke into an embarrassed smile. I sat down beside her.

"What's the problem?" I asked.

She laughed. "Okay, this is a little weird, but a year or two ago I made the mistake of reading some of Joyce's love letters, thinking they would be really beautifully written and lovely and sweet."

"No?"

She shook her head forcefully. "The opposite," she said. "They might be the most vulgar things I've ever seen."

"Very graphic?"

"Yes, but also not even erotic graphic; more just, like, gross and weird graphic. Very TMI. It kind of ruined Joyce for me," she said, laughing.

"Jesus. How bad could they have been?"

"*Bad*. But I've been assigned this for a course."

"I might have to look up these letters."

"Don't," she said. "No one should have to see those things. They should be burned. I'm joking, but I'm also not joking."

"Well, don't worry, I promise my letters will be much nicer than his." I said the sentence unthinkingly. She smiled at my clumsy attempt to flirt. "Oh—I didn't mean . . . Sorry, that sounded different in my head," I said quickly.

"I think you're setting yourself a low bar," she said. "And, by the way, Christopher, that was very forward," she teased. "I barely know you, and you're already talking about sending me a love letter?"

"Hang on a minute. Who said anything about a love letter? All I said was *letter*. There are many, many different types of letters. I could have been referring to a thank-you letter . . . a condolence letter . . . a cease-and-desist letter. You really shouldn't be so presumptuous."

"As long as it's not a chain letter, because then I'll have no choice but to forward it on to between fifty and twenty of my closest friends, family members, and/or business associates. I'm very superstitious with a particular weakness for chain letters."

I blinked. "Wow," I said. "You really shouldn't have told me that."

"Oh no . . ."

"You see where this is headed, right?"

"Please tell me it doesn't involve James Joyce's dirty mind and the chain letter format," she said. "I would actually kill you."

"I'm not making any promises."

"I swear to God, Christopher." She hit me on the arm and I pretended to wince.

"Okay, fine," I said. "No chain letters."

"You promise?"

"For now."

"Good enough," she said. "So you're in this class, too?"

"Which class?"

She laughed. "I guess not."

"Should I be taking it?"

"You should. It's Helen Vendler's class. My mom gave me her new book for Christmas."

"Oh, sure. Right," I said. I had no idea who Helen Vendler was. "What's her class called again?"

Harriet produced a syllabus from her bag. "The name of the course is," she said, pausing to clear her throat, "Aesthetic and Interpretive Understanding 20: Poems, Poets and Poetry."

"You're taking a class called poems, poems, and poems?"

She laughed. "It's better than Joyce, Joyce, and Joyce."

"Fair. How was your break, by the way?"

"It was nice. Relaxing," she said, after a pause. "I spent most of it at home. A lot of naps. A lot of Netflix. Super exciting." She laughed. "Oh! I did go to Palm Beach for New Year's. That was super fun. How about you? What'd you do?"

"Palm Beach . . . That's Florida, right?"

"Yep! About an hour north of Miami. My roommate Isa lives down there. She invited me to stay with her for the week before New Year's."

"Isn't it, like, all old people in Florida?"

"Also meth heads and crocodiles. But, yes, generally old people. Plus me and Isa. We were big hits at the water aerobics class."

"I bet."

"I'm also extremely good at bridge now," said Harriet.

"And bingo?"

"Can anyone be *good* at bingo? It's random."

"Spoken like someone who's not very good at it," I said.

"Anyway, it was super fun. A lot of young people go down for New Year's. There was a different black-tie party every night. I told Isa she should invite a bigger group next year. You should come if she does. For New Year's Eve we went to this big party called The Coconuts—"

"A coconut party?" I interrupted. "Curious. Was it coconut themed? Or only for coconuts?"

"The latter." Harriet laughed. "It's the world's biggest party only for coconuts. Coconuts as far as the eye could see. All in black-tie. Thousands of them. Plus me and Isa—of course."

"Theme of the trip."

"So," she said. "How was your break?"

"It was good. But definitely involved fewer coconuts than yours."

"Well, like I said, all the coconuts were down in Palm Beach. They're like snowbirds. They migrate south every winter."

"Ah, yes, the famous March of the Coconuts."

"Exactly," she said. "So, besides not hanging out with coconuts, what else did you do over break?"

"I was mostly at home, too. Painted a lot but also had some nights out in New York City. Met up with Lucien and his girlfriend. Went to her debutante ball at the Waldorf, and . . . Have you been to this place called Riff Raff's?"

She shook her head. "I don't think so."

"You should go. It's a cool spot. I think it just opened."

"It's a restaurant or . . ."

"Oh, it's a nightclub. There's sort of a tiki-jungle theme. Everyone wears face paint."

"Face paint?"

"Yeah, they do it so it kind of looks like war paint. Or how football players have it."

"Oh, that's disappointing. I was picturing a kid's birthday party kind of vibe. You with your whole face painted like a tiger."

"Or a butterfly."

"Yes. A purple one. With sparkles."

"Sadly not," I said. "I did ask the bottle girl if she could paint my face to look like Spider-Man, but she said—and I quote—'Get the hell away from me, you absolute weirdo.'"

"What a shame." She laughed. "That does sound fun, though. Where was my invite?"

"I didn't know you were around!"

"You didn't ask!"

"Okay, well, next time," I said. "For sure."

"Don't make promises you can't keep. If I'm not there the next time you get your face painted, I'm warning you . . ."

"You'll be furious."

"You have no idea."

"Oh, wait," I said. "Okay, two-part question. One, what are you doing Friday night? And, two, how do you feel about French electro?"

"French electro?"

"As in the music."

"Oh, um, French electro music . . . I would say I am . . . undecided. I have also never listened to that before, but it sounds very avant-garde."

"Well, we're going to a concert if you want to come," I said.

"Is it a French electro concert?"

"Ding, ding, ding. Ten points for Gryffindor."

"Wooo!" she said. "Um, I'll think about it. I'm more of a Rihanna kinda girl, to be honest. But, um, maybe? I bet that would be a lot of fun. I still need to figure out my classes, and I'm also trying to comp the *Lampoon*. Let me see how on top of my work I am."

"I've heard the *Lampoon* is hard."

"I think it is," she said. "There's just so many people trying to get in. The line for the first comp round went all the way down Mount Auburn to UHS."

By this time a small crowd of students had assembled outside the classroom and were waiting to go in. The door cracked open and a teaching assistant poked her head out and signaled with a wave that we could begin filing in. Harriet gathered her things.

"Are you coming?" she asked.

"Sure, why not? I'll check it out."

I followed her in and headed straight for the back row of seats, securing two. Calling out to Harriet, I pointed to the empty seat next to mine. She hesitated, tilting her head to the side, her arms crossed. "I'm going to sit closer—to see," she said, pointing to her eyes.

I nodded and watched Harriet walk to the front of the class, where she took a seat in the second row.

"Dammit," I said, under my breath. How had I managed to screw that up? Of course she wouldn't want to sit in the back row. I considered moving closer to Harriet, but the room quickly filled up and I lost my chance.

I spent most of the class staring at the back of Harriet's head, daydreaming and replaying the conversation we'd just had. I felt a quiet thrill as I realized I'd stumbled upon the perfect opportunity to get to know her better. I imagined us working together on group assignments, spending late nights in Lamont studying for the midterm, discussing essay prompts over breakfast at Annenberg. I pictured the two of us alone on a common room sofa, a book of poems in her hands, her head resting against my shoulder.

The next week I turned up for class ten minutes early, hoping to run into her again. But she didn't show up. And she didn't show up the next time we had class, either. By the third week of the semester there was still no sign of Harriet. She must have dropped the course. She told me later she'd been placed into an Expos section at the same time and was unable to switch out of it. The worst thing was the course turned out to be ten times harder than I'd expected. We were required to memorize a whole poem before every class—no haikus allowed—and to ensure we did, the professor would pick a student at random to stand up and recite it in front of the entire room.

My other courses were a joke. At the start of the semester, someone sent an email over the Hasty Pudding LISTSERV containing an inventory of the easiest courses on offer that semester—or, as they were informally known, gems. Gems typically had no attendance requirement, no regular homework assignments, and only one or two major papers or tests. The ideal gem would have a take-home final exam and a generous grade distribution. The courses were often given jokey nicknames. For instance, Science of the Physical Universe 36: Microbiology and Interplanetary Life became "Aliens"; Anthropology 1097: Introduction to the Classical Archaeology and Customs of Nordic Antiquity was shortened to "Vikings"; and Biology 118: Understanding Life at Twenty Thousand Leagues Under the Sea was far more commonly known as "Sea Monsters."

The professors who offered these classes knew exactly what they were doing. The goal was to attract a large enrollment. Teaching a class at Harvard with a thousand students enrolled could result in a certain level of prestige and fame. It might lead to a book deal, or media appearances, or a feature piece in *The New York Times*. I remember seeing one article in a major publication with the title "Why Are Hundreds of Harvard Students Studying Ancient Chinese

Philosophy?" with the subtitle "The professor who teaches Classical Chinese Ethical and Political Theory claims, 'This course will change your life.'" What the journalist either didn't know, or failed to mention, was that the Confucius course had a single graded assignment: a take-home exam at the end of the semester.

I signed up for two gems: Primitive Navigation and Pharaohs. Primitive Navigation was exactly what it sounds like: a course designed to teach Harvard students how to navigate using the same tools Christopher Columbus had at his disposal. Pharaohs, an anthropology course on ancient Egypt and early writing systems, turned out to be far more difficult than advertised. A new professor had been brought in to teach the course, and she'd thrown out the prior year's syllabus and replaced it with one of her own making. About three weeks in, I discovered we were expected to learn to read, write, and translate Egyptian hieroglyphs. Much of the spring term of my freshman year was spent drawing tiny pictures of ibises and memorizing the azimuths of stars.

But deciphering ancient symbols was the least of my problems. There was an expectation—a social pressure—to excel without breaking a sweat. It was cool to be smart and cooler to be brilliant. But it was not cool to have good grades because you spent every night in the library. If you went to office hours too often, or answered too many questions in section, or even seemed too interested in whatever it was you were supposed to be learning, you were labeled a "section hero," or a "tryhard." The key to fitting in at Harvard was to do well *without* trying hard. I wanted to fit in. And so I did what everyone else did.

CHAPTER 12

It was Valentine's Day and the Pudding was holding a date event. There was a play on at the College Theater, and the idea was that each member would invite a date to the show and then to a party at the clubhouse after. I'd invited Harriet a week earlier and she'd said yes. Neither of us were able to make it to the actual play, which began at seven. I had a late class, and she had a meeting scheduled with her advisor. Steinway and Isa were in a similar situation. He suggested we come by his room in Adams for drinks while everyone else was at the play.

After a few gin and tonics, we set out for the Pudding at half past eight. The initial plan was to walk, but it was cold, and a frosty wind whipped snow crystals off the top of drifts and through the air against the girls' exposed legs. A unanimous decision was made to redirect to the taxi stand. Harriet took my arm and I held her close as we crossed icy patches where snow had melted into slush and then refrozen.

We were the first ones to arrive. The play hadn't finished yet and the clubhouse was empty except for the catering staff. We ordered drinks at the bar and went upstairs to play pool while we waited for the others to arrive. Harriet and I played against Steinway and Isa. We lost three quick games.

"I think we should retire," said Harriet.

"You're abandoning me?"

"We're not very good at this."

"Just like you did in poetry class."

"I told you! It conflicts with my freshman seminar!"

"I'm kidding," I said. "I agree. This clearly isn't our game." I heard voices downstairs. "Should we go?"

Half a dozen couples milled about, making small talk while a Katy Perry song played faintly in the background. Two sophomores stood by an open window, sharing a cigarette.

I felt a hand slap me on the back and heard a familiar cackle. "What's Gucci, savage?" Xander was wearing a black suit with a white T-shirt underneath. His date, a tall girl with tousled blond hair, was wrapped in a black bandage dress. "Melissa, you know Atlas, right? Lucien's boy. This guy is king savage."

I shook her hand and introduced Harriet. "How was the play?" I asked.

"Bro, you came straight here? Fuck. We should have done that."

"It wasn't good?"

"It was fucking wack. Horrible. Like maybe the worst play of *all time*. It was all dudes dressed up as chicks, chicks dressed up as dudes. I didn't get it."

"I think it's a tradition," said Harriet. "The Theatricals, I mean. They always do their show in drag."

"I'm telling you, bro, the whole thing was wack. I'm never going again. So, what's up with this party, huh? It's fucking dead. We should go into Boston. My boy Faisal has a table at Bijou. You've met Faisal, right? The guy's an animal. Loves to rage. Anyway, let me know if you want in. Lucien said he was down. We're probably going to bounce soon."

"I think we're okay," I said. I looked at Harriet. "Unless you want to go."

She shook her head and smiled. "I'm having fun here."

"I feel you, I feel you," said Xander. "I'll hit you up late night, then. We can postgame in Weld. My homie from the city brought up some dank-ass weed. This shit is *elite*." Xander spotted someone over my shoulder. "YO, CORTLAND!" he yelled. "You want to hit up Bijou tonight?"

Xander trundled off followed by his date. I caught Harriet's eye and we both laughed. "What interesting friends you have," said Harriet.

"*Friend* is a strong word in this context. I might use the phrase *lunatic who knows my name*," I replied.

Toward the end of the night, Harriet took my hand and led me upstairs to the Krok Room. She stopped before one of the black-and-white photographs mounted on the wall. It was an old Hasty Pudding Club class photo from the 1920s. There were about twenty people in the photo, all young men dressed in suits. She stood silently before it, so I studied it but couldn't find anything extraordinary about the photograph. It was one of dozens of old class photos on the wall. I looked at Harriet, puzzled.

"Look closer," she said.

"What am I looking for?"

"Back row. In the middle. It's weird. I probably shouldn't have showed you this. You're going to think I'm really weird."

I leaned in closer. There *was* something off about the people in the back row. They didn't look natural. And then suddenly I saw it and burst out laughing. In the center of the back row, Harriet's face stared out from the picture. To her left was Abraham Lincoln, and to her right was a young Justin Timberlake. I also spotted her roommate Isa at the end of the row.

"That's amazing!" I said. "How did you do that? Or are you secretly a hundred years old?"

"Isa and I scanned one of those old pictures and photoshopped it. And then we printed it off and put it in a frame on the wall."

"Incredible."

"Oh God. You don't think I'm weird now, do you? It's a weird thing to do. We thought it'd be funny," said Harriet.

"Oh, I think you're incredibly weird. You might be the weirdest person I know," I said. "Relax. There's an eight-foot crocodile on the wall downstairs. That's way weirder than anything you could do."

"What is it with this school and dead animals? My friends from home see my photos on Facebook and they're all like, *Why is every wall at Harvard covered with dead animals?* Have you been to the Fly? They have a big room where their dance floor is. They call it the trophy room and it's full of stuffed animals. I feel so weird partying next to dead reindeers and mooses. Is it *mooses*? *Meeses*?"

"I'm going to go with *meeses*," I said. "Definitely *meeses*."

"If it's not a real word, it should be," Harriet said, nodding thoughtfully.

"It sounds much less intimidating than *moose*, doesn't it?"

"What does? Meeses?" Harriet asked.

"Yeah. I mean, if you were trampled to death by a moose, that sounds all right. That's an honorable death. But being killed by a herd of rampaging meeses . . . well, that sounds a little embarrassing."

"I suppose it does."

"What do you tell your friends?"

"About what?"

"All the animals."

"Oh, I've been telling them Harvard has the best taxidermy program in the country. I even picked it as my minor."

"Do they believe you?" I asked.

"Some of them do. Which is slightly concerning. I don't know if that says more about them or me."

The party was winding down and the house had emptied out. The music from downstairs stopped playing and all at once the room became quiet. Our eyes met, and this time neither of us looked away.

"You're not what I expected," said Harriet.

"What did you expect?"

"I don't know. You're just different."

"Good different?"

"Yes," she said. "Good different."

"You're not what I was expecting, either," I said.

"How so?"

"I thought you were going to be really charming and interesting and beautiful."

She laughed. "Little did you know . . ."

We fell into a comfortable silence. I wanted very badly to kiss her. From the look in her eyes I had the feeling she wanted that, too, but I wasn't sure. What if I was wrong? What if she turned away? Everything would be over before it even had a chance to begin. I couldn't risk it. And so I let the moment slip away.

"Can I walk you home?" I asked, breaking the silence.

"You can walk me part of the way," she said.

She took her coat and we went outside. It was a cloudless night. The wind had fallen away, and the air wasn't as cold anymore. I walked with Harriet until we came to the place where our paths diverged. We stood under a streetlamp and I said good night. She didn't say anything back. I said good night again and leaned in and put my hand on the small of her back and kissed her on her cheek. I started to pull my face away from hers but then I stopped because I felt her breath on my neck and realized she hadn't moved away. So I leaned in closer, lifted her chin with my hand so that our lips were almost touching, and paused. I felt her shallow, warm breath on my lips. And then I kissed her.

CHAPTER 13

For the next few days, the memories of that night—of that kiss—played in my head on an unending loop. No detail, no moment, was too insignificant to relive a hundred times. I replayed every joke, every laugh, every witty riposte.

We began texting back and forth every day, seeming to continue just as we'd left off. One afternoon I was thinking about the conversation we had outside that poetry class when an idea came to me. I opened up Microsoft Word on my laptop and began drafting a letter to Harriet. I wrote it in the style of a "personalized" form letter with blank spaces to be filled in by hand.

[MONTH] _February_ [DAY] _28_ [YEAR] _2011_

Dear [NAME OF RECIPIENT] ___Harriet___,

I had a very special time with you at [DESCRIPTION OF DATE] _the Hasty Pudding date event_ on _Valentine's Day_. You were a(n) _wonderful_ date, and I can assure you that was not a(n) [SELECT ONE:] a) day, b) afternoon, c) evening, d) experience I will forget anytime soon. I especially enjoyed our conversation about ___taxidermy___, and also that joke you made about college life that made us both laugh very hard.

The truth is I knew from the moment I met you

that you were not just another girl, but someone special. Although we've only known each other for <u> a few months </u>, and that was only our <u> first </u> date, I feel as though we have already developed an incredibly unique and deep interpersonal connection.

I would love to take you out again sometime. How do you feel about [INSERT ROMANTIC ONE-ON-ONE DATE ACTIVITY HERE] <u>   skydiving   </u>? Or perhaps we could ~~catch~~/(grab) a: film, meal, (drink) or coffee sometime soon.

For your convenience, I have included here a link to my personal website where you can find a current list of available days/time slots and select one most amenable to your schedule: *www.atlasnovotny.com/datingcalendar*

In any case I hope you enjoyed this romantic, personal letter. Looking forward to seeing you again, [NAME OF RECIPIENT] _____.

Yours,
~~Atlas~~
Christopher

Once finished, I read the letter over. It was definitely a gamble. Would she get the jokes? Would she even remember our conversation about the Joyce letters? I decided to wait until the morning to send it. Maybe I would change my mind after sleeping on it.

Morning came, and in a spurt of impulsiveness I sealed the letter in an envelope, addressed it to Harriet, and dropped it in the school mail. Within half an hour I was second-guessing the decision. But by that point it was already too late to do anything about it.

Several days passed without a response. Harriet also never mentioned it in our text conversations, and so I began to wonder if she'd even received it. And then one day I checked my mailbox and found a return letter from her. I stuffed it in my backpack and hurried home to open it in private. Standing over my desk, I unfolded the letter and began to read.

Harriet Anderson & Company, Inc.
Straus Hall
Cambridge, MA 02138

March 5, 2011

Dear Applicant,

Thank you for your thoughtful submission. Despite finding you a charming and attractive candidate, Harriet Anderson regrets to inform you that, at present, her feelings for you are deeply conflicted. While she greatly enjoys spending time with you, she is unsure if a romantic relationship between the two of you is the wisest course of action at this moment in time and will thus be passing on your tantalizing offer to tandem leap out of an airplane at ten thousand feet. She wishes to add that she too had a wonderful time at the date event and found your letter highly amusing (while also appreciating the distinct lack of vulgarity).

Ms. Anderson remains extremely fond of you and hopes you will understand her current position. She has no doubt there will be a very long list of girls eager to take her place by your side as you hurtle toward earth at terminal velocity.

*Fondly yours,
Name of Recipient*

I folded the letter into a small square and placed it in my pocket, feeling disappointed and confused. I went to my studio and tried to draw to clear my head, but I couldn't take my mind off the letter and its cryptic message. Lucien was home when I returned. I explained her response to him and asked him what he thought.

"You guys are sending letters to each other?" he asked, in a tone that suggested he was wildly unimpressed. "What is this, a Jane Austen novel?"

"It's an inside joke. Whatever. That's not important."

"If I understand this correctly, she said she likes you, but she doesn't know if it's a good idea for you guys to date?"

"Date or take this further—whatever. Oh, and she said she thinks I'm attractive," I added.

"I thought she said an *attractive candidate*."

"Yeah, but that's just part of the joke."

"Okay," said Lucien. "And she doesn't say why she thinks it's a bad idea?"

"She doesn't say it's a *bad* idea; she says she doesn't know if it's a good idea."

"Atlas?"

"Yes?"

"If something is *not a good idea* . . . what does that make it? That makes it a . . ."

I sighed. "A bad idea."

"A bad idea. Exactly." Lucien thought for a moment. "Well, I'm not sure what to tell you. She didn't give you a straight no, but it's definitely not a yes. And in my experience, not a yes is effectively the same thing as a no. If I were in your shoes, I would just move on. Plenty of girls out there. No reason to get hung up on this one. You can waste a lot of time chasing a girl who isn't into you."

I considered the advice for a moment and then rejected it. "But I think she *is* into me," I said. "We have this weird connection."

Lucien held up the letter. "Yes, Mr. Darcy, I am well aware of this connection, and it is certainly weird."

"I'm close. I know it."

Lucien shrugged, already bored by the conversation. "Whatever, man. It's your life."

The more I analyzed Harriet's response, the more certain I became that I could still win her over if I was patient. I decided she must be worried about it ending badly or about her getting hurt. I wasn't sure how I could change her mind about either of those things, but perhaps if I tried I could make her want me badly enough to overcome her concerns. That same thought was going through my mind a few days later when Lucien convinced me we should throw a party of our own.

"A massive one."

"What for?" I asked.

"What for? . . . For fun."

"How many people are you thinking?"

"Everyone. We'll make it black tie and open bar and we'll get the band from Cantab. It'll be legendary."

"How much would that cost?"

"We need a good theme," Lucien said.

"I thought you said black tie."

"I've changed my mind. We need a theme. What about '80s *Wall Street*? You know the vibe: Gordon Gecko, Patrick Bateman, French cuffs, mountains of cocaine, the whole deal. Ooh, wait. We could do *Eyes Wide Shut*. With the masks and everything."

"Isn't that movie about a secret underground sex cult?"

"You think that's too aggressive? Fair. Might weird some girls out. I like the masquerade idea, though."

"But where would we do this?"

"We'll rent a venue."

"Like a big common room or something?"

Lucien stared at me and shook his head in wonderment. "A common room? You know . . . sometimes I worry about you, Atlas. A venue means a club or a bar. Bijou. The Estate. Splash. We're not doing this in fucking Weld Basement. Jesus Christ."

"Won't that cost a fortune?"

He waved me off. "It's fine. We'll figure it out. Depends on the open bar. Now shut up and tell me what you think of this." He cleared his throat. "*Carnival of the Animals*."

"Okay," I said. "Well . . . what the fuck is that?"

"For an artist, you really are bizarrely uncultured. *Carnival of the Animals* is a famous piece of classical music. Look it up. And the timing's perfect. Carnival is right around the corner. Hey, you know that animal party they throw in the Hamptons every year?"

"No."

"Oh," he said, looking surprised. "Well, they have one. And it's massive. Everyone dresses up in an animal theme. We could do a hybrid of that and a Mardi Gras slash Carnival theme."

"What would that even look like?"

"Simple. You either wear a Carnival mask or dress up as an animal."

"In black tie?"

"I told you, forget black tie. Get creative, Atlas."

"How are we going to pay for this?"

"Can you relax, please? It'll be a few grand. It's not the end of the world. I'll just sell that painting you did during the holidays."

"I didn't paint that so we could blow it all on a party. That's going to pay for my summer, remember?" In the back of my mind was the loan I'd taken out from Harvard in the fall.

"Who said we're blowing it? This is an investment, Atlas. It's an investment in our future. This is for punch next year. We'll invite all the older kids. It'll make us look sweet. Everyone will be talking about our party. We'll walk into whatever club we want next fall."

"Dude, we're not even twenty-one. What if the party gets busted for underage drinking and we get in trouble with the school? I owe Harvard money. What do you think is going to happen if they find out I'm running around renting out clubs?"

Lucien collapsed into his chair, leaning back, putting his hands behind his head. He kicked his feet up onto his desk. "You know what? You're right. Maybe it's better if I do this without you. I was thinking this could help you out with Harriet—impress her, make you seem cool, etc. But I don't want to do this with one hand tied behind my back. If I'm going to do it, I'm going to do it properly and throw an epic fucking party. You can still come, of course. It just won't be *your party*."

We were both silent for a moment. I felt the creep of FOMO. "Can I still invite people?"

Lucien shrugged. "I'll give you a couple invites, sure. But if I'm paying for it, I'm controlling the guest list."

"Okay," I said. "Actually . . . screw it. I'm in."

"You sure?"

"Yeah. But only if we get enough from the Vlaminck."

"*Wunderbar.* I'm heading to New York this weekend. I'll take it with me."

Just as I had educated myself on the methods and techniques necessary to create realistic forgeries, Lucien had learned all he could about the art of faking provenance: inventing a false history for each of our paintings backed up by fraudulent documents. Before he left for New York, he showed me what he had come up with. I was impressed. The Vlaminck fake was accompanied by two falsified records of sale, a real exhibition catalog from 1962 doctored to include a page with an image of my Vlaminck, and a forged letter from Harvard professor Henry L. Bloom on official department letterhead giving his expert opinion that the piece was indeed genuine. The letter from Bloom was a masterstroke. Not only had he been considered one of the world's foremost experts on the Fauves, but he'd died five years earlier—a fact that made verification of the letter impossible.

With Lucien away I had a quiet weekend, spending most of it in my studio. I'd recently begun working on a new painting—a narrative piece inspired by Adam and Eve's departure from the Garden of Eden to accompany my now-finished *Trinity*. I planned to put the two paintings together as a diptych. I'd become interested in the idea of what it must have been like to have to walk the earth, having been banished from Eden. Knowing that you'd once had perfection and would never have it again.

I didn't want to paint a literal scene of Adam and Eve leaving Eden but rather something conveying their loss and hopelessness. I discussed a few different ideas with Marcus and began work on the painting Saturday morning. It wasn't until I returned to our room late Sunday night that I realized I'd heard nothing from Lucien since Friday.

I sent him a text checking in. He didn't reply. He should have been back already. I gave him a call but it went straight to voicemail. I texted Gardner and Zola to see if they'd been in touch with him. Neither of them had. I called him again and sent him another text, this one more urgent.

What if something had happened when he'd gone to sell the painting? What if he'd been arrested? An image of Lucien being guided into the back of a cop car drifted through my mind. I tried to stay calm. Maybe Lucien had decided to stay another night. Maybe he was out drinking. But why hadn't he sent me a text—or any sort of update—after he'd made the sale?

There was nothing I could do other than wait. Time ticked by. Each passing second added weight to my fears. Ten became eleven. Eleven became eleven thirty and still no word from Lucien. At midnight I began to panic. I cursed myself for being so stupid as to agree to all this. I started looking up lawyers. I thought about turning myself in. I almost called my mother at two in the morning to confess everything. I sent Lucien several more texts and emails. At four a.m. I still hadn't heard from him. I fell asleep sitting on my bed, staring at my phone screen, praying for a text from him to appear.

A few hours later I was shaken awake. It was Lucien.

"Morning, Atlas," he said, cheerfully. "I've got big news, buddy."

I shot up in bed. "Dude, what happened? Why didn't you text me back? I sent you, like, a million texts."

Lucien stared at me like I had lost my mind. "All right, chill out. What are you, my girlfriend now? I left my phone in a cab Friday night and haven't had time to pick up a new one yet."

"I thought you got arrested."

"What?" Lucien laughed. "Arrested?"

"What happened with the painting?"

"Oh, it went super well. Give me a minute and I'll show you." He slung his duffel bag onto my desk and started rummaging through it.

"Goddammit, Lucien! I've been freaking out all night, thinking you got arrested."

"Calm down. Nobody got arrested. Everything went fine. In fact, it went better than fine. It went fucking amazing. Check this out."

Lucien rummaged through his bag and pulled out a yellow envelope. He dumped the contents out onto my bed. Thick stacks of cash. Crisp $100 bills secured in neat bundles by paper bands.

"And that's just your cut," said Lucien.

I stared at the money. It seemed like an impossible amount. I began adding up the denomination markings on the paper bands. Two thousand. Two thousand. Five thousand. Another five thousand. It was too much. "That's all for me? How much did you sell it for?"

Lucien held out a magazine. "Here, look at this," he said. I reached for it, feeling dazed. It was a Sotheby's catalogue for an upcoming auction. I flipped to a page that had been dog-eared and my heart almost stopped. Right there in the middle of the page was my painting—the Camoin; the one we'd sold to the Winslow Gallery back in December. I looked up at Lucien, my mouth agape.

"This is Sotheby's, Lucien. This is bad. This is really bad. Someone's going to notice."

"Atlas, don't you see what this means? It's not bad. This is good, mate. If it's in the catalogue, it's already been accepted for auction. It's already passed their test. And once it's been sold by Sotheby's, we're golden. That's the ultimate establishment seal of approval. No one will dare question the authenticity once Sotheby's has put their name behind it."

"Is that true?" I asked, wanting to believe it was.

"Yes," he said. "Now will you let me tell you what happened? I was flipping through some of these auction catalogues on the train down to New York. You know, to get a better understanding of prices and what I should try to get for the painting. And I'm flipping through when all of a sudden this Camoin painting catches my eye. At first, I wasn't positive it was yours, but then I looked at the provenance and it's a complete match. Look at the listing: *Winslow Gallery, Boston, acquired from a private collector.* The dates, everything is the same."

"Of course it's the same. It's our painting."

"Look at the estimate: seventy to eighty thousand. That guy bought it off us for thirteen. I thought the most he could get out of it was, like, forty grand. But he's making double that! He ripped us off!"

"He didn't rip us off. It's a fucking fake."

"Agree to disagree. The point is I'm sitting there on the train, thinking to myself there has to be a better way to do this. I mean, the more paintings we put out there, the higher the probability one of them gets discovered as a fake, ipso facto, the higher the probability we get caught, yeah?"

I nodded.

"If that's the case, then it makes more sense to try and make a lot of money from a couple paintings rather than a little bit of money from a lot of paintings."

"Assuming . . ."

"Provided we can do that without exposing ourselves to a stupid amount of risk. I was thinking all this through and then it hit me: if your painting is good enough to pass the bar at Sotheby's, it must be an amazing forgery."

"So?"

"So we might as well be selling more expensive paintings," said Lucien. He was in full flow now, pacing the room, gesturing with his hands like a professor delivering a lecture. "Look, if a young kid shows up out of the blue claiming to own a Cézanne, people are going to ask questions. But take the same piece and give it to an established, legitimate dealer with a roster of private collectors, and he's going to have no trouble offloading it."

"What are you saying?"

"I'm saying what we really need is a partner."

"*A partner?* We never discussed that."

"And I found the perfect guy."

"No. No way. We agreed we were going to keep this small. Just us. We don't need to be selling million-dollar paintings. Please tell me you haven't brought someone else in on this. Please, Lucien."

"Hear me out. I met this art dealer at a party Grace's parents threw back in January. Swiss guy. His name's Florian Jaeger. Look him up: he's a big dog. You know Nikolay Orlov, the Russian oligarch? He's the billionaire who just bought that de Kooning at Sotheby's for, like, a hundred million. Jaeger is *his* guy. He's mega-connected, mate."

I put my hands over my eyes and groaned. "Lucien, Lucien, no..."

"We had a good chat at the party, so he agreed to meet me for coffee on Saturday. We get to talking, and I'm asking him all these questions about where he finds art for these collectors, and how he deals with authentication and all that jazz. And he makes it very clear he doesn't care to ask a lot of questions. He says it's not in his interest to ask questions. I tell him I actually have a painting I'm trying to sell. A Vlaminck. Would he mind taking a look at it? He says fine, bring it by my office tomorrow. So I do, and he's looking at the painting, and looking at the provenance documents, and then he looks at me and asks me point-blank how I managed to get my hands on such a good fake."

I stared at Lucien, wide-eyed. "What did you say?"

"I say, *Fake? What the hell are you talking about?* He holds up the Henry Bloom letter and says, *I knew Dr. Bloom very well, and he never typed anything. His letters were always handwritten.* Always. *The man didn't even own a computer.* But then Jaeger tells me that it's one of the best fakes he's ever seen. And he asks me if there are more where it came from."

"And you said yes?"

"We worked out an agreement. That's how I was able to get so much for the Vlaminck. He gave us $25K. Amazing, right? By the way, how are you with Matisse? He has a client who wants a Matisse. He agreed to give us thirty percent of the profit."

"Matisse? Are you crazy?"

"What's the big deal?"

"What's the big deal?? You're talking about a five-to-ten-million-dollar painting."

"Uhh . . . I'm well aware of that. And he's going to give us thirty percent of the upside. How unreal is that?"

"That's too much, man. I didn't sign up for this," I said. I pointed to the cash on the bed. "Give it back to him. We're not forging a Matisse."

"No, Atlas. We *are*," he said. There was a firmness in his voice.

"Well, I'm not," I said. "You can do whatever you like, but I'm out."

"Oh, come on. Don't you realize we could walk away with a million or two each? Think about that!" said Lucien. He flashed a playful smile. "Think about what you could do with a million bucks in play money. Mate, we could be ripping it up in Vegas every weekend. Bottles and models, baby."

"I don't want to go to Vegas every weekend."

"Okay, fine. The Caribbean, then: Bahamas, Aruba, BVI—wherever you like. Picture it. You, me, a mega-yacht, some babes. We could do that. That could be us," said Lucien. "Or who's that girl you're obsessed with? Harriet. You could fly Harriet to Paris for lunch, Tokyo for dinner. First class all the way. Hell, you could even fly private if you wanted."

"You're not listening," I said, growing annoyed. "And it kinda pisses me off that you would agree to this without even thinking to check with me first. Like, what the fuck, man?"

"Are you actually angry with me?"

"A little, yeah," I said.

Lucien wore the surprised, injured look of a child who didn't quite understand what they'd done to land in trouble. "But I did this for *you*, mate. *I* don't need the money. I thought you'd be thrilled. I said we'd do it because I knew it would solve all your problems. This will set you up for life. If we do this, you won't have to worry about funding your career. You'll have all the freedom in the world."

"Yeah, or maybe I'll end up in a federal penitentiary."

"What's the alternative? We keep doing rinky-dink sales for ten thousand here, twenty thousand there, versus one big score and we walk away with all the money we need? Atlas, this is a layup. Jaeger already has a buyer sorted. It's a client he's advised for years. The guy trusts him. If Jaeger tells him the painting is legit, he'll take his word for it. No one is going to check. Honestly, it's way less risky than what we've been doing."

"*Less* risky?"

"Yeah. It's one and done."

"Pass."

"What do you mean, *pass*?"

"I mean pass. I'm out. I'm not doing it."

"You have to."

"I don't have to do shit."

There was a brief pause. "Yeah," said Lucien. "You do. You have to do it."

I glared at him. "Who the hell do you think you are? Are you going to break my legs if I say no?"

"It's not up to me. *We* have to do it."

"Why?"

He reached into his pocket and pulled out a small, gold key. "Because of this," he said.

"What's that?"

"This key opens a safe-deposit box at the Chase branch on

Seventy-Second and Madison. There's a hundred grand in there. It's a deposit for the Matisse. I said yes. I took his money."

"A hundred grand?"

"We're committed, Atlas. You have to do it."

"Just give it back. Give it all back."

"I can't. Before he gave me the money he said, *If you waste my time, I'll turn you in for the Vlaminck.* He knows my name. He knows who I am."

"And you didn't think to check with me?"

"I didn't think I had to! I assumed you'd be thrilled."

"Fuck, Lucien."

"You're looking at this the wrong way," said Lucien. "Don't you see how lucky we are? He could have called the police the second he realized the Vlaminck was a forgery. Instead, he's given us this massive opportunity."

I held up my hands. "I'm sorry, man, but I'm not doing it. End of discussion. You got yourself into this mess; I'm sure you can find a way out. Just give the guy his money back. He's not going to care as long as you do that."

Lucien gave me a cold, unfriendly look. "So that's how it is, yeah? I'm on my own."

I shrugged. "I guess you are."

"Are you seriously going to screw me over like this?" asked Lucien. "You're supposed to be one of my best friends."

"I'm not screwing you over," I protested. "Talk to the guy. I guarantee you he only cares about his money."

"No. You are screwing me over. Well, guess what, buddy? I didn't give him my name. I gave him yours. So fuck you," snapped Lucien. "And good luck with that."

I stared at him, stunned. "You're lying," I said.

"Wanna bet?"

"There's no way. You wouldn't do that."

Lucien ignored me and made for the door.

I jumped up and reached for his shoulder. "Lucien! Wait. Did you really?"

He threw me off. "Leave me the fuck alone. I need some air."

"Stop. Stop. Don't go. Let's talk."

"I'm done talking."

"I'm sorry, okay? I shouldn't have said it like that. I shouldn't have told you that you're on your own. I'm going to help figure this out."

"You're gonna do the painting?"

"I'm thinking."

"What's there to think about? I told you, we don't have a choice."

"What I'm trying to say is that we're in this together, okay? Whatever we decide to do. Whatever the consequences, I'll be right there with you."

"What changed, Atlas? A second ago it was every man for himself. Funny how you're all about sticking together when you're the one on the hook."

"I don't believe you really told him that. It doesn't make any sense. You said you met him at a party with Grace and her parents. So, what—you were going around a party with your girlfriend's parents pretending to be me?"

"Maybe that's not how I met him," said Lucien. "Maybe I was lying about that."

"Were you?"

Lucien shrugged. "No. Fine. You're right. I didn't tell him your name. Are you gonna back out now?"

I shook my head. "No, but I want you to promise me that we'll do everything possible to get out of this situation without giving him the painting. Promise me you'll try to get him to take the money back and let us off the hook."

"Okay, that's fair. I can try."

"Lucien . . . if I do this . . . it's not for the money. I'd be doing it for you—for us. Because I had to."

Lucien nodded. "I'll see what I can do."

He left early the next morning without announcing that he was leaving or saying where he planned to go. I was still in bed half asleep when I heard his door open and close. And later when I got up, I went into his room and saw that his laptop was gone. The charger, too. His toiletry kit wasn't in its usual place on his dresser. I checked his closet and found no sign of his weekend duffel bag.

I sent him a text asking if he'd gone back to New York to see the dealer, but he didn't reply. I didn't think too much of it. It wasn't unusual for him to take spontaneous trips to New York for a random party or dinner or just to see Grace.

It was only when it had been a couple days and he still hadn't responded to any of my texts that I began to wonder if I should be more worried. Finally, on Wednesday afternoon I received a text back from him. But it raised more questions than answers.

> Sry. With parents. Can't talk. Family issue. Will explain later.

Friday rolled around and Lucien was still missing. We were both in Primitive Navigation and had section together every Friday afternoon. At the end of class, I caught up with our TF and asked if she'd heard anything from him. She looked at me, puzzled.

"Aren't you his roommate? I believe he's still at the hospital," she said. "Unless you've heard different?"

I felt a stab of shock. "The hospital?"

"He didn't tell you? His mo—" She caught herself before she finished the word and paused to reconsider what she was about to say. "Don't worry, he's fine. One of his family members is very ill." She spoke haltingly, parsing the information out in short bursts of deliberately chosen words.

"Did he say who?" I asked.

"I'm sorry, I shouldn't have said anything. I assumed you knew. Please don't repeat that. I could get in a lot of trouble. If he hasn't told you, I'm certain he wants to keep it private."

The next day I received a letter in the mail postmarked:

PAR AVION—PRIORITAIRE

I ripped it open, recognizing Lucien's handwriting straightaway.

HOTEL D'ANGLETERRE
GENEVA

17/3/2011

Atlas—

You must have been wondering where I've been this past week. I'm afraid my absence has been due to rather unfortunate circumstances. It's my mother. She had an accident skiing in Verbier. She hit a bad patch of ice going too quickly, lost control, and went into a tree. She had to be airlifted out

> *and has been in the ICU since. Thankfully her spine is okay. But she's had very severe internal bleeding and has required a number of blood transfusions.*

The sentences crashed into me, one after another. I felt sick.

> *Luckily I'm the same blood type as my mother (AB–). It's quite rare and the hospital does not have a lot in reserve, so they've been taking the blood from me. It seems to be helping her. The doctors say they've managed to stop the bleeding and her vitals are stabilizing (although she's still quite weak). I'm optimistic. She's a fighter and I know she will make it through this one, too.*
>
> *I'm sorry I didn't tell you before I left. There wasn't a lot of time. My father arranged a flight to Geneva and I had to go straight to Logan. Please don't say a word of this to anyone. Father is worried about it getting out in the press. I'm only telling you, Atlas, because you're my closest friend in the world and I know I can trust you.*

I paused and read that last sentence again. Was I really his closest friend? I felt a swell of pride and growing sense of responsibility. I read it again, again, over and over. *I know I can trust you.* The letter went on:

> *I've thought more about our last conversation, and I'm so sorry that I lashed out. The whole thing is entirely my fault. You were right that I should have checked with you before agreeing to anything. I can't believe how thoughtless and careless that*

was. I never would have done any of that if I'd known you were against the idea. Honestly, I thought I was helping you out. That's all I wanted to do. But instead I've landed us in a real jam, and I can't tell you how sorry I am about that.

I spoke with Jaeger—like you asked. The good news is he's willing to drop the whole thing for the right price. The bad news is he wants 200k—double what he paid us.

The way I see it, we have two ways out. The first is that we fulfill our side of the bargain. He agreed to give us until August to deliver the painting—which means you would have the whole summer to do it. The second is that we figure out a way to pay him back. My parents have money, but I'd have to go to my mother and ask her to hide it from my dad. He can't know. If he finds out he'll disown me. I just know it. Mother will understand, though. She's been in and out of consciousness since the accident, and even when she's awake she doesn't seem all there. But I'll try and find the right time to bring it up if I can find a moment alone with her when she's lucid. That is, of course, if you think that would be the best course of action.

Let me know how you want to proceed.

Your Brother,
Lucien

I ran home and rushed out an email asking Lucien not to bother his mom about the money. The most important thing was for her to recover. We could figure out the Matisse situation ourselves.

CHAPTER 14

Lucien returned the day after spring break looking as though he had aged ten years overnight. We discussed his mother only briefly. He told me her condition had improved but she was still fragile and had lingering neurological damage. Wrinkles had appeared on Lucien's forehead and his lips drew tight together. He looked tired. I asked him a few questions, but his answers were clipped and short. I sensed he would rather not go into further detail and so I didn't press him. He asked me again not to mention the accident to the others. I promised I wouldn't and I told him to let me know if I could help in any way. He thanked me and then said the best thing I could do was to keep him distracted from thinking about her.

He seemed down, and I wanted to cheer him up. A thought occurred to me. "What about that party you wanted to organize?"

"I thought you were against the idea," said Lucien.

"I never said that."

"You didn't sound very keen."

"I am keen," I said. I wasn't lying. I'd started to come around to the idea during Lucien's absence. It had been a while since I'd seen Harriet, and I figured the party was something to invite her to—another chance to see her. "Let's do it. It'll be fun."

"Yeah? Okay. Well, we should get on it," said Lucien brightly. "There isn't much time."

He was suddenly reinvigorated. He rose to his feet and began pacing back and forth between his desk and bed, running through all the things that needed to be done. I'd wanted to ask him about how we intended to repay Jaeger, but the moment didn't seem right. I would find another time.

Over the next days, Lucien threw himself into planning his party with such focus and energy that he must have had little time to think about anything else. But that was the point. He secured a concert hall in Central Square with a capacity of three hundred for the last Saturday in March. He had special invitations made up on heavy cardstock at the printshop in the Square. Embossed in large, shiny golden letters were the words *The Carnival of the Animals*. At the very bottom was a line that read, *April 9. Attire: Wild. By Invitation Only.* And that was it.

"You forgot to put the address," I said. "It doesn't give a time, either."

"That's intentional."

"Is the new plan to throw a party no one comes to?"

"They'll come."

"Not if they don't know where to go, they won't."

"If they want to find out, they'll figure out a way to find out. The point is to provoke their curiosity. People love mysteries. The key is that last line: *By Invitation Only*. Exclusivity. You make a few people feel special, and everyone else will be desperate for an invitation. Just watch. This is all anyone is going to be talking about for the next week."

And he was right. Word soon spread about the underground party with the secret location. Rumors multiplied as people traded on gossip and tried to figure out who had been invited. Lucien nurtured the growing hype by feeding selective pieces of information and misinformation into the gossip pool. And then he quietly allowed it to be known that he was the mastermind. By then everyone wanted to go.

In the days leading up to the party, hundreds of people asked if they could get on the list. Lucien gleefully announced it was already at capacity. But I told them to come anyway. I knew what it felt like to be left out.

Over four hundred people showed up—not only freshmen but upperclassmen, too. The concert hall was decked out with green and gold streamers. Fake palm trees were imported, as were inflatable exotic animals: flamingos, monkeys, elephants. A huge disco ball twirled above the dance floor. Everyone came in costume. There were a few Tarzans, lots of girls dressed as black cats, and one guy who wore a full mascot-style panda costume. Lucien wore a tuxedo and a lion hat and went around telling people he was king of the jungle. I found a store that sold Venetian carnival masks and bought a white bauta mask that reminded me of a Pietro Longhi painting.

The mask hid my face, making me unrecognizable, so after about ten minutes I flipped it up on top of my head. I doubt I knew more than thirty percent of the people who came to the party, but everyone seemed to know me—once I'd removed the mask, of course. Throughout the night people I'd never met came up to me and acted as if we were long-lost friends. The same girls who would have blown me off months earlier now tried to dance with me. Even guys like Xander who had once treated me like a pariah hugged me and slapped my back. This new popularity was so foreign that it felt as if it were happening to someone else. I'd always felt anonymous at parties, and now I couldn't go three steps without being treated like a hero.

A couple hours into the party I realized I was exhausted. It was tiring being Atlas. It took energy to stay in character—to keep up that façade and be confident and funny with every interaction. I needed a break. I pulled the bauta mask back on and felt myself turn invisible. At last I could breathe. I found a drink and wandered through the crowd unnoticed. With the mask on I felt a sense of remove, as though the party were taking place on the other side of a one-way mirror. I could see other people but they couldn't see me.

For all the people who came that night, there was only one I really cared about, and she wasn't there. Harriet had gone home for the weekend. It was her mother's birthday and they had long-standing plans to spend the time together. I understood, of course, but it was disappointing all the same.

I hadn't seen much of Harriet since Valentine's Day. She didn't go out much and she spent a lot of time in the library. I invited her to a couple parties, but she always had a reason she couldn't make it. The only times I really saw her were the handful of occasions I ran into her in Lamont or Annenberg.

We still talked pretty much every day. We traded Facebook messages and texts, our conversations mimicking the irregular rhythms of a tennis match: short, rapid-fire skirmishes interwoven with longer, more thoughtful rallies. We dealt mostly in absurdities, developing a unique dialect of inside jokes and memes and links to YouTube videos of strange people doing stranger things. To anyone else it would have appeared nonsensical, but to us it made sense.

The only exception came during two weeks in the middle of April, just after our party, when I heard nothing from her at all.

Not only did she cease responding to my texts and messages, but she also vanished from her usual spots in Lamont.

And then one day, all of a sudden, she texted to ask if I wanted to grab a coffee that afternoon. We met at Café Algiers on Brattle Street. I was a few minutes late and when I arrived she was already sitting down at a table with two lattes.

"She lives!" I said.

"I know. I've been MIA. There's a good reason for it, though. I have some exciting news."

"Tell me."

"I got into the *Lampoon*!"

"You mean the world's only humor magazine that isn't funny at all?"

"Hey!"

"I'm kidding," I said. "That's amazing! Congratulations! It's super impressive. You got in for writing?"

She nodded. "Thank you. We just finished initiation. That's why I've been off the map."

"Ah, don't they, like, kidnap you for a week?" I'd heard rumors that they locked the initiates down in the basement of the *Lampoon* castle for days at a time as part of an elaborate initiation process.

"Something like that," she said. "I'm not supposed to talk about it."

"It's classified. Got it." I raised my cup to make a toast. "Here's to you, Ms. Anderson. Congratulations on your success. I look forward to reading your jokes and not laughing at all."

"Thank you very much, Mr. Novotny. And I look forward to upholding the *Lampoon*'s long-standing tradition of exclusively publishing inside jokes that no one outside the *Lampoon* understands. By the way, I brought you something." She reached into her backpack and withdrew a worn book in a cracked yellow dust jacket.

"What's this?" I asked.

"Do you know W. H. Auden?"

I shook my head.

"Oh," she said. "I thought you might have covered him in class. He's one of my favorite poets. I saw it in a bookstore and thought of you. Because of the title," she clarified. I glanced at the cover. *The Shield of Achilles*. "It seemed appropriate given your affinity for Greek mythology."

"Great. More poems," I said. "This is exactly what I needed. Thank you. Not only have you tricked me into taking a poetry class, you've now started giving me homework."

She laughed. "If you don't want it, I'll take it back."

"No way." I cradled the book against my chest. "It's mine now."

"Read it," she said. "You'll like it. I promise."

"I'll give it a go."

"So, what are you doing this weekend?" she asked. "Anything fun?"

"I'm actually going to the *Gatsby* party at the Fly on Saturday."

"How come they're letting freshman guys go?"

"It's a pre-punch thing," I said. "I think they've invited, like, twenty of us."

"Pre-punch? Look at you."

"I'm fairly sure they just invited me because they want to score points with Lucien. I've heard they want him to join next year."

"And you're supposed to bring a date?"

"Yeah."

"Do you have one?"

"Um, not yet," I said, surprised by her question.

"You should take me," said Harriet.

"Yeah?" I asked.

"What? You don't want to?"

"I didn't say that."

"I think we'd have fun," she said.

"Okay. Well, I'll think about it," I said, unable to hide my smile. "You know there's a long list of interested applicants and . . . no, I'm kidding. I'd love to go with you. Let's do it."

"Great," she said. "What should I wear?"

"It's white tie with a sort of 1920s theme."

"Fancy!" she said. "Good thing I brought my tailcoat from home."

CHAPTER 15

I stood on Mount Auburn Street and waited for Harriet by the steps of the Lampoon Castle. It was twilight, and the evening was cast in a scattered blue light. A band was playing, the music bright and swift, and the sounds of laughter and revelry flowed over the brick walls of the Fly garden and out onto the street. I watched as couples, dressed in clothes from a past era, drifted onto Mount Auburn and toward the party. The combination of the antiquated costumes and the blue light of the dying day enchanted the scene, untethering it from time.

"I hope this counts as acceptable attire," said Harriet. She came toward me in a deep navy dress, a string of pearls falling loose and careless around her neck. A single pale feather was tucked into a hairband, tilting backwards like it might fall. She looked different—her eyes more shadowed, her lips a touch more red. She smiled, and for a moment I almost forgot to breathe.

I kissed her lightly on the cheek and held her hand as we walked the short distance to the Fly. The air swelled with gossip and laughter. As we passed through the gate, a waiter handed us each a flute of champagne. Everyone was gathered in the garden. Strings of lights affixed to the trunk of a tall tree ran down to the garden walls like maypole ribbons, creating the illusion that the entire party was sheltered beneath a circus tent of lights. A man in a striped blazer and a straw hat sat at a piano on the veranda while one of his bandmates plucked a double bass and the other sang a song I'd never heard before.

Lucien and Grace were talking with Mark Brockton, a tall senior in the Fly. Brockton was from Greenwich and had gone to a school Gardner considered second-tier. He wasn't exactly the smartest guy in the world, but what he lacked in mental acuity, he made up for in self-confidence.

"The Andover Shop is infinitely superior," Brockton said. "J. Press is dust."

"J. Press has a better tie selection," Lucien said.

"That's true. Their ties are solid. Where do you get your clothes done?"

"We have a tailor on Jermyn Street. New & Lingwood."

"Jermyn Street, huh? Where is that? D.C.?" Brockton asked.

"London," Lucien said.

"London," Brockton repeated, nodding knowingly. "Yeah, that sounds right. You know, I'm pretty sure there's one in D.C., too."

"Babe, you should take your things to my dad's place in the city," Grace told Lucien. "Huntsman. I've told you about it before. They made suits for Churchill and Reagan."

"Ronald Reagan?" asked Brockton, impressed.

"Well, I'm wearing Theory," said Harriet brightly. "I've heard it was Mrs. Churchill's favorite."

I stifled a laugh. Grace glared at Harriet. She turned her attention to Lucien, placing her hand on his forearm.

"Babe, can you get me a drink? Belvedere with soda."

Lucien winked at me. "Back in a tick."

"So, Atlas, what are you getting up to this summer? Finance?" asked Brockton, pronouncing *finance* with a long *a* so it sounded French: *fin-aaance*.

"Uh . . . no. I'll be here, actually. I'm painting," I said.

"Painting?" His eyes narrowed. "What do you mean?"

"I won a summer artist fellowship. Harvard's giving me a grant to paint over the summer."

"Oh, like *painting* painting. Interesting. I didn't know you were into that. Well, that's a fun way to spend a summer. You're only a freshman. I wouldn't sweat it. I did a Euro trip with my block mates freshman summer. We started in Paris and ended up in Croatia for yacht week," he said. "Everyone always makes a big deal about freshman summer internships, but I don't think they're all that important. Sophomore internships are the ones that really matter. You still have time. There's always next year."

"I mean, the only reason Vermeer ended up a painter is because he failed the banking exam," said Harriet.

"Is that right?" asked Brockton. "Fascinating. Well, it does happen from time to time. There was a Fly guy couple years back, Ollie McKay, failed his Series 7 test twice. Some people just aren't cut out for it."

"I'm sorry. I was kidding," said Harriet. "I have a terrible habit of making very bad jokes that no one understands. Anyway, I'm excited for Christopher. Those fellowships are really hard to get. My friend in the *Advocate* said a lot of them applied and none of them got it."

"Yeah, well, the *Advocate* is the least relevant organization on campus. No offense," said Brockton. He frowned. "Who's Christopher?"

"She means me."

"Oh," said Brockton. He wore the confused, unsettled look of a man who doesn't fully understand what is going on in front of him. It was the kind of look, I decided, that Brockton's face was probably quite used to making. Unable to make sense of Harriet's comment, he returned to his two favorite subjects: the Fly Club and himself.

"You know," Brockton droned, "one of the great things about the Fly is that our grads literally run Wall Street. Credit Suisse, Goldman, Citi, Deutsche—tons of Fly guys. We get job offers forwarded over the email list all the time. There was one yesterday. This Fly grad, class of '97, sent an email round. He just set up a private equity shop in Back Bay and was looking to hire interns for this summer. I don't know if he's interviewing freshmen, but I can give him your info if you want. He offered me a full-time job but I'd already accepted an offer."

"Where are you working?" I inquired and immediately wished I hadn't.

"At this totally cool boutique PE shop specializing in emerging markets and leveraging nontraditional growth strategies in the technology space," Brockton said, a little too quickly. "I love it because it's right at the intersection of finance and tech. That's the sweet spot. That's where you want to be."

He paused and looked at me expectantly, clearly waiting for me to ask him to explain what *leveraging nontraditional growth strategies in the technology space* meant. He seemed disappointed when I didn't take the bait.

"Lucien and I are summering in Europe," Grace said. "I have an internship with *Vogue* Paris. My dad is lining something up for Lucien, too."

"Do you speak French?" Harriet asked.

"*Oui, bien sûr.* We've gone every summer since I was five. Saint-Tropez mostly."

Lucien returned with Grace's drink.

"Paris. That sounds epic," Brockton said. "What will you be doing there?"

"I'll be in Condé Nast's corporate strategy division," said Lucien. "Looking at potential acquisitions. New media. That kind of stuff."

"Oh my God, I can't wait. I'm so excited," Grace said. "I have to take you to this restaurant that our family friend owns. It's so good. It has three Michelin stars. I went there during Fashion Week last year, and, oh my God, I literally almost died, it was so good. Wait—I took a photo. Let me find it."

There was a drawn-out pause as we waited for Grace to scroll through pictures on her phone.

"Here! See? How amazing does that look? And this was the dessert. They set it on fire! Literally right in front of you." She offered a glance of her phone to Harriet. "Lucien, we should go this summer. I think Tarek keeps his boat in Monaco," said Grace. She started scrolling again. "I'll text him now."

I noticed Harriet's glass was empty. I touched her on the arm and tipped my head at the bar. She nodded.

"We're going to grab a drink," I said. "We'll be right back." We walked over to the bar and traded the champagne glasses for highballs. Harriet pointed to a wooden bench beneath a red maple.

"Do you mind if we sit for a second?" she asked. "My feet are kind of killing me. I made the mistake of walking all the way here in heels."

"Let's sit down," I agreed. "This is exactly why I never wear heels. Well, that and for purposes of general agility."

"Of course." She nodded solemnly. "Maintaining a minimum standard of agility is very important."

"Hey, the good news is you only have"—I glanced at an invisible watch—"several hours left."

We sat down.

"How does Lucien know that girl?" she asked.

"Grace? He met her in New York City. Through Xander, I think."

"You must go to New York a lot."

"Not really. He does. I've only been twice," I said.

"She's very beautiful," said Harriet.

"I guess so. Between us, I'm not her biggest fan," I said. "I find her pretty tough to talk to."

"You don't like talking about tailors?" she asked, a look of pretend shock on her face.

The band reached the end of a song and there was a brief interlude as the singer unpacked and tuned a violin. He played a short riff heavy with vibrato and then the pianist came in with the openings chords of "It Don't Mean a Thing."

We flitted around the party, dipping in and out of conversations beneath the darkening sky. Hours skipped by like nothing. At ten the band moved inside and the president of the Fly announced that everyone should do the same. We went in through a side door and up a short staircase to a barroom.

"I thought you said this place was full of taxidermy animals," I said.

"Come with me. I'll show you," said Harriet. I followed her into a wood-paneled banquet hall hazy with cigar smoke. Adorning the walls were perhaps a dozen trophy mounts: bison, elk, antelope, and one or two animals I couldn't name.

We went back to the bar and ordered drinks and stood talking and laughing for maybe an hour and then I took Harriet to the dance floor and started dancing with her and kissing her and after a while I asked if she wanted to go home with me and she said she wanted to stay at the party a little while longer.

As the night was winding down, a group of us decided to go swimming in the pool at the athletic center. The building was locked at night, but one of the girls was on the fencing team and had a key card that gave her round-the-clock access to the building. She let us all in through a side door and we followed her down a series of dark corridors to the center of the deserted building and the Olympic-size pool. Harriet grabbed my elbow and pulled me aside.

"Is this a good idea?" she asked. "What if we get caught?"

"Come on. It'll be fun. What could go wrong?" I took her hand and pulled her with me, drunk on fearlessness.

I could feel her eyes on me as I stripped down to my boxers. Someone let out a whoop and jumped into the pool. I jumped in next, and the rest followed.

I swam over to where Harriet was resting with her arms draped over a lane rope. Her makeup had bled into blurry dark circles around her eyes. I swung an arm over the lane rope and it sagged in the water under our combined weight, inadvertently bringing us closer together. Suddenly the beam of a flashlight hit the water from above. I looked up and saw the dark outline of a man looking down on us from three stories above.

"Security guard!" someone yelled out. "We gotta go!"

A collective panic descended over the group and we all made for the pool's edge at a pace that would have impressed at the Olympic trials. We snatched our clothes and shoes and scattered in different directions. The building was a labyrinth of corridors and underground passageways. Hurtling down a hallway, with Harriet following close behind, I turned a corner and almost ran straight into the security guard. I was so shocked that it took my brain a moment to register what it meant. "Hello," I said without thinking. A millisecond after those words left my mouth, my brain kicked into gear. "Oh shit!" I said, turning and running as fast as I could in the opposite direction.

"Other way! Other way!" I shouted to Harriet, and quickly reversed course. We ran down the corridor and up a flight of stairs, which by some miracle led directly to a building exit. I flew through the green door and out into the cold night air. Harriet followed, half a step behind. I caught her and the two of us burst out laughing, gasping for air.

"It'll be fun. What could go wrong?" she said, imitating my voice. Her eyes were lit up with adrenaline.

"I never said we wouldn't get caught."

"I hate you."

"We should probably keep running."

"Agreed," she said. "But to where?"

"Come back to mine?"

"Not tonight."

"Another night?"

"Maybe. I don't know."

"I can live with maybe."

CHAPTER 16

April rains gave way to the bright, clear skies of May. There was a week or two of garden parties, which then came to an abrupt halt, and we found ourselves in the middle of exams. A semester spent coasting through with minimal effort finally caught up with me. The only class I did well in was my studio art course. I received a B in Poets and was embarrassed to register B minuses for Primitive Navigation and Pharaohs. That the latter two were supposed to be easy classes made it even worse.

With our freshman year over, Lucien and Grace disappeared to Paris. Zola surprised everyone by announcing he would be spending the summer in Beijing, learning Mandarin. Gardner played it safe and found an internship and an apartment in Manhattan, while Kane returned home to Australia to earn some money over the summer working construction and doing odd jobs.

I remained behind in Cambridge. I'd arranged to sublet a studio apartment on Brattle Street from June until August. Staying close to campus allowed me access to the Carpenter Center and free use of the school's art supplies. And renting my own apartment meant I had a private space in which to work on the Matisse painting Lucien had promised Jaeger.

Every year following commencement, Harvard held a week of alumni reunions with events staffed by undergrad students. The word was you could earn easy money from the generous tips alumni often lavished on the student staff. Harriet was signed up to be a bartender. I tried to do the same, hoping that we might share some shifts, but could only find an opening as a babysitter for alumni kids. The pay was decent, and a few times I was slipped a $100 tip for my assistance. But the main reason I worked reunions was to have another week with Harriet before she vanished to Europe to spend the summer studying Italian at a language institute in Florence.

Over the final weeks of the school year, our relationship had developed into something of a tentative, fledgling romance. We still hadn't slept together or agreed to be a couple, but I wasn't seeing anyone else, and neither was she. Twice she stayed over in my room but both times she kept her clothes on and we only went as far as making out. She wanted to take things slow. I didn't mind. I wasn't in a rush.

But I did hope to make her my girlfriend before she left for the summer. I felt good about my chances. We hung out every evening during reunions, often just the two of us. One night we even talked about dating long distance and how we'd only be apart for a couple months. I suggested visiting her in Florence. She seemed to like the idea.

But just before reunions came to an end, I noticed a sudden change in her attitude. She became very cool toward me, taking longer than usual to reply to my texts, offering noncommittal responses when I proposed plans. But I could tell she was doing it despite herself because every evening she caved and asked me if I wanted to meet up. I wasn't sure what to make of it. I had no idea what prompted the change. I certainly hadn't done anything to warrant it. It was as if she'd had a sudden realization that she'd allowed us to grow too close and was determined to restore a level of distance between us. I wondered if she was nervous about spending the summer apart.

The Pudding had a party on the final night of reunions. It was a warm evening, and the party was at overcapacity; the clubhouse felt like a sauna. Harriet and I climbed the fire escape up to the roof to get some air. From our perch we could see all the way down Garden Street to the last intersection before the Square. We had been taking turns inventing fictional biographies for the pedestrians who passed along the street below us. It was my turn. Harriet pointed to an overweight man in cargo shorts and a Boston Bruins T-shirt. As she pointed, her hand grazed the top of my knee, sending a flutter of excitement through my body.

"What's his story?" she asked.

"That's Brian," I said. "We have pottery class together."

"I didn't realize they offered pottery at Harvard."

"It's very popular," I said.

"Tell me about Brian," she said.

"In his spare time he enjoys computer coding. Hopes to one day invent the next MySpace. He's not very good at pottery, by the way."

"Isn't Facebook the next MySpace?" she asked.

"I don't have the heart to tell him about Facebook."

She laughed. "He's never heard of it?"

"Apparently not," I said.

"What else can you tell me about Brian?"

"He recently applied to be on *The Bachelor*. Still waiting to hear back."

"Oh, he's single?"

"Would you like an introduction?"

"I would have to see how bad his pottery is first," she said.

"Honestly, *pottery* is too generous a word to describe what Brian does to clay. He takes a misshapen lump and manages to make it look worse. It's borderline impressive. And besides, I think to be on *The Bachelor* you have to be a—"

"Bachelor."

"Exactly." I leaned into her gently. "You wouldn't want to ruin his chances, would you?" I turned and met her eyes. She was smiling. I leaned over and kissed her. She kissed me back, but only for a moment or two. And then her body became very tight and rigid and her jaw locked up. She pulled away.

"What's wrong?" I asked.

"Do you think this is a good idea?"

"Us?"

"Yes."

"No, I think it's a great idea."

She smiled, but it was a sad smile. She was quiet for a second before speaking again. "I don't know what we're doing," she said. "Or where this is going."

"How do you mean?"

"I like you. I really do. But I don't know if this is ever going to be serious to you. I don't want to get hurt."

"It *is* serious to me."

"You don't always act like it."

"Harriet, I can't stop thinking about you."

"Why did you hook up with Layla, then?"

I blinked. "Layla?" It took me a second. I hadn't thought about that night in months. A classmate, a party in December, too much to drink. We'd spent the night together but nothing had happened.

I hadn't thought of it as something that would matter. She ran in the same circles as Harriet, but I didn't think they were close.

"You know we're friends."

"That was forever ago. That was back in December. I barely knew you then."

"You'd already asked me out."

"But I didn't realize you two were friends. I wouldn't have done it if I knew . . ."

"If you knew I would find out?"

"No. If I thought it would hurt you," I said. "It only happened once. I was really drunk. Honestly, I barely remember anything from that night."

She didn't say anything.

"I'm sorry, Harriet. I really didn't—"

"It's fine."

"I meant what I said. I want you. Only you."

"I don't know whether to believe you," she said.

"Why wouldn't you believe me?"

"Sometimes I feel like I don't really know you," she said. "With me you're one way, but then I hear stories about you, and it sounds like a completely different person."

"Stories? What are you talking about?"

"You know what I mean."

"I don't. I really don't," I said.

"With other girls. You're always out partying with Lucien and those boys. I know the things they get up to."

I sighed. "I know that you don't like Lucien."

"I just wish you guys weren't so close."

"You don't know him like I do," I said.

"I know enough about him. The drugs, that whole rich-city-kids scene he's into. I knew guys just like him in high school. They're all the same. All they care about is partying."

"What does that have to do with me?"

"I just worry that you're going to turn into him. It's obvious how much you look up to him. I don't want to date someone with those values."

"What values?"

"That girl he was with at the Gatsby party—that was his girlfriend, right? Are they still together?"

"Grace? Yeah, they're still together."

"Then why is Lucien always hitting on my friends? Especially Isa. You should see some of the texts he sends her. It's so inappropriate."

"He's just being flirty."

"He has a girlfriend!"

"That's just how he is. He would never actually do anything, though."

"He hooked up with Isa a month ago."

"He did?"

"Yes," she said.

"I didn't know that," I said. "He and Grace were kinda on-and-off at one point. They were probably split up whenever that happened."

"Even if that's true, he shouldn't still be texting her."

"I agree with you," I said.

"And what about the cancer thing?" she asked. "You've heard about that, right?"

"What cancer thing?"

"Apparently he made up some crazy story about his mom having cancer to get out of a midterm this spring," said Harriet.

"What?"

"And it was a complete lie."

"Wait. What? Who told you that?"

"My friend was in section with him."

I shook my head. "That's not what happened," I said. "His mom was in a skiing accident. A bad one. I don't know where that cancer rumor came from, but she was in the ICU. She almost died."

"Christopher, my friend was *in the class*. He heard Lucien say that."

"Who is this friend?"

"Why does that matter?"

"I'm just asking."

"Reed."

"Reed Turner? Oh, come on, Harriet. He hates Lucien. He probably made that up."

Harriet shook her head. "Reed would never make that up if it wasn't true. Besides, I've heard it from other people, too."

"You have?"

"Yes." A pained expression came over Harriet's face. "You don't believe me?" she asked.

"I believe you. I just think maybe the story has gotten mixed up. His mom was in really bad shape. I saw the whole thing go down. It wasn't cancer but Lucien had to leave school and was with her in the hospital for, like, two weeks. It really shook him up. They're very close."

"I don't know, Christopher. Reed wouldn't just make that up."

"But he might have the story wrong."

Harriet shrugged. "You should talk to him about it if you don't believe me. He heard Lucien say his mom had cancer. Multiple times. There was a big blowup when the TF found out he was lying."

"Lucien wouldn't do that."

"You have so much faith in him. I don't know why. He lies to everyone."

"Not to me."

"You don't know that," she said. "If he lies to his girlfriend . . ." She trailed off. "Whatever."

Harriet sniffled and I looked over at her and saw with surprise that her eyes were damp. I put my arm around her and tried to pull her close but she shook me off.

"I don't know if I want to do this anymore," she said.

"Why? Because I'm friends with Lucien?"

She shook her head. "No, it's not that."

"Then what?"

"I think you still have some growing up to do. And that's fine. I understand boys need to run around after girls for a while and get that out of their system. But I don't want to be collateral damage."

"What? Harriet, no. That's not fair. I don't want to run after other girls. I want you. Only you."

Harriet was silent. "I want you, too," she said softly. "But now isn't the right time for us."

"Why, though? We're so great together."

"Christopher, I'm not saying no. I'm saying not now," she said.

"So, what do you want?"

"I think we should try just being friends for a while."

"I don't know if I can do that," I said. "I spend all day texting you, thinking about you. The thought of you with someone else just kills me."

"I know," she said. "Maybe we should take a break from talking, then. Just for a while. So we can get some distance."

I fixed my eyes on a point in the distance and tried to make sense of what was happening, but my mind refused to work. "I don't want that," I said finally.

"I don't, either, but that feels like the grown-up thing to do," she said. "I'm going away for the summer. It's a natural break. We should just hit pause here."

I watched the traffic light blink from yellow to red, and then I looked up at the night sky. One by one, my visions of the future began plummeting to earth, not in a great, fiery blaze but in a sad, noiseless way like birds who'd suddenly forgotten how to fly.

"I don't think I can hit pause," I said. "I'm going to miss you too much."

"I'll miss you, too," she said.

I felt tears gathering in my eyes and tried to blink them away. Harriet rose to her feet. I reached out a hand. "Don't go," I said.

"I'm sorry, Christopher," she said. "I hope you figure out who you want to be. Don't let Lucien decide for you." And then she climbed back through the window and into the house.

I sat alone on the roof for a while longer, staring at the ground but not really looking at anything at all. The breeze fell away, and the sounds of a traffic jam—angry car horns arguing in the distance—overwhelmed the music coming from inside the house.

After some time I caught sight of Brian again, walking back the way he had come. Only now he had stopped being Brian. Now he was just another stranger in the night.

CHAPTER 17

A sluggish gray sky blew in overnight and settled over Cambridge as if to rest for a while. It rained until late in the afternoon in a gentle, steady pattern, with big, heavy drops that clung to the window. I spent the day in bed, listless, passing in and out of consciousness to the crash and boom of distant thunder and the trickle of water down a gutter pipe.

Harvard emptied out in a hurry. The alumni disappeared first, melting away under the cover of crimson umbrellas held by volunteers hoping for one last tip. The huge marquee outside the science center was disassembled and packed away, the class banners affixed to Widener's columns were brought down, and the ocean of folding chairs in front of Memorial Church vanished in a single afternoon. With each day the number of remaining students and staff dwindled until there were only a handful of us left.

I spent the next week feeling pretty low. Harriet asked me not to text her for a while. I did my best, but one night I went out with friends and got drunk and texted her that I missed her. She didn't reply. The next day I deleted her number from my phone to make sure it wouldn't happen again, but not before writing it down on a piece of paper and hiding it in my desk drawer.

I tried not to think about her but it was impossible not to. Had I made a huge mistake? Or was it unfair of her to expect me to turn my back on Lucien because of a few rumors? I tried to convince myself that it didn't matter. We were going to be apart for the summer anyway, and maybe it was best not to be so attached to a girl a whole ocean away. She would be back in the fall. I could try again then. I would show her that she was wrong about me—that I *was* the person she'd thought I was. And maybe if she got to know Lucien a bit, too, she would realize that he wasn't such a bad guy after all.

To distract myself from thinking about her, I buried myself in work. I decided to get the Matisse out of the way first. Our debt to Jaeger had been hanging over me the past few months. The sooner I had it behind me, the better.

Through Lucien, Jaeger had provided elaborate, detailed instructions. He didn't want an original done in Matisse's style but rather an exact reproduction of a painting called *Seated Woman*, which had gone missing during the Second World War. Because it had disappeared so long ago, all I had to work from were a few grainy images from old French exhibition catalogues. The biggest challenge was getting the colors right. All but one of the images were in black-and-white, and the lone color photograph was faded with age. My best bet was to study other paintings he made during that period to get of a sense of his palette and then go with my best judgment.

The way Matisse drew his lines was similar to Marquet and Camoin. All three had been students of Gustave Moreau in Paris and received the same classical education in technique. But I found Matisse's drawings deceptively complex. People often confuse his line drawings with simple sketches, but they contain a depth and a quality of emotion rarely found in sketches. His delicate interplay of light and shadow creates the illusion of warmth, atmosphere, and movement. This complexity didn't happen by accident. It was the result of a rigorous process. For every drawing he completed, Matisse would first make a half dozen studies in a medium like charcoal. These drawings represented, in his own words, "the purest and most direct translation of my emotion." I circled that line and found myself reading it again and again.

I set about replicating his process as best I could. I had no live model to work with, but I was used to working off photographs. Still, I've always found faces the hardest part of the human body to portray. It was one of the reasons I tended more toward abstract figures. Marcus in particular had very high standards when it came to faces. He always said that a well-painted face should be both intimate and mysterious, expressive yet elusive.

As an exercise, Marcus once had me study a collection of mug shots mixed in with professional headshots. The headshots, he explained, were façades. They were like masks that people wore—a projection of the version of self they chose to display to the outside world. The images were sterile and contrived. In a sense they were dishonest. The smiles were forced and fixed. There was nothing genuine in the emotion. The mug shots were the opposite. They showed people at their lowest and most vulnerable moments.

He asked me to write down my observations. What could I learn from studying someone's face? What did the lines and creases around their mouths tell me? What about their eyes? Did they have scars or imperfections? What did those mean? What did the happy faces look like when they were sad or angry? And what about vice versa?

Matisse was a master of reducing that complexity to simple lines. And in dissecting and reengineering his work, I felt as though I was able to grasp an understanding of how he did it, like a watchmaker taking apart a watch and rebuilding it piece by piece.

Perhaps it was the poor quality of the images I had to work from, but I found *Seated Woman* itself to be a rather unremarkable Matisse. The painting featured a woman dressed rather demurely in a floral-patterned blouse and a beige floor-length skirt, sitting in a brown armchair in the corner of a living room. Its palette was more muted than his earlier fauvist period, and the painting lacked the wild, rapid brushstrokes I associated with his more energetic pieces.

I spent longer than I wanted working on *Seated Woman*, in part due to my own carelessness. About a week after I started painting, I realized I had to start over. I'd been using a pigment called titanium white. Today, it is perhaps the most common pigment on the market. But titanium white wasn't commercially developed until 1930; *Seated Woman* was painted in 1921. Matisse would have relied on different pigments, either flake white or zinc white. It was the kind of error that would instantly reveal the painting to be a forgery—an anachronism that would destroy the illusion.

A few times I thought I had finished, only to come back to it a few hours later and decide I needed to rework a certain detail. My perfectionism stemmed from a deep distrust of Jaeger. There was something about him that reminded me of the dealer who had ripped us off when I was a kid. I'd tried digging into his background, but there was almost nothing about him online. I couldn't even find a photo. I did find a few articles that mentioned him in passing as a dealer to the mega-rich. And then, deep in the search results, I came across an article that referenced a rumored settlement between Jaeger and a former client. Apparently, he'd been taking cuts of transactions without his client's knowledge. Lucien might have trusted Jaeger, but I certainly did not. If something went wrong, he'd find a way to pin everything on us. I couldn't afford to make any mistakes.

Jaeger supplied me with a specific canvas for the job. The wooden frame was stained in places, and the tacks were old and rusted. The back side of the canvas was spotty with black mold. All I had to do was match the painting to the rest of the canvas so that it told a coherent story of wear and neglect. To lower the tone of the colors, I brewed a pot of tea, and after it cooled, I took a mop brush and spread a thin layer of the liquid over the finished painting. I let that dry and then I emptied a vacuum cleaner onto the canvas, showering it in dust and debris. The soot seeped into the cracks and valleys in the paint, mimicking what fifty years in a dust-filled attic would do to a painting. I ran a dry flat brush over the whole canvas a few times and then shook it to dislodge any loose particles. Then I stood back and took in the whole work. With a great sense of relief, I realized I was done.

Over the course of my research, I'd noticed a disturbing pattern in the biographies of forgers. Many of them had begun as I had: young, talented painters who had resorted to forgery to remedy financial difficulties. At first it was about survival, about having enough money to live. But over time these artists were seduced by greed and became accustomed to the lifestyle their forgeries could support. Whenever they wanted something, they just sold a forgery. It was like having a cheat code or access to a secret ATM that dispersed free money. It was a shortcut to the life they wanted, but it came with a hidden cost.

Two artists stood out as cautionary tales. First, there was Han van Meegeren, the Dutch painter who gained infamy after several of his spectacular Vermeer forgeries were discovered in the personal collections of the Nazi high command. In his youth van Meegeren was seen as an exceptional talent. He won a gold medal from the Netherlands' top university, awarded to one art student every five years, and went on to study at the world-famous Royal Academy of Art in The Hague. After encountering a handful of early setbacks in his artistic career, van Meegeren turned to forgery. He earned tens of millions selling fake Vermeers but never achieved anything of note under his own name. Instead, he developed addictions to alcohol and morphine and wasted his income on a life of pleasure. At his own trial he declared that his success as a forger was the defeat of his career as a creative artist. Two years later he died of a heart attack, aged fifty-eight and bankrupt.

Elmyr de Hory was a similar case. A former protégé of Fernand Léger, de Hory painted more than a thousand forgeries, many of which wound up in major collections and museums. Shortly before de Hory died, he claimed there were dozens of his forgeries on display at the Louvre still undetected as fakes. The forgeries were how he paid for a wild jet-set lifestyle. He spent years living in ritzy hotel suites in New York, Los Angeles, Miami, and Rio. He was friends with Zsa Zsa Gabor. He owned a villa in Ibiza. But he lived on the run, and he was always looking over his shoulder, waiting to be caught. His work brought him into contact with unsavory figures who manipulated him and ripped him off and threatened to turn him in to the authorities if he didn't acquiesce to their demands. He suffered from depression and never fulfilled his own potential. In his final years he was reduced to forging the work of his former classmates from Paris. These were the same classmates he'd once towered over. While awaiting extradition for his crimes, de Hory swallowed a bottle of sleeping pills and took his own life.

There were others just like them. Beltracchi. Hebborn. Bastianini. It was the same story over and over: talent wasted, a life unfulfilled. None of them intended to become what they did. They fell into it gradually through a series of thoughtless decisions and poor choices. Like a hiker who strays from the path, confident in his ability to find his way back, they'd stumbled farther and farther into the woods, only realizing they were lost once it was too late.

I knew myself well enough to understand that the same thing could happen to me. I, too, was drawn to the bright lights, and I saw the danger of allowing someone like Jaeger into my life. I was being pulled into the orbit of a world that would be hard to escape. If I didn't get out now, I might never have the chance again.

The canvas was ninety-six inches square, primed and ready for paint. It was the largest I'd ever worked on. I'd spent the past week drawing the entire composition onto the canvas in light pencil, using a tape measure and grid system to ensure the spatial organization was exactly right.

Propped open on a table behind me was the collection of Auden's poetry Harriet had given me. She'd been right. I did like it. I hadn't really expected to, but the language was beautiful and the poems sounded nice when you read them aloud. One moment they were playful, the next profound. After a semester reading the schizophrenic nonsense of Gertrude Stein and the cut-up gibberish of Burroughs, it was nice to read a poem or two that actually made sense.

My favorite was the title work, "The Shield of Achilles," a reimagining of the passage in the *Iliad* in which Homer describes the intricate design on Achilles's shield. Hephaestus forges the shield at the request of Achilles's mother, Thetis. On it he works five concentric circles depicting a microcosm of existence. In the centermost circle are the sun and stars, the moon and Earth. The second ring shows a city at peace and a city at war, besieged and encircled by invaders. Further out are representations of life during peacetime: men and women dancing, farmers plowing a field, a shepherd guarding his flock, the gathering of the harvest. In the outermost ring is the ocean.

Auden's poem recasts the shield to reflect the reality of the world he experienced during his own lifetime. Thetis watches over Hephaestus's shoulder as he works, expecting to see the familiar, idyllic scenes from the *Iliad*. But Auden's landscape is bleak. It's a gray nuclear wasteland defined by the death and destruction of two world wars and the splitting of the atom. In Auden's world the fields are strewn with barbed wire and choked with weeds. Nothing grows. Columns of troops march off in clouds of dust, and crowds of townsfolk gather to witness firing squads. It is a world stripped of all beauty, compassion, and empathy, in which once-decent men and women have become numb to atrocity and blind to humanity.

In high school I'd fallen in love with the epic allegories painted by Dutch masters like Hieronymus Bosch and Brueghel the Elder. I was blown away by the encyclopedic nature of their compositions and the grotesque, almost cinematic quality of their works. I'd always wanted to try my hand at something similar in scale but had never been brave enough to try. I proposed the idea of a large-scale allegorical work in my fellowship application, thinking I would do something biblical, but one day while turning over ideas I considered Auden's poem.

The shield had been a popular subject for artists throughout history, most recently during the wave of neoclassicism in the nineteenth century. Benjamin West and François Gérard had both painted well-known scenes of Thetis delivering Achilles his armor. As far as I knew, no one had ever painted Auden's shield.

But Auden's pessimistic vision didn't reflect the reality of what had come to pass. The world had not devolved into nuclear war, and ours was quite different from the one depicted in Auden's poem. It would be more apt, I thought, to come up with my own version of the shield.

I began by working out thumbnail sketches of possible scenes. I had to figure out how I wanted the painting to look stylistically, in particular how to incorporate elements of the modern world while maintaining a balance with the ancient. What was the painting's message? If the scenes in Auden's poem did not reflect our world, what would? Should I paint the shield alone? Or a scene showing Thetis giving it to Achilles? I considered a triptych: Thetis with Hephaestus at his forge, Thetis and Achilles, Achilles and Hector. I threw that idea out because it drew too much attention to Achilles. I wasn't painting the story of Achilles; I was painting the allegory written on the shield.

I landed on a theme I called the paradox of modernity. I wanted to show a society that contradicted itself: one that was both prosperous and impoverished; a society in which technology had advanced and humanity had regressed; a civilization that was founded on and doomed by a gospel of growth and consumption.

Ideas for the painting came to me a little at a time, when I was in the shower or walking to get a morning coffee. I got ideas from articles and stories I heard on the news. I spent a lot of time looking at neoclassical art and reading about the designs on Greek shields. By July my sketchbook was filled with hundreds of sketches and preparatory studies. The hardest part was deciding what to include and what to leave out.

The shield itself would be gold, centered on a light blue background. I'd decided to keep certain elements of the original design, painting the sun, the moon, and the stars in the innermost circle. I also kept the outermost ring as the ocean, but it wasn't the same ocean that Achilles and his Myrmidons would have known. I painted in polar ice caps at six and twelve o'clock, with great chunks of glacier sliding off into the sea, and I painted cargo ships and cruise ships and the *Deepwater Horizon* oil spill and the Pacific trash vortex. Instead of a city at war and a city at peace, I painted a city of dreams and a city of despair. The city of dreams featured a gleaming skyline, clean, well-lit streets, and manicured parks. The people were smiling and happy, well-dressed and healthy. The city of despair was closer to Auden's vision, a city from which hope had long since departed. It was gloomy and dark, with narrow streets and barred windows and boarded-up houses. The citizens of despair looked forlorn and isolated. Their skin was anemic and blotchy, their bodies aching and joints arthritic. In a tribute to Auden, I added in the ragged urchin mentioned in his penultimate stanza. The final ring contained a series of panels depicting elements of modern society: a smokestack spewing ash to the sky; a great field worked by automated machines; a crowd of tourists paying homage to a golden statue of a charging bull; the crowded cityscape of Pudong illuminating the night sky. In other panels I painted yachts in the Monte Carlo harbor, a vacant main street with empty storefronts, the debutante ball at the Waldorf. And for the final panel I painted the man committing suicide on the steps of Memorial Church.

That summer I kept to a regular routine. I woke up at six a.m. and painted until noon. I would break for lunch and go for a run along the bank of the Charles. I worked for another hour or two in the afternoon before calling it quits for the day. Evenings I spent alone for the most part. I did a lot of reading. I had a few friends who were working in Boston that summer, and I saw them on the weekends, but they were busy with their jobs during the week. It was a solitary existence, but I enjoyed it.

On the nights I did go out to bars in Boston I would occasionally spot a dark-haired girl across the room and think for a second that it was Harriet. It never was, of course. She was thousands of miles away.

I followed her summer via Facebook. Even though I knew it was a bad idea, I visited her profile from time to time and clicked wistfully through her photos, dragging up a deep longing I'd done my best to bury. She seemed to be having a nice time in Italy. She uploaded a few albums showing her with the other students in her program doing touristy things, going to bars, having adventures. It looked fun. I wished I could be there with her.

Every now and then we exchanged messages. I tried to get us to slip back into our usual, familiar banter. But it wasn't the same. Our conversation felt suddenly unbalanced. Her responses lacked the same enthusiasm, the same level of engagement and energy, they'd had during the school year. I got the sense that she was replying to be polite.

About halfway through the summer I noticed that there was one guy who seemed to be popping up in a lot of her photos. He was blond and good-looking and had his arm around her in a couple photos. At first it was mostly group shots. And then in August she uploaded a few where it was just the two of them. I clicked on his profile. He was swimmer at Yale studying neuroscience. I felt sick. I tried to persuade myself that he might be gay and just a friend. But then I saw a photo of her sitting on his lap, her arms wrapped around his neck. I read the comments her friends had written below and I realized with great sadness that she was gone.

I didn't really date anyone that summer. Without Lucien around I didn't feel as much pressure to chase girls or go out all the time. In fact, the longer I spent apart from him, the more I realized how his physical presence—the gravity of his charisma—had a way of distorting reality. I began to reflect on the events of the past year and view them in a different light. I realized how much sway he held over me, over my actions. Everything we did was his idea, not mine. I thought back to the moments when he'd presented me with a choice, and I recognized that in almost every instance it was not so much a real choice as the illusion of choice. He was there all the while, an invisible hand guiding and steering me to the outcome he desired.

It was hard, too, to put Harriet's story totally out of my mind. I didn't take it as the gospel truth, but even if a fraction of the details were true, that was still disturbing enough. I did believe that something must have happened between Lucien and Isa over break. I didn't know what exactly. But it was believable enough that he would have hooked up with her. I didn't like that. I realized there was a high probability that it would have occurred while Lucien was staying with Grace at her parents' house. It made me uneasy that he would be so duplicitous with Grace, who loved him.

If he was willing to lie to her, then would he really think twice about lying to me?

I was due to meet Lucien in New York in the last week of August to deliver the forged Matisse to Florian Jaeger. As the day of our reunion drew nearer, I spent a lot of time asking myself if I could really trust Lucien when it came to our dealings with Jaeger. I recalled our argument when he first told me about the deal and how he hadn't been totally up-front with me about everything. It was only after I refused to do the painting that he told me about the safe-deposit box with a hundred grand in it. I knew there might be other pieces of information Lucien had left out or strategically forgotten to mention. He would have his own agenda. That I was sure of. I had to take matters into my own hands. I needed my own plan—my own way out. I couldn't leave it up to him.

CHAPTER 18

A cool breeze drifted down West Broadway, tickling the back of my neck. It was the middle of August, a few weeks before we were due back at school, and I'd arranged to meet up with Lucien in New York.

A maître d' appeared. "Ah, Signor Lucien," he said. "How lovely to see you again. Will your mother be joining us today?"

Lucien shook his head. "She was hoping to," he said. "But unfortunately something came up."

"What a shame. It's been too long since we saw her. Please give her our best, will you?"

"Of course. Thank you, Fede. We're here for another week, so I'll make sure to come by with her for lunch another day."

"So just two of you, then?" he asked, motioning to me. "Do you want your mother's usual table?"

"Wonderful."

The maître d' led us outside to a sidewalk table and we sat down, shielded from the midday sun by the restaurant's lemon-yellow awning. Lucien had been in the city for a week already. He'd come with his mother, who was in town for medical reasons. Ever since the accident she'd had difficulty with motor function on her left side, and she'd come to New York to see a specialist at Mount Sinai. I was due to meet her later that afternoon. They had a suite at the Plaza and she'd invited me to stay with them for the weekend.

I glanced at the table next to us. A dark-haired woman wearing oversized sunglasses and a wide-brimmed hat sat with her legs crossed, staring at her phone while she sipped on a glass of white wine. Across from her a young boy, perhaps six years old, knelt on his chair and drew stick figures and tanks on the cotton tablecloth with his mother's red lipstick.

A waiter in a white coat arrived carrying a basket of bread and a silver ice bucket on a stand. Like the boy's mother, he ignored the child and asked us if we wanted still or sparkling water. "Tap's fine," I said.

"We'll do sparkling," corrected Lucien. "That's okay with you, right?"

"Just tap for me."

The waiter nodded and produced two menus. I felt my stomach turn when I saw the prices.

"This is kind of elaborate for lunch, don't you think?" I asked.

Lucien frowned. "Elaborate? Here? Oh, I picked it because it's easy. We come here loads. My parents are quite good friends with the family. Giuseppe came to their wedding. The food isn't spectacular, but it's just easy, you know?" The waiter returned holding a frosted bottle of San Pellegrino. *"Allora . . . possiamo prendere due Bellini?"*

"Certo, e da mangiare?"

"Hmm . . . ," said Lucien. He glanced up at me. "You like fish, right? *Il branzino per due.*"

"Qualcos'altro? Something to start, perhaps?"

Lucien ran his eyes down the menu a final time before snapping it shut. "We'll take the carpaccio. One order. Two plates." He winked at the waiter. "Summer diet."

We were momentarily distracted by the incoherent cursing of a homeless man as he rattled his tarp-covered shopping cart past the restaurant. Lucien reached for the bread basket and tore off a piece of focaccia. "Where was I?"

"You were telling me about Monaco," I said.

"It was incredible. You should have been there. I've never seen so many Ferraris and Lambos in my life. You walk down the street and it's like Ferrari, Ferrari, Aston Martin, Maserati, Bugatti, Ferrari. *Occasionally* you see a shitty car. Oh, also, it's super small. The streets are tiny. I was surprised."

"I thought you'd been there before."

"Monaco? No. My parents think it's very tatty. Which it is. It's all new money. Tax exiles. Russians. You know the sort."

I nodded and tried to picture the kind of person he was referring to. The best I could do was an image of Le Chiffre, the Bond villain from *Casino Royale*.

"What were you doing there again?"

"This was for Tarek's birthday. He invited fifteen of us to spend a week on his family's yacht. They keep it there for tax purposes. He's actually quite close with the Casiraghis."

"Who?"

"Pierre and Charlotte."

I shook my head. "I don't think I know them."

"The royal family of Monaco . . ."

"Oh."

"But, Atlas, this yacht. This thing was like a fucking aircraft carrier. There was a movie theater, Jet Skis, a helipad. The chef used to work at Eleven Madison Park. And, dude, they had a full-time masseuse! Anytime you wanted a massage, you just pressed a button. It was unbelievable. Hands down the best week of my life. You can google it. They have pics online. Search *Elysium yacht Monaco*—it should come up."

"Tarek . . . Is he the one whose dad is an arms dealer?"

"No, no, no. That's Alexios. He's a total psycho—loads of fun but completely mad. Tarek's Egyptian. His family owns, like, the fourth-largest company in Africa. It's some sort of industrials slash construction conglomerate. They've basically built everything in North Africa since the pyramids. Tarek's a great guy. You'd love him."

"Let's hope they've started paying their workers," I said.

It took Lucien a second to get my joke. "Oh. The pyramids. Slave labor. Got it," he said. "I was exaggerating. They've been around since the fifties. The granddad was tight with Nasser."

"Was anyone I know on the trip?"

"I doubt it. It was a very Euro-heavy crowd. You haven't met Leander, have you? Or Cosima?"

I shook my head.

"Oh, you know who came for a few days? Mischa Barton."

I stared at Lucien, unsure if I'd heard him correctly. "Mischa Barton—like *the* Mischa Barton? Are you serious?"

Lucien laughed. "One of the guys is pals with her. Alex Da Silva. He's from the Bacardi family. Anyway, she was on holiday in Antibes, and we were passing by, so we sent the tender to pick her up. She only stayed for the afternoon."

"Did you talk to her?"

"Yeah."

"What was she like?"

"A little weird. Quite guarded."

"Two Bellinis, and carpaccio alla Cipriani," announced the

waiter. He set the carpaccio down in the center of the table and handed us champagne glasses filled with a bubbling, pinkish liquid.

"What is this?" I asked Lucien, after the waiter was gone.

"It's like a peach mimosa. Try it. They're delicious."

The drink was cold, and sweet. I could see why Lucien liked it. It seemed like the kind of drink you might sip on a yacht with Mischa Barton. I tried to imagine myself in that situation. What would I say to her? I had no idea. She belonged in the category of people I'd always thought of as having a kind of theoretical existence. She existed on bedroom posters, and DVD covers, and the pages of magazines sold in supermarkets. She existed in the same way that distant wars exist in newspapers, or galaxies and black holes exist in textbooks. She was real but also not. And Lucien had hung out with her.

"Good, right?" asked Lucien, holding up his Bellini. "I knew you'd like it. Oh, I haven't told you about Marrakech yet, have I? It was unreal. We rode ATVs to this random spot in the desert and spent, like, two hours shooting AK-47s. I shot a chicken with an Uzi!"

A gap opened in the clouds and the sun glinted off a passing car. From the table next to us came the sound of cartoon gunfire and airplanes whooshing through the skies. The young boy had transformed the salt and pepper shakers into Spitfires and Messerschmitts and appeared to be relitigating the Battle of Britain over his bread basket. I held my breath as the saltshaker clipped a water glass as it zoomed past, threatening to knock it over. The glass teetered but then stabilized. I looked back at Lucien. "Can I ask you something? How much does all that stuff cost?"

"What stuff?"

"The yachts, the crazy trips, the clubbing—that stuff. How much do you think the Monaco trip cost?"

"It didn't really cost anything. Tarek hosted us. We only went clubbing one night. Fede paid for the table."

"That yacht must cost millions."

"Two hundred."

"Two hundred million?"

"Apparently."

"Christ. And the crew, the gas, the food, the alcohol, the elite chef—how much do you think that all costs for a week? A hundred thousand? More? It's kind of obscene, isn't it?"

"Not really," he said, tight-lipped. He was irritated. "It's their money. They can spend it how they want."

"But for a kid's twentieth birthday party?"

"Who the hell are you to tell them how to spend their money?"

"No offense, Lucien, but these kids sound like rich douchebags."

"Is that right?" Lucien crossed his arms. "Is that what you think about Grace, too?

"That's not what I said."

"Or me? Am I a rich douchebag?"

"Lucien, come on," I said. "That's not what I meant. Forget it. I'm sorry. Forget I said anything."

The waiter brought our main course. We ate in silence until the tension was suddenly broken by a loud gasp followed by the shattering of glass. I turned and saw the young boy frozen in his seat, eyes locked on the broken wine bottle flooding the table. His mother exploded out of her chair, drenched and furious. She unleashed a torrent of abuse at the child—who started crying—hauled him out of his seat, and dragged him to the exit.

Lucien watched them leave and then turned to me. "You see that?" asked Lucien. He raised his eyebrows. "That kid is going to have *a lot* of issues. Future rich douchebag right there."

I laughed.

"So tell me about the painting," he said. "It's good, yeah? You did everything just the way he asked?"

"It's good. I spent a lot of time on it."

"Where is it?"

"It's with my bags. I found a luggage storage place by Penn Station."

"You left it in a luggage locker? Are you serious?"

"What's the big deal? I mean, we have plenty of time, right? I didn't want to be carrying a suitcase around all afternoon."

"*What's the big deal?* Dude, what if it gets stolen? We should go get it right now."

"It's not going to get stolen. It's wrapped up in brown paper. It looks like a random package."

Lucien seemed antsy. He waved for the check. "Let's go now. Shit gets stolen from those places all the time."

The waiter arrived with the check. Lucien glanced at it and put it back down on the table. "By the way, do you mind getting this?" asked Lucien. "Is that all right? My card was declined earlier and I haven't had a chance to call my bank. They must think I'm still in Europe."

"Uh—yeah, sure," I said. I looked at the check and recoiled when I saw the total. I reluctantly put my card down and the waiter took it away.

"Cheers, dude. I'll get you back," said Lucien.

We left and took a cab to the storage facility. We retrieved the painting but left my luggage, planning to return after our meeting with Jaeger. We had a couple hours to kill before we were due at his office, so we decided to walk down to Chelsea to check out some of the art galleries.

Our first stop was a Jeff Koons show at Gagosian on West Twenty-Fourth Street. We were passing by a series of balloon animal sculptures when Lucien started giving me looks.

"What?"

"Koons is a total fucking genius," he said.

"I wouldn't go that far," I said. "The guy makes balloon animals."

"Exactly! The art is total shit. And yet people pay tens of millions for his shitty sculptures. People are such idiots, aren't they? He doesn't even make anything himself. It's all done by his army of employees. I mean, you have to give him credit. He's pulled it off."

"I guess. I don't know if he's good for the art world, though—or for artists, at least. A $30 million Popeye statue makes it seem like art is only about money."

"Isn't it, though? Most of these collectors don't give a shit about art. What do hedge fund guys care about? Having more money than anyone else and making sure everyone knows it. So they go to Art Basel and say, *I'll take one of whatever other people want the most*. Someone shows them a Koons and they say, *Great, fine. Is it expensive?* And the dealer says, *Very expensive*. And they say, *Even better*. And so they buy it and they put in their apartment because when their friends come over they can point to it and everyone knows they're looking at a ten-million-dollar sculpture. So really they're just pointing to a big pile of cash and saying, *Fuck you, I have more money than you*."

"That's only part of the market," I said. "I've met collectors who know a lot more than I do."

"Bullshit."

"It's true."

We stopped by a few small, unremarkable galleries before walking into the Robert Ryman exhibit at Pace. Lucien actually burst out laughing when he realized every one of Ryman's works was nothing more than a canvas painted white.

"Mate! Are you joking?" He put his arm around me and leaned close. "Now, this is what we should have been forging." He broke away and winked at me. "Watch this," he said.

"Lucien, don't do anything stupid," I said, but he had already walked away. I followed him past several partitions and into the main gallery, a cavernous space with stark white walls and a smooth floor of polished concrete. He made for the wall on the far side of the room on which three square canvases were arranged. But instead of examining Ryman's paintings, Lucien studied a section of the empty wall. He tilted his head sideways and crossed his arms and put a hand on his chin, looking as though he was deep in thought. I realized what he was trying to do, and I rolled my eyes, thinking it wouldn't work. But about fifteen seconds later, another person wandered over and stood behind Lucien. And then a third, and a fourth, and soon there was a small handful of people staring at the wall. Lucien slipped away. I could tell he was trying to hold back a laugh.

"Let's go. I'm dying."

"I can't believe that worked," I said.

"Honestly, even *I* didn't think that was going to work. Oh my God. I think I heard someone say *Staggering* under their breath."

We turned south and a few blocks later arrived at a tired, charmless office building. It was an unremarkable structure, the kind one could reasonably assume would be home to a variety of middling law firms, accountants, and orthodontists. It was not the sort of building I associated with the world of fine art.

"Are you sure this is it?"

"Yeah, why?"

"I thought he had a gallery."

"It's just an office. I've been here before."

I followed Lucien through the revolving doors and into the lobby. An elderly security guard wearing headphones sat behind a desk, ostensibly keeping watch over the comings and goings. He paid us no attention. We walked past him and into an open elevator. Lucien pushed "27."

The elevator opened onto a hallway as drab and generic as the rest of the building. The walls were an ugly sandstone color, and a dingy, faded green carpet ran the length of the corridor. I followed Lucien past a psychiatrist's office, and then a podiatrist's, and finally to a door marked *Renaissance International & Company*.

Lucien pressed a doorbell and a buzzer sounded inside the office. A small, thin man with a receding hairline opened the door. He was dressed in a gray suit and had on a pair of wire-rimmed glasses. He blinked several times.

"You're early," he said. "I have a telephone call. You may wait here." And with that, he closed the door, leaving us standing awkwardly in the hallway.

"Well, that was weird," said Lucien. "He was much nicer last time I saw him."

"Was that him?" I asked. "Was that Jaeger?"

The man reappeared and opened the door. "Come in, please." He looked at me and nodded. "You must be Mr. Novotny. Please, sit."

His office was a single room. A small room. There was space for a desk, a handful of office chairs, and little else. There was a telephone on the desk, one of those standard-issue business phones, a clock, a task lamp, and a small stack of papers. To my surprise, the walls were bare.

Nothing about this was right. The office looked like it had been rented that very morning. Shouldn't he have art on the walls? Were we being set up? Was this some sort of sting? I scanned the room to see if I'd missed anything. A red light was blinking on the smoke detector on the ceiling. Could that be a camera?

"I take it you have the delivery?" Jaeger asked.

"The painting," Lucien said. "Yes, it's right here."

"Very good," said Jaeger. He pulled on a pair of white gloves. "May I examine it, please?"

Lucien took out the painting and handed it to Jaeger. He carefully unwrapped the canvas and propped it up against the wall. He took a step back. The room became very quiet. I could hear the ticking of the clock on his desk. Somewhere down the hall a door slammed shut. Lucien started to say something, but Jaeger held up a finger, silencing him.

"I'm sorry," he said, "but I require complete silence. Would you mind stepping out for a moment? I'll be with you in a few minutes."

Was he asking us to leave? I looked at Lucien, unsure of what to do. He nodded. "Sure thing," he said. "Take your time. We'll be outside."

We retreated to the hallway and left Jaeger alone. I walked down the hall to the corner and motioned for Lucien to follow.

"What is going on?" I asked. "This whole thing . . . something isn't right."

"What are you talking about?"

"All of this. Are you not getting a weird vibe? I mean, where the fuck are we? What the fuck is this place?"

"You're being paranoid. Jaeger is mad legit. His clients are serious people."

"Does this look legit to you? Do you think billionaires come here to buy art? This feels like the kind of place where people go to get budget Lasik surgery."

"Jesus, Atlas. You always get like this. Can you calm down and try to relax for once?" He crossed his arms and leaned against the wall. An electric shock ran through my body and I resisted the urge to shake him.

"No! I can't! Like, what the hell is *Renaissance International & Company*?" I asked. "That's not even the name of his company. I looked him up. His business is Jaeger Art Associates."

Lucien yawned. "It's called a shell corporation, Atlas. Read about it. This is how it's done."

I shook my head. "I don't like this."

"Plus he's buying a forgery—"

"Quiet!" I hissed.

Lucien dropped his voice to a whisper. "You think he wants us walking into his main office with that thing?"

"I want out," I said.

"It's too late, mate."

"It's not," I said. "I have a way out for us."

"No, no, no," said Lucien. I detected a slight note of angst in his voice. "Don't fuck this up, Atlas. Please don't fuck this up. Just smile and nod. Okay?"

Jaeger's head appeared in the doorway. When he saw us halfway down the hallway, a measure of mild annoyance came over his face. "Boys, please. I'm on a tight schedule."

"Coming," Lucien said. He shot me a sharp glance as if to say, *Whatever you're thinking, don't do it.*

Jaeger closed the door behind us and then he locked it. I looked at Lucien and raised my eyebrow.

"You're not about to mug us, are you, Florian?" Lucien laughed.

"What?" The joke went right over his head.

"Oh, nothing. I just meant with you locking the door—Never mind."

Jaeger frowned. "For privacy," he said. He pronounced *privacy* with a short i sound, the way English people say it. "It is a sensitive matter. You understand."

Jaeger's attention turned to me. "The painting is superb. You have a most wonderful gift. Tell me, have you ever considered pursuing this in a professional capacity? It was very kind of your friend, Lucien, to introduce us, but perhaps we could work out a direct relationship moving forwards. It could prove very lucrative."

Lucien perked up. "I'm sorry—a direct relationship?"

Jaeger ignored him. "The timing is right. The demand for the kind of work you are capable of producing has never been higher. With my network and expertise, I would be able to substantially reduce your risk of exposure. Money can be made to be untraceable. It would be most simple to accomplish."

"Whoa, whoa, whoa," Lucien attempted to cut in. "We're a team. You deal with both of us or neither."

"I'm not interested," I said.

"Take some time to consider the proposal. I'm amenable to a partnership arrangement with an equitable split of proceeds. You can reach me at my private number." He held out a business card. It was bare save a phone number printed in the center.

"I'm sorry but I'm not interested."

The look of irritation returned to Jaeger's face. He had the air of a man who was used to getting his way. "A pity," he said. "As for the painting, there's one issue I need resolved."

"What's the problem?" Lucien asked.

"There's no signature," Jaeger said. He looked at me. "I take it you didn't merely forget. It's rather an important detail."

"You'll have to find someone else to add a signature," I said.

"That was not our arrangement."

"I'm changing the arrangement."

"Atlas, just paint a fucking signature on it," Lucien said. "I apologize for this. He'll do it. It'll take him two minutes."

"No," I said. "I'm not painting the signature. Also, I want you to sign this." I held out a document I'd prepared for this very moment. It was a contract formalizing the purchase of an authentic reproduction of Matisse's lost work, *Seated Woman,* for the price of $100,000. The purchaser was listed as Florian Jaeger, the seller, Christopher Novotny.

"What is this?" Jaeger asked, studying the document.

"Atlas, what are you doing?"

"And why would I sign this?" he asked.

"Did you read the purchase price?"

"Yes—one hundred thousand dollars. That's quite a lot of money for an *authentic reproduction*."

"Under the original arrangement we were due thirty percent of the profit, right?"

"Correct," said Jaeger.

"If you sign the contract, we agree to waive the thirty percent," I said.

"What? No we don't!"

"Sign it, we walk away, and the painting is all yours," I said.

"Time out," Lucien cut in. "What are you doing?"

"We give him the painting and we walk away. It's all over."

"Why?"

"Do you need a moment?" Jaeger asked.

Lucien grabbed my arm. His eyes seemed to take up half the room. There was a wildness in his glare. He wasn't in control. He looked desperate.

"Listen to me." His voice was low and seemed to come from a place deep inside his torso. "Thirty percent means millions."

I lifted his hand off my arm. "Trust me," I said to him. "This is how we get out."

Jaeger held up the contract and waved it in the air. "Do you think this will protect you? You drafted this yourself, no? You should have gone to a lawyer. I'm willing to sign it, but I do feel obligated to tell you that this document will be nothing short of worthless in a court of law."

I felt a knot form in my stomach. I *had* drawn up the document myself. I'd considered hiring a lawyer, but I was worried they might ask too many questions. So I found a template online and adapted it. I figured it might offer us a modicum of protection— the illusion of plausible deniability—but in truth I had no idea. It was too late now.

Lucien gripped the arm of my chair. There was a feral look in his eyes. "Atlas, what the fuck are you doing? Have you lost your fucking mind?"

"Do we have a deal or not?" I asked.

"Ignore him," Lucien said to Jaeger. "He's being an idiot. We go back to the original deal: one hundred grand advance, thirty percent of the profit. We'll bring the painting back to you tomorrow *with* a signature."

"I don't think so," Jaeger said. "No. I like this deal better."

He produced a pen from his jacket pocket and signed the contract. Then he handed me the pen and I signed it as well. Lucien stormed out, slamming the door behind him. I folded up the contract and tucked it into my wallet.

"Can I ask you something?" I said to Jaeger.

Jaeger shrugged. "Why not?"

"Why this painting?"

"I have a client who desires a special Matisse," said Jaeger.

"But this one was stolen by the Nazis."

"Yes."

"I thought there were laws about paintings stolen by the Nazis."

"There are," he said, looking at his watch. "I apologize, but it's time for you to leave. I have another appointment."

Jaeger held the door for me, and as I walked out he pressed his card into my hand. "Keep it," he said. "Call me when you change your mind."

I rode the elevator down alone. When the doors opened to the lobby, Lucien was waiting for me with his arms crossed, his face twisted with anger.

"That was some trick you pulled in there," he snarled.

"What are you talking about?"

"You just threw away our lottery ticket. You fucking idiot." Lucien closed his eyes and pressed his hands together, touching his fingertips to the space between his eyes. "I can't do this right now," he said, dropping his hands to his side. I placed an arm on his shoulder, but he threw me off and barreled through the revolving doors and out into the street.

I followed close behind. "Hey!" I called out. "Would you wait a second?"

Lucien continued to walk away. I jogged to catch up and when I did he ignored me. His eyes looked straight ahead. "Are you really *that* pissed?" I asked, bewildered by his reaction. "What the hell is wrong with you? Hey! I'm talking to you!" I pushed on his shoulder.

That got his attention. He stopped dead in his tracks and rearranged his body to loom over me. His face was a dark cloud. Without warning, he jabbed me in the chest, hard. "Do you realize how stupid that was?" He jabbed me again. I staggered backwards. "The only reason we took the risk of working with Jaeger was the upside. That was the whole fucking point. Before it was high-risk, high-upside. Now it is high-risk, *zero* upside. Do you see that? Or are you too fucking stupid?"

My heart raced, pumping blood to my cheeks and ears. "We made a hundred thousand dollars, Lucien. And we didn't do anything illegal. It's not a forgery until you add a signature."

"He's going to make millions on that painting. *Millions!* I bet he sells it to some oligarch for twenty mil. You just threw away six million dollars, Atlas. How does that feel?"

"Don't be naïve," I protested. "He was never going to pay us six million dollars."

"Naïve? I'm being naïve? How about your stupid fucking contract? That thing looked like it was drawn up by a five-year-old. I was surprised it wasn't written in crayon."

I felt a swelling in my throat. I'd thought my plan would

impress Lucien. I'd imagined him saying what a clever idea it was. But he didn't. And somehow I'd become the bad guy? How was this my fault? He was the one who had put us in this situation. All I wanted to do was help.

"I'm sorry for trying to look out for us," I said. "I'm not the one who got us into this mess, Lucien. You are. I did the best I could in a bad situation."

"*Mess?*" Lucien shot back. "A six-million-dollar payout is a *mess*? Listen to yourself!"

"He was never going to pay us!"

"You literally have no idea what you're talking about," he said. "You don't even realize how stupid you sound."

"We could go to jail, Lucien! Do you not understand that?"

"Keep your fucking voice down," snarled Lucien. "Are you stupid or what?"

I tried to resist the wave of bitterness and resentment rising inside me. And then I snapped. "Why do you care so much, rich boy? You're loaded."

Lucien's eyes narrowed. "Six million dollars is a lot of money no matter who you are," he said. He pushed his hair back, closed his eyes, and let out a long breath. "I can't believe you just did that." He began to say something else but caught himself and stopped.

"If you have something to say, then say it."

"I don't want to say something I'll regret. But what you did in there . . ." He shook his head. "Friends don't do that to each other."

With that, he turned and began walking away. I remembered then that I was supposed to go with him to the Plaza and had nowhere else to stay in New York.

"Lucien!" I yelled after him. "Wait! Where are you going? Dude, I'm staying with you."

He didn't even turn around. He just kept walking until he disappeared into the crowd, leaving me alone on the corner.

I waited an hour before trying to call him, hoping that he'd cooled off. But he didn't pick up my calls and he didn't respond to any of my texts, either. Finally, when a few hours had passed without a reply, and with nowhere else to go, I collected my bags from the storage locker and boarded a train back to Boston.

CHAPTER 19

Two weeks later I returned to school for the fall term uncertain of where my relationship with Lucien stood. I was supposed to room with him again. We'd managed to secure a three-room double in Eliot House, on the same floor as Zola and Gardner. But with the way we left it in New York, I wasn't even sure that we were still friends. My texts to him went unanswered. I began to dread the beginning of school. What if he wouldn't speak to me? What if he made me find a new roommate?

But when he finally showed up to campus, swanning into our room with a twelve-pack of Heineken under one arm, he embraced me with the other and acted as if the incident in New York had never even happened. His coolness took me by surprise. Maybe he was embarrassed about the way he'd behaved. I decided to play along with the charade. If he was going to pretend it hadn't happened, then I could do the same. Happy to avoid further conflict, I accepted the truce and his unspoken offer to return to how things once were.

It was the fall of our sophomore year, which meant punching season for upperclassmen final clubs and the whirlwind of activity that went along with it. The first punch invitations arrived our second week at school, and the events began not long after that. I was punched by five of the eight male final clubs: the Porcellian, the A.D., the Spee, the Fly, and the Delphic. Lucien received all eight.

It was around that time that the Harvard Student Art Collective put on their fall show at Gallery 224 in Allston. My *Shield of Achilles* painting was accepted and even chosen as the cover art for the show's program. Marcus loved the painting and had gone so far as to convince a friend, the senior director of the Marian Goodman Gallery in New York, to come up to Boston for the opening of the show. Marcus had had a solo show at Goodman in London the year before.

It was a big deal. Goodman represented Gerhard Richter, Joseph Beuys, and a number of other serious heavyweights.

On the day of the opening, I met them outside Gallery 224. Marcus's friend was wearing black Persols with a neat white T-shirt and crisp olive trousers. Circling his wrist was a gold watch with a light brown leather strap. He was the kind of person it was easy to imagine owning a cool, vintage Porsche.

"Arthur," he said. I shook his hand and introduced myself.

"All right, lead the way," said Marcus.

They followed me into the second room, where my painting hung on the back wall.

"Oh, marvelous," Arthur said. He removed his sunglasses to take a better look. And then he just stared at the canvas in silence. Finally, he turned to Marcus. "Is there somewhere close we could go for a drink?" he asked.

We walked back across the bridge together to Shays Pub. Arthur ordered a round of Stellas.

"It's very promising," Arthur said. "I want Marian to see it. Is there any chance we can get it down to New York?"

"The show only lasts two weeks. I could send it after," I said.

"Marian leaves for Paris next Wednesday. I'd want to get it in front of her before then."

"She's still traveling?" Marcus asked.

"It's remarkable. I don't know how she does it. The woman's almost ninety. You'd never know."

"Do you think they'll let me send it before the show is over?" I asked Marcus.

"I'll talk to them," Marcus said. "It'll be fine."

"Good. I think Marian will want to see this," said Arthur.

"Outstanding," Marcus said. "That's outstanding. You see? I told you this kid was worth the trip."

"Chris, who have you worked with in the past?"

"Do you know Julian Roland at Ernst?"

Arthur frowned. "No," he said. "I can't say I do."

"It's a small gallery."

"Well, listen, I can't promise anything, but Marian has the best eye for talent in the business. Developing talent is what we do best."

We finished our beers and Arthur picked up the tab. They were having dinner with an old friend in Back Bay. I walked with them to the taxi stand in the Square, hardly believing how well it had gone, and waved goodbye as they climbed into the back seat of a cab. As I watched it disappear down Eliot Street, the corners of my mouth lifted up into an involuntary smile. I felt a kind of soaring giddiness, as though I'd just inhaled an entire tank of helium and hardly weighed anything at all.

Back at Eliot, I found Lucien lying on his bed, reading a book of Warren Buffett's letters to shareholders.

"There you are," Lucien said. "How was the opening? I stopped by but I couldn't find you." The expression on my face must have given something away because he looked closer at me and said, "Wow, that good, huh?"

"I think Marian Goodman wants to take me on."

"Seriously? They're major-league, right?"

"This would be so huge. God, I hope it happens."

He closed his book and sat up. "This calls for a celebration."

"It's not a done deal."

"Oh, come on. Don't be a bore."

"No, seriously. I don't want to jinx it. He said he couldn't guarantee anything. We can celebrate if it happens."

"*When* it happens," said Lucien. "Not *if*. Think positively, Atlas. Haven't I taught you anything?" He yawned and stretched out, leaning back with his arms behind his head. "That reminds me," he said in an offhand manner, "have you ever tried imitating Raoul Dufy?"

"Dufy? Yeah, a couple years ago. Wasn't hard."

He pushed up onto an elbow. "Do you think you could paint one for me?"

"I thought we said we were done with that," I said.

"We said we were done working with Jaeger."

"Oh," I said. "No, when I said I was done, I meant, like, I'm never doing that again."

"I know. Of course. But I was thinking it wouldn't hurt to have a little extra walking-around money. A nice Dufy would be easy to sell, and—I mean—it would take you a week? Maybe two, tops? It could be worth it."

"What about all the money in the safe-deposit box?"

"I've been meaning to talk to you about that," he said, sitting upright. He went over to his desk drawer and took out a gold key and tossed it to me. "Here's the other key. There's about sixty thousand left. I want you to have it."

"What? All of it?"

He nodded. "All of it."

"Why?"

"A gift to make up for the whole Jaeger debacle. I've been thinking it over, and you were absolutely right. I feel awful for putting you in that position. *Mea culpa*, Atlas."

"You don't have to do that."

"Of course, I don't *have to*," he said. "But I want to. You might need it one day. Think of it as a rainy-day fund." He patted me on the back. "Do me a favor and just say yes. You're my closest friend. I want to make things right."

"You're sure?"

"I just ask one thing in return. Paint me a Raoul Dufy. Something to do with Paris."

"Look, man, I'm finished with that. No more forgeries."

"No, no. This isn't a forgery. It's not like that at all," he said. "I just want something to give to Grace for her birthday. It's in two weeks. And Dufy did those amazing paintings of Paris with the Eiffel Tower in the background. She'd love one of those. We spent the summer there."

I hesitated. "I don't know. How about something else?"

"This would be so special. She'll absolutely die when she sees it. I'd love you forever if you could just do this one thing for me."

It was a reasonable request, but I didn't want to do it. What if this was a ploy? What if he followed this small request with a larger one? What would I say then? He was so good at getting me to do whatever he wanted. I wasn't sure that I could trust myself to say no. But more than that, I didn't want to find myself in another situation where I had to decide whether or not I could trust him.

Lucien must have sensed my unease because he pulled out his

phone and started going through his photos. When he found the one he was looking for, he flipped the phone around and offered it to me. It was a picture of him with Grace in front of Raoul Dufy's gigantic mural, *La Fée Électricité*.

"This is at the Musée d'Art Moderne. That's his mural—the famous one. It was Grace's favorite thing we saw in Paris."

He went to his texts and showed me a string of recent messages from Grace telling him about an upcoming Dufy retrospective at MoMA. So he wasn't lying.

"Okay," I said, nodding. "I can do the painting."

"Amazing! Could you do it properly and make it look old? I'll tell her you painted it—of course. But it'd be funny to make her think it was real at first. Just as a joke."

"As long as you tell her it isn't real," I said. "You *will* tell her, right?"

"Cross my heart," said Lucien.

And just like that, I agreed to something I never wanted to do. I completed the painting in a matter of days and then put it out of my mind. It was, I'm glad to say, the last forgery I ever painted. I didn't even consider it to be a forgery. But, of course, that's what it became the second I put it in Lucien's hands.

Two weeks later, Lucien and I were in New York for a punch dinner with the A.D. Club. We had some time before the dinner, so Lucien suggested we go over to Grace's house for a drink. She lived in a six-story mansion on East Seventy-Third Street, a block from the park. A maid let us in and led us up a winding staircase to the library on the second floor. It was a beautiful room with rows of books and a huge stone fireplace. Lucien made himself at home, pouring whiskey over two glasses filled with ice. Grace came in.

She wasn't drinking, she said. She had a paper to write. We sat there chatting for a while. Lucien excused himself to go to the bathroom and I was left alone with Grace. The conversation died, and I searched for something to talk about.

"So, what did you think of the painting?" I asked.

"What painting?"

"My painting."

She gave me a searching look.

"The one Lucien gave you for your birthday," I said.

"He didn't give me a painting," she said, frowning. "He gave me a necklace from Bulgari." She saw something in my reaction, and her eyes lit up. "Wait—is it a surprise? Did he get me something else?"

I recovered, smiling apologetically and tapping myself on the head as though I'd just forgotten something obvious. "Of course. Sorry, I got mixed up. He gave you the necklace. And then the painting was for his mom's birthday."

"Oh," she said, disappointed.

When Lucien returned, he must have sensed something was off, because he gave us a mock frown and said, "Not talking about me, I hope?"

"All terrible things," I said.

After the punch dinner, we were led by a group of A.D. grads to a dive bar in the West Village. Once everyone had gotten in and ordered drinks, I pulled Lucien aside and asked him about the Dufy. He didn't answer right away but took on the focused expression of a chess player confronted with a double attack. I could see his mind performing permutations, working its way through the splintering branches of a decision tree. And then, just like that, the look was gone. And in its place returned the easy, confident smile I knew all too well.

"Honestly, I decided I had to keep it," he said. "It was too beautiful. I wanted to give it to her, but I liked it too much. I had it shipped home. It's not a problem, is it?" Before I had time to respond, he continued. "I'm going to have it put up in my bedroom at home. I was going to tell you, but I was a bit worried you might think I had sold it or something. The painting would have been wasted on her, mate. I love the girl to death, but she doesn't know the first thing about art. Hey, I have to take a slash. I'll be right back."

I wanted to believe him, but his hesitation, that brief moment of recalibration . . .

CHAPTER 20

As the semester rolled on deep into the fall, the darkness that sometimes gathered around Lucien returned in full force. His behavior became increasingly erratic and unpredictable and his mood swings more frequent and intense. He would get low and depressed over things that seemed completely inconsequential. But then just hours later he was bouncing off the walls. I hardly ever saw him sleep. Some nights he wouldn't come back to the room until four or five in the morning. Other nights he didn't come home at all. Usually he would turn up at some point the following afternoon in a bizarre, confused state that I chalked up to him being sleep-deprived or still messed up from the night before. I called them his walkabouts. If I asked him where he'd been, he would invariably claim not to remember. I didn't know whether to believe him or not.

It wasn't just the walkabouts that had me worried. He began having these weird memory-lapse episodes that I found very concerning and difficult to explain. The only way to describe them is like random blackouts. I'd have a conversation with him in the middle of the day and then an hour or two later he would have no recollection of what we'd discussed. One time he called at two in the afternoon and told me he was in New Haven and had no idea how he'd gotten there. I urged him to see a doctor, but he brushed me off and told me it wasn't a big deal. He just needed to catch up on sleep, he said.

I found my own explanation for his strange behavior. Over

the summer he'd picked up a cocaine habit from hanging out with Grace and her friends. At first he only did it now and then. But soon it became a regular part of his going-out routine. Sometimes I would even hear him doing lines in the morning before going to class. The drug made him hard to be around. He became aggressive and irritable, occasionally even violent. There was one incident in particular that really scared the hell out of me.

It was around the middle of November. We'd been out at a club in Boston and Lucien had overdone it and gotten really fucked-up. Just after one a.m. he was thrown out of the club and I had to drag him home, half carrying him into a cab. As we got in, the cabdriver—a Haitian guy who didn't speak great English— told us he only took cash, no cards. That was fine, I said: we could stop at an ATM on the way back. Lucien mumbled something and passed out.

He came to as we sped down Soldiers' Field Road. I saw him reach into his jacket pocket for the small glass vial he never left behind. I tried to stop him. He brushed me off.

"Dude, enough," I said. "It's almost two."

He snorted off the back of his hand. I looked up and saw the cabdriver glancing at us in the rearview mirror. "Lucien."

"What?"

"He can see you."

"Congratulations to him." Lucien prepared to do another bump.

"Yo—put it away."

"Just go . . . just go fuck yourself, Atlas."

"He's looking right at you."

"The driver? So the fuck what?"

The cab jerked left. We veered across two lanes of traffic and up an exit ramp. The driver pulled off to the side, slamming to a stop on the shoulder. "Hey!" he yelled, twisting in his seat. "Not in my car! Out! You get out now!"

"The fuck is this guy saying?" slurred Lucien. "Hey, relax, mate. Just take us home."

"Out!"

"Sir, sir, please. I'm sorry for my friend. He's had too much. We're close."

"Out! You get out! Both of you—out!" He looked furious. I realized we weren't going to talk our way out of this one.

"Okay, okay, fine," I said. "We're getting out. We're getting out. I'm sorry." I reached for the door but felt Lucien grab my jacket.

"Where are you going?" Lucien blinked. He was upright now and alert. "Fuck this guy. I'm not getting out here. We're in the middle of fucking nowhere. He can take us home. Hey, mate? How about you chill out and get back on the road? I'll pay you double."

The driver got out, came around, and yanked open Lucien's door. He reached in and grabbed Lucien by his jacket collar. "What the fuck— *HEY!*" Lucien tried to shove him off and kicked out at the driver. The driver grabbed his leg and pulled him out of the back seat.

There was a sudden blur of motion and they spilled onto the road, locked in a tangle.

"Yo, stop!" I yelled, jumping out after them.

It all happened so fast. By the time I got around the car, Lucien was already on top. He was much bigger than the driver and had him pinned down, shoving the man's cheek into the asphalt. The driver flailed, throwing wild swings that didn't land.

I saw Lucien draw his elbow back and pause for a split second before releasing it in a single, violent motion. And then I heard the crack of Lucien's fist going through the man's jaw.

He must have hit the man at least three more times before I could pull him off.

I don't know what happened to the driver. We left him there that night, lying on the side of the road, dazed and bleeding. He was conscious when we left. I made sure of that. But I think his jaw was broken. I still remember the look of fear in the man's eyes when I bent over him to check that he was alive. He whimpered and raised his forearm to protect his face. And then our eyes met, and I don't know if I'll ever forget that look.

It was around that time that Lucien started having issues with money. The first sign of it was when I caught him listing a few of his Hermès ties on eBay. I wouldn't have thought much about it, but then his credit cards started getting declined. It happened at least three times when we were out to dinner together and I had to spot him because none of his cards were working. He claimed it was a security issue. He'd been the victim of several large fraudulent transactions over the summer, and, ever since, his bank him flagged for every little charge. I didn't really believe that. Not fully. I figured there was probably some truth to it, but I knew the real issue was that he was burning through his weekly allowance on partying and drugs.

It started with cocaine, but it soon became other things, too. Adderall for studying. Ambien for sleeping. Xanax to chill. Oxy to take the edge off. Those were the ones I could keep track of. He accumulated a small pharmacy in his desk drawer, purchasing orange pill bottles from other students with prescriptions. The transactions took place in the library, at the backs of dining halls, sometimes just outside our window in the Eliot House courtyard. I think Lucien thought he was being discreet but I could see what was going on.

I was torn over what to do. Most of my friends found Lucien's antics entertaining, funny even. They told stories about him when he wasn't around: tales of epic evenings spent partying until daybreak; how he would go to class without getting any sleep at all. I pulled Zola aside and asked him if he thought Lucien had gone off the rails. He rolled his eyes and told me Lucien knew how to handle himself. Gardner took a similar view.

But they didn't know everything I knew. Lucien was good at compartmentalizing, at hiding things from people—even from Zola and Gardner. They weren't around him as much as I was, so they didn't see all the things I saw. Lucien made me swear not to tell anyone about his walkabouts and his memory problems. And I never told a soul about the cabdriver.

After the incident with the cabbie, I sat Lucien down and attempted a kind of intervention. I told him I thought he had a serious problem and I pleaded with him to quit.

"You know what they say about problems, right?" he asked.

"What?"

"If they aren't yours, don't worry about them."

"But, Lucien, you could have killed that guy."

"Oh, don't be so dramatic. He was fine."

"You broke his jaw."

"No I didn't. Do you know how hard you have to hit someone to break their jaw? My hand would be in a cast."

"What if he'd hit his head? What if a cop had seen?"

Lucien shrugged. "It was self-defense. He attacked me first. You can't just go around assaulting passengers."

"I can hear it when you rip lines in the morning. The walls are thin."

"What?" He laughed. "Are you serious? Oh, come on, Atlas. Even I'm not that much of a degenerate."

"But, dude, all these pills . . ."

"What pills?"

"Don't treat me like I'm an idiot, Lucien. We live together. You think I don't see what's going on?"

"I don't know what you think you see."

"Lucien . . ."

"Fine. I take an Adderall every now and then to crush out a paper. So what? So does half the campus."

"Look, man, I'm only saying this stuff because you're my friend and I care about you. This can't be good for you. It's not healthy."

"You're being incredibly melodramatic, Atlas."

"What about the New Haven thing?"

"What about it?"

"You don't think that's a red flag?"

Lucien groaned. "I never should have told you about that. It was midterms. We had punch shit every single night. I basically hadn't slept in four days. I got a little loopy, but so what? I slept for sixteen hours that night. The next day I was totally fine."

"I'm just trying to look out for you."

"I appreciate the concern, and I mean this in the nicest possible way, but worry about yourself, all right? You're not my dad. I'm a big boy. I can look after myself."

"Fine."

"How's this: I'll stop once punch is over, okay? I just need it to get through to the end of punch. You know how crazy it's been. I haven't had a night off in two weeks. It's exhausting."

"You don't have to go to everything. You can say no. You can drop the clubs you're not interested in. This is your health. It's more important than punch."

"Yeah, but punch is fun," he said, then paused. "Maybe you're right. Maybe I'll drop the Fox and the PSK."

At one point I considered contacting Lucien's parents and telling them I was worried about him. But in the end I decided I couldn't do it. I knew what it meant to tell his parents. They would pull him out of school and send him to rehab. He would never forgive me for blindsiding him. Neither would our friends. They would see it as a complete overreaction on my part and a betrayal to boot. And so I didn't tell his parents about his problem.

When he came to me and threw his arm over my shoulder and asked me to give him the Matisse studies I'd done in preparation for Jaeger's painting, I told him no. I knew why he wanted those drawings.

"Hey!" He snatched my arm and yanked me backwards. His fingers pressed into my bicep, finding the space between bone and muscle. I tried to shake him off, but his grip was tight.

"Why are you being such a prick?" he asked.

"Let go of me."

"Just give me the drawings."

"No," I said.

"Why the fuck not?" His grip on my arm grew tighter still, his nails digging into my skin. I felt a sharp stab of pain as his fingers found a tender spot in the muscle.

"Ow!" I yelled. "Get the fuck off." I jerked my arm away again and this time he let me go. "What is wrong with you? I threw them out, okay? I don't have them anymore."

Lucien stared at me, a searching expression on his face. His blue eyes were flared, seeming larger and brighter than usual. "You're lying," he said. "You think I'm going to sell them, don't you?"

"Because you are."

"You ungrateful little shit! I ask you for *one* favor and you can't even do that." He was furious. Spittle flew out of his mouth with every other word. I recoiled. "After everything I've done for you! You were a fucking loser before I found you!" Lucien cast his eyes downward and his rage suddenly disappeared. He sniffled and rubbed his nose with the back of his hand. When he looked up again, his eyes were damp. "I wouldn't be asking you for this if I didn't need it," he pleaded. "Do me this one favor. Please. I'm asking you as your best friend. You're like a brother to me, Atlas."

"Dude, I'm not jeopardizing everything I've worked for just because you've spent all your pocket money on drugs."

Lucien gave me a long, searching look. "Is *that* what you think this is?"

"What is it, then?"

He sighed. "Things aren't great with my dad. They haven't been. Not for a while. But it's gotten worse. And I'm just a little short of cash at the moment. It's nothing major. I'm just not in a position where I can ask my dad for more and I need to make it through until the end of term. Please, Atlas." He placed his other hand on my opposite shoulder and pulled me toward him, bringing us face-to-face. I noticed the dark rings under his eyes and the faint creases that lined an otherwise perfect forehead. A lock of hair fell across his face and I saw strands of silver amid the blond. He looked exhausted. "Atlas, please."

I shook my head. "I'm sorry."

His eyes fell and his face dropped. He nodded. "It's okay," he said. And then he did something I didn't expect. He put his head on my shoulder and started to cry.

"It's all falling apart," he said, weeping. His breaths came in staccato intakes. "My whole life—everything—I'm losing it all. I need a little help. Just a little help. That's all."

"What's going on with you? I can't help if you don't talk to me."

He drew backwards and composed himself. He wiped his eyes. "You promise you won't tell anyone? You swear?"

I nodded.

"My parents are done," he said. "My father's been seeing some whore. Apparently, it's been going on for a while. We had a big row before I saw you in New York. I hit him. Broke his nose. I shouldn't have done that. But fuck it, he deserved it. He's cut me off. Stopped paying my tuition. Said he never wants to see me again." The words came out clipped.

"Is that why . . ." I began.

"Yeah," said Lucien. "That's why I've been acting like a lunatic lately with all the drugs and booze. Real mature, I know."

"Dude, I'm so sorry. I had no idea."

"Look, I need to pull myself together. I know I do. And I'm going to. I just need a little help right now to get through to the end of the semester and then I can figure everything out. It's just a few more weeks."

"The drawings are gone, Lucien."

"Can you lend me some cash, then?"

"How much do you need?"

"A few thousand?"

I thought about it for a minute.

"I'll pay you back," said Lucien. "It's just a short-term loan."

"Yeah," I said. "Of course. Just promise me one thing."
"Anything."
"No more coke, okay? That's my one condition."
"Easy," said Lucien.
"I mean it."
"I know. No more coke."

Lucien walked me to the bank right then and there, and we did the transfer before I had a chance to change my mind. That weekend I saw him staggering around, coked out and blackout drunk, and I knew I'd made a mistake.

By the tail end of November I was more than ready for punch to be over. The process had been a lot of fun, but it had completely taken over my life. We had events almost every night. There were the four official functions for each club, but there were also the dozens of smaller, informal events like the grad dinner in New York. We were taken on trips and out to concerts, to Celtics and Bruins games at TD Garden and to karaoke nights with girls from Boston College. I was going out five or six nights a week and was hungover so often, it felt like my head was trapped in a permanent fog. I wasn't doing well in my classes, and my painting was suffering, too.

In the final week of punch, the Delphic Club tapped me and three other guys to go on their annual trip to Atlantic City. The trip was sponsored by an alumnus named Roy Simon, an infamous real estate billionaire. The rumor around campus was that every year Simon flew a small group of Delphic members and punches on his private jet to Atlantic City or Las Vegas for a secretive weekend of gambling and partying. This trip occupied its own place in Harvard folklore. It was one of those things—like the secret blackjack team or the tunnels that supposedly ran beneath Harvard Yard—that oscillated between fact and myth, depending on who you spoke to. Even I didn't quite believe it was real until we arrived at the private air terminal and saw a matte-black Gulfstream emblazoned with a cursive letter *S* in glossy white paint.

Simon was waiting for us on the jet, settled into a plush leather chair accented with gold. He was shorter than I'd expected. He had thick black hair flecked with gray and was severely overweight. His rounded face gave the impression of someone who had never lost their baby fat, with ample cheeks that blended right into wide jowls and a double chin. It was hard to tell where his face ended and his neck began. He wore a gray suit, a navy Delphic tie, and brown tasseled loafers. Before the plane took off, he had the stewardess bring everyone a tumbler of whiskey and a "survival kit" containing toiletries, Advil, some snacks, a pack of condoms, and $200 in casino chips.

A stretch limo picked us up at the Atlantic City airport and took us to Simon's very own hotel-casino, the Babylon. There were fourteen of us in total: seven punches and seven Delphic upperclassmen. As we walked through the doors into the lobby, we were met by a troop of receptionists and handed key cards to our own suites. A concierge appeared and instructed us to follow him. He led the way, guiding us on a twisting, snaking path across the casino floor, down aisles of slot machines with flashing lights, and through a pair of double doors into a labyrinth of hidden corridors and back stairwells. We followed him three levels down, emerging in a subterranean cavern where a long table was set for fifteen.

Simon took his place at the head of the table and motioned

for us to find our seats. The resulting dinner was something of a carnivore's dream. First, they brought out trays of crab cakes and bacon-wrapped scallops. Next came plates loaded with caviar, bone marrow, and carpaccio. Simon warned us not to touch the Caesar salad that came next lest we fill up before the main courses arrived. Arrive they did: platters of butter-soaked lobster tails, thick cuts of bacon, and the biggest porterhouse steaks I've ever seen, sizzling on skillets taken right from the oven. There were baskets of truffle fries and plates of steamed green beans and buttered corn on the cob. To wash it all down, we had four separate glasses—one for red, one for white, one for champagne, one for a negroni—plus a shot glass to be filled from the bottles of Pappy Van Winkle's bourbon placed around the table. At the start of dinner, Simon decreed no glass should ever be empty for more than ten seconds. Anytime this occurred, he told the waiters, he would deduct $100 from the tip.

As they took away the main courses, Simon rose again and toasted the Delphic, declaring it the most influential organization he had ever been a part of. Then he launched into stories about his time in the club, most of which concerned a litany of female conquests. Everyone laughed along with him, courtiers eager to please the king. They even cracked up at the stories, which sounded more like admissions of guilt. Simon lapped it all up, glowing from the thrill of adulation.

The waiters cleared away the mess of plates and refilled the table with tiramisu and Irish coffee. Simon took out a stack of business cards and instructed the punchmaster to give one to each dinner guest.

"When it comes to the Delphic, I will always take your call.

But don't you dare fucking call me about anything else," said Simon to scattered laughter. "I'm serious. You think I'm kidding? Do you think I really have time to hang out with college students? Let me tell you something. I don't. I'm so fucking busy you wouldn't even believe. But for the Delphic, I *make* time. That ought to tell you something about how special this club is."

I turned the card over in my hands, feeling the weight of the heavy cardstock.

ROY SIMON
Founder & Chief Executive Officer
Orcus Capital Partners

Orcus. It had to be a coincidence, right? Could it really be the same company that had gone after my mom? I stared at my half-eaten tiramisu, suddenly feeling very full and heavy and sick. I'd eaten too much. I pushed the plate away, unable to take another bite, and then I lifted my eyes to Simon and watched him hold court from his seat at the head of the table. He did strike me as the kind of person who would have no problem shaking down poor people for money. But would a guy who owned casinos also be in the business of low-income housing? I wasn't sure if that made sense. And besides, the names of the companies were similar but not identical. Maybe it was a coincidence, I reasoned, but something in my gut told me it wasn't.

Simon must have noticed me looking at him because he stopped in mid-sentence and pointed at me. "What's up with this guy?" he asked. "Hey, kid. Stand up."

I found myself on my feet, the room suddenly much quieter.

"What's your name?" Simon barked.

"Atlas," I said.

"You want to be a Delphic man, Atlas? You don't look much like one to me," said Simon. He turned to the punchmaster, seated to his right. "I thought I told you no scrubs. Don't tell me this is one of our top guys." There was a quiet tittle of awkward laughter around the table.

"Oh, come on, Mr. Simon," said the punchmaster. "Atlas is a real beauty. He's the artist we told you about."

"An artist? What is this? The Delphic Club for wet blankets? What's next, theater kids? You guys are killing me," said Simon. He stared at me with his black eyes and I stared right back, refusing to be flustered or fazed. He waved a dismissive hand and I sat back down.

My memory of the rest of that night is of a grotesque dream. After finishing his speech, Simon shouted at a subordinate to "start the show," and a moment later the opening bars of a Frank Sinatra tune thundered from speakers mounted on the walls. And then strippers came in—perhaps a dozen—a parade of sequins and spray tans greeted by wild whoops and hollering. Two strippers draped themselves over Simon and he obliged them by pressing his face into their breasts. The rest performed a kind of cabaret show that was vaguely reminiscent of the Rockettes, only dirtier. After half an hour Simon became bored and announced it was time to go to House of Gold, the night club on the hotel's second floor.

He led a procession of college kids and strippers through the hotel lobby and up the escalator. I trailed along at the back of the group, wanting to be anywhere else and yet lacking the courage to leave.

I could hear the bass thumping all the way from the lobby. A long line stretched from the top of the escalator to the club's entrance. We walked straight to the front of the queue and past a small army of bouncers into an explosion of light and sound. Just inside the doors I felt a cool rush and was enveloped in a cloud of cold white vapor that seemed to come from nowhere. Once it had cleared, I turned to a Delphic kid and shouted in his ear.

"What the fuck was that?"

"CO_2!" he yelled back. "They shoot it from the walls."

A hostess guided us through the throng of people on the dance floor to a roped-off area in the back. Strobe lights flickered overhead, giving the scene a strange stop-motion quality. I was hit by another blast of CO_2 and got momentarily lost in the fog. I bumped into a tall, muscular man, who shoved me back with disproportionate force. A senior in the Delphic came to my defense but I waved him off.

"It was my fault," I shouted.

Two servers wearing tight black dresses waited for us by a table with bottles of vodka and tequila encased in ice. The Delphic punchmaster offered me a shot of tequila. I was beginning to feel nauseous, so I tried to refuse the shot but he pressed it into my hands anyway. I tipped it back, holding the liquid in my mouth, and when he turned away I spat it back into an empty cup.

I watched Simon flirt with a stripper. He took out a cigar and a lighter and a $100 bill and he lit the bill on fire and used it to light his cigar. A bouncer came over and told him he couldn't smoke inside. Simon got to his feet and gave the bouncer a dressing-down. Didn't he know who he was? He owned this fucking place and he could do whatever the hell he wanted.

At that moment, as I watched the billionaire scream profanities at an employee who had only been doing his job, I was overcome by revulsion—not just toward Simon but toward everything around me. Toward the impossibly loud music and the Delphic members acting like animals. Toward the barely dressed bottle girls parading through the club with $2,000 magnums of Dom Pérignon lofted above their heads. I counted a dozen bottles of alcohol at our table. How much did that all cost? Ten, twenty thousand? I realized it was all being paid for by people like my mom, and I felt sick. What was I doing here? This wasn't me. This wasn't who I wanted to be. What would Harriet think if she could see me now?

Someone floated another shot of tequila in front of my face. This time the smell alone was enough to make me gag. I barely made it to the bathroom before vomiting the entire contents of my stomach into a trash can.

Five minutes later, my eyes watering and my throat burning with acid, I shuffled over to a sink and flapped at the motion sensor. Water trickled into my cupped hands for two seconds and then stopped. I groaned. *Fuck these sinks.* I splashed water onto my face and looked up at the mirror and recoiled.

The face looking back at me belonged to someone who was very sick. He was unshaven and his skin was sallow and puffy, his eyes yellow and dull. His lips were crusted with dried vomit. Everything was bloated. He looked lost—a drunken mess. I wanted to look away, but instead I forced myself to stare at the image in the mirror, committing it to memory.

I walked out of the club without saying goodbye to anyone and the next day I dropped out of the running for the Delphic.

CHAPTER 21

On the morning of December tenth, Arthur called out of the blue to ask if I could have a painting ready for a group show at their New York gallery in March. Marian had liked my painting and wanted to include me in the dozen or so artists to be featured in their annual Young Artist Spring Show. Of course, I told him. Since finishing *The Shield of Achilles*, I'd continued with the mythology theme and was close to completing a painting inspired by the myth of Sisyphus. I promised to send Arthur photos of the work and then I hung up the phone., elated. *It's true what they say*, I thought. *Good things come to those who work hard.*

I'd returned from Atlantic City a few weeks earlier determined to get my life back on track—to rediscover the drive and sense of purpose I felt I'd lost in the past year and a half. I taped a pair of quotes to the back wall of my studio. The first was something Marcus was fond of saying: *An artist without discipline is just a bum with a paintbrush.* Beneath that was one I'd come across in my philosophy course: *Discipline is choosing what you want* most *over what you want* now.

Next, I took out a pen and a pad of paper and wrote down two lists.

What I Want Now	*What I Want Most*
• *To be popular*	• *A successful career as an artist*
• *To have fun at parties*	• *Financial security for my mom*
• *To be in a final club*	• *To achieve something meaningful*
• *To get girl*	• *To be with Harriet*

I circled the list on the right and studied it for a while. I knew none of those things would happen unless I made them happen. It was up to me and no one else. I had to make changes to my life. And so I did.

I've never worked harder than during the six weeks that followed the Delphic trip. Free from the burdens of punch, I felt like I had all the time in the world. I started getting up early in the morning so I could spend a few hours every day painting before class. I did all the reading for my courses and I stopped skipping lectures. I started participating in class and going to the gym. I spent pretty much all my free time in the studio. I forced myself to go even when I was tired or felt more like watching a movie in bed. I knew the key was just getting myself to the studio: once I found myself in front of a canvas, it would come easily like it always did.

The change in my behavior didn't go unnoticed by others. Marcus was thrilled with my newfound dedication. Lucien and the other guys were more confused than anything. They still couldn't wrap their heads around the idea that I'd decided not to join a final club. I tried explaining it to them several times, but they still didn't get it. Gardner in particular thought I was nuts. But they were so busy with punch and then their initiation processes that I hardly saw them during that time anyway. And besides, I didn't care so much about what other people thought anymore. I was on my own path. I had goals and I was working toward achieving them. Everything else was noise. When Arthur called, it felt like a validation of my turnaround. I was already thinking about how cool it was going to feel to be able to invite Harriet to a show of my work at a major gallery in New York.

And then the very next day my whole life fell apart.

I was leaving my philosophy section when I saw six missed calls from Marcus.

Sorry was in class. Everything ok? I texted him.

His reply came through seconds later: Come to my office ASAP.

I could tell from the curtness of his text that something was wrong. I ran over to his office filled with trepidation. He was waiting for me when I arrived, pacing behind his desk, muttering to himself. He looked pissed.

"What's going on?" I asked.

"You have anything you need to tell me?" I looked at him blankly and said nothing. "I'm waiting. Now's your chance."

"I don't understand," I said.

"I'm not messing about now, Christopher. This is serious."

"I'm sorry, I—"

Marcus lifted a magazine off his desk and tossed it at me. It bounced off my chest and fell to the floor. I bent down to pick it up and saw it was a catalogue for an upcoming impressionist and postwar art auction at Phillips. It was earmarked to a page at the back. My stomach dropped and I suddenly became very aware of the beating of my heart.

"Go on, open it," said Marcus.

Somehow I already knew what I was going to find. I flipped to the page at the back and, sure enough, there was the painting I'd given Lucien.

The listing read:

>*Property from a private estate.*
>*Raoul Dufy, 1877–1953*
>La Capitale
>*Signed Raoul Dufy, lower right.*

I felt like I couldn't breathe.

"Explain," he barked. "Right now."

"This isn't what it looks like. I didn't do this. I promise." The words rushed out. "This is the first time I'm seeing it. I had no idea he would do this."

"Which one is it? It's not what it looks like? Or you didn't do it? Because I saw you paint that with my own eyes not thirty meters from here."

"Marcus, please, you have to believe me. I didn't—"

"This is what you been up to, huh? This is how you been paying for all your partying and carrying on—for those new fancy clothes I've seen you walking around in. Christ above," he said, shaking his head. "Ripping people off . . . stealing hard-earned money like some low-down, common crook. And you're sitting here at Harvard with all the opportunity in the world. It's disgusting. Disgusting. Your mom didn't raise you to be like this. You ought to be ashamed."

"No! I didn't do this. I swear to God."

"Is this not your painting?"

"It is. That's not what I'm saying. Yes, I painted it. But I gave it to a friend. It was a birthday present. It was all supposed to be a joke. He never said he was going to try to sell it. Obviously I wouldn't have done it if I'd known."

"A joke?"

"He told me he was going to put it up in his room and tell girls it was real."

"And you believed him?"

"Why wouldn't I believe him? He does stuff like that. He likes to mess with people. But selling it at an auction? Are you kidding?

That's crazy. Do you really think I would go along with something so stupid? The canvas was brand-new. It doesn't even look old." This last bit wasn't true, but Marcus didn't know that.

Marcus didn't respond right away. He put his hand over his mouth and looked me right in the eye. His stare made me uncomfortable, but I knew I couldn't look away without seeming guilty. I could tell that he wanted to believe me.

"You swear you had nothing to do with the auction?"

"I swear to God."

"Don't be lying to me, Chris. I'll find out the truth in the end. You know it."

"I'm not lying."

"What's his name, then? The friend."

I hesitated. "I can't tell you that."

"You sure as hell can. And you better, too."

"Do you promise he won't get in trouble?"

Marcus snorted. "I'll do nothing of the sort."

"But I'll get him to pull the painting. This doesn't have to be a big thing. I can make it all go away."

"We're way past that point, Chris. This isn't me catching you with a joint. This isn't kids being young and stupid. This is a proper crime. This is fraud. I'm a member of the faculty, Chris. I have to report him. It's my duty."

"But we can still pull the painting."

"What if I found your friend selling stolen laptops? What if I saw him trying to steal a car? Would you expect me to let that slide? *Oh, just put it back. No harm done, son?*"

"Of course not. This is different, though. It's not the same as stealing."

"That's exactly what it is," he said. "Show me the listing." He took the auction catalogue from my hands. "Look at the estimate: fifty thousand to sixty thousand dollars. It should say zero. The painting is worthless. Where I come from, if you deceive someone into giving you sixty grand for something that's worth nothing, we call that stealing. It's the same as if I sold you a house that doesn't exist and then I ran off with your money."

"But what if they kick him out?"

"Kick him out? Chris, he might go to jail. Who knows what else this kid is up to? He's sure as hell not getting off the hook for this. And if you're not being honest with me and it turns out you're more involved than you're saying, there are gonna be consequences for you, too. I can't protect you," said Marcus. "Especially not if you lie to me. And trust me, we're going to get to the bottom of this one way or another."

I felt my heart flooding with resentment toward Lucien. How could he have done this? How could he have lied to my face again and again? I was a fool for trusting him. I saw that now. He wasn't my friend. He was just someone who used me. I thought of how hard I'd worked to get into Harvard, of all the sacrifices my mom had made to get me to where I was, to give me this opportunity. Lucien had fucked us. And for what? Some bottles at a nightclub? A new Hermès tie? Another necklace for Grace? Why was I protecting this guy when he clearly didn't give a shit about me?

"Let's start at the beginning," said Marcus. "How many other paintings are there?"

"None," I said.

"Is that the truth?"

"This is the only one. I made a mistake. I trusted this guy and

I shouldn't have. I thought he was my friend. I thought I could trust him."

"I need a name," said Marcus.

"What if I talk to him? I'll get him to come see you."

"A name," repeated Marcus.

When I finally left Marcus's office sometime later, I was still furious with Lucien and went straight to Eliot to confront him. I bounded up our entryway stairs and burst in on him reading.

"You promised you wouldn't sell it."

Lucien glanced up, confused. "What?"

"You lied to me. You swore you weren't going to sell it. And then I asked you about it in New York and you lied to me again."

"Atlas, slow down."

"Do you realize what you've done?"

"Slow. Down. Okay? Now tell me what this is all about."

"What the fuck do you think this is about? The Dufy."

"I didn't sell it! I told you. I had it sent to our house in Paris. It's literally hanging above my bed at home. I can show you if you really want. My mum sent me a picture."

"Lucien. I saw the Phillips catalogue. You put it up for auction." I watched for his façade to drop, waiting for that telltale sign of fluster or guilt. But it didn't come. He was unfazed.

"Auction? No I didn't." He smirked. "Atlas . . . it's in my bedroom at home. What don't you understand about that? You're acting really crazy, you know that? You obviously just saw a different painting."

Such was his self-assurance that I even began to doubt myself. But only for a fraction of a second. And then I snapped out of it. "What the hell is wrong with you? Stop fucking lying!"

"I'm not!" said Lucien.

"You think I can't recognize my own painting?"

"I'm saying you're confused, that's all."

I was staggered that he would continue to lie even now. "Lucien . . . I saw the fucking auction catalogue. Do I really have to do this?" I took out my phone and found the auction website and pulled up the listing for the Dufy. "Here," I said, thrusting the phone in his face. "Can you cut the shit now, please?"

Lucien sighed. "Okay, so what if I did? What's it to you? The painting was a present. You gave it to me. It's mine."

"Lucien, why?"

"I don't see what the big deal is. How is this different from the other ones?"

"He knows. He fucking saw it."

"Who?"

"Marcus."

"Marcus knows?" For the first time Lucien looked rattled. "What exactly does he know? What did you tell him?"

"He saw the painting in the catalogue. And knows I painted it. He literally watched me do it."

"What else does he know? Did you say anything else?"

"No."

"Think, Atlas. This is important."

"Hey, screw you. How about you fucking apologize, huh? *Hey, Atlas, sorry for lying to your face and ruining your life.* How about that?"

"Don't be so dramatic. What else did you tell him? Does he know I'm involved or not?"

"I didn't tell him shit. I said I had nothing to do with it. I told him I gave it to a friend as a gift. Which is true, by the way."

"Did you give him my name?"

I looked away and shook my head. "No," I said.

"Atlas, did you give him my name?"

"I just said a friend, all right?"

"Okay. Okay," said Lucien, nodding his head. "Good. That's very good. I knew you were solid. I knew I could rely on you. You're like a brother to me. Haven't I always said that? Okay, I think we can make this work. I'll withdraw the painting from the auction and everything should be fine. We can explain this. We'll say it was all a big misunderstanding. You can talk to him, right? You can do that. He's known you since you were a kid. He doesn't want to see you get in trouble."

"You don't get it. He's reporting this to the school. Maybe to the cops."

"The cops?"

"He said we could go to jail unless we come clean."

"What do you mean, *we*?" asked Lucien. "Look, no one is going to jail. That's fucking mental. Number one: you didn't do anything wrong. Number two: unless Marcus took a photo of you with the forgery, then he doesn't even have any hard proof that you painted it. It's your word against his. And number three: he doesn't know who you gave it to. I consigned the painting under a different name. They can't trace it back to me. We're going to be fine."

"No, Lucien . . . it's over. We have to come clean. Let's just go to him and tell him the truth. That's our best option."

"That's not happening. Deny. Deny. Deny. We admit nothing."

"I have to give him a name, Lucien. I have to."

"You don't have to give him anything."

"He said I'm going to get kicked out unless I give him a name."

"Well, make one up," he snapped.

"You know that won't work."

He stared at me with contempt. "What the fuck are you suggesting, then? You're gonna snitch on me? Really?"

"I'm not getting kicked out for this, man. Not for something *you* did."

"Something *I* did? Who painted the fucking thing? Who aged it? Not me! What if I claim ignorance? What if I say you told me it was real? How about the other paintings? Maybe I'll tell Marcus about those."

I stood there motionless. "You wouldn't do that, would you?"

"I might," said Lucien. "You want to sit there and pretend to be all innocent. Give me a break. You're the whole reason we got into this. You asked me to do this for you. You literally begged."

"I did what?"

"I'm in this situation because of *you*," said Lucien. "And this is my thanks. This is what I get for trying to help *you*. First sign of trouble and you want to throw me to the wolves."

"When did I ever ask you to do to this?"

"*Lucien, can I have some money please?*" he whined in a high-pitched voice. "*Can I borrow your clothes? Will you spot me for dinner? Can you pay my Pudding dues? Pleeeeeaaassse, Lucien. I don't have any money, Lucien.*"

I looked at him and said nothing. I could feel my eyes brimming with tears, but I refused to look away. He shifted into a state of penance.

"I'm sorry," he said, embarrassed. "I didn't mean that. I'm just stressed." He sat down on his bed and ran his hands through his hair. He looked up at me with pleading eyes. "Don't give him my name. Please, Atlas. You don't understand. It will ruin everything. I'll be finished."

"You'll be fine, Lucien. Your parents have money, lawyers. I don't have anything."

"They won't help. My father will use this as an excuse to disown me. I'll lose my inheritance—everything," said Lucien. "Please, Atlas, just take the fall for this one."

I blinked. "Take the fall? Me?"

"It wouldn't be so bad."

"What the fuck? You want me to say *I* did it? I'm not doing that."

"Please, Atlas. I'll be forever in your debt. Tell Marcus you did it to help your mum. Say she needed money and it was a stupid mistake and you'll never do it again. He'll go easy on you if you say that. He'll get over it, I promise."

"But, Lucien—"

"You won't get kicked out. You know that. Not for good. They never kick anyone out for good. At worst, you'll have to withdraw for a year. It's not that big a deal. I could sort out a job for you through my parents. Or you could travel! Yeah, I could pay for you to travel! You could go to Paris. Or to Rome! Wouldn't that be fun? We could go together. It would be an adventure. Just take the blame for this and I can help you. Say you did it. Marcus doesn't have to know about me. It's better for both of us if he doesn't."

"Lucien, stop."

"Please, Atlas. You don't get it. I'll pay you. How much do you want?"

"It's not about money."

"Twenty grand? Fifty? Fifty and I'll cover your travel."

"I already told him," I said, unable to contain it any longer.

There was silence. I watched Lucien's face shift from confusion to anger. "You did what?"

"I'm sorry. I had to. I didn't have a choice."

"You told Marcus? About me? You fucking told him? Are you serious?"

"Look, I'm sorry. I had to."

Lucien put his hands on his head and turned his back to me. He let out a long, deep breath and rubbed his eyes. Then he walked over to his desk and picked up an empty water glass. He stood there for a moment with the glass in his hand and then without warning he wheeled around and launched the glass at my head. It came screaming past my ear before impacting the wall behind, showering the room with glittering fragments.

"You piece of shit!" he yelled, advancing toward me. His face was dark and seething and I felt afraid. I took a step backwards. And then another.

"Lucien! You have to understand. I didn't ha—"

"Shut the fuck up!" Lucien shoved me with both hands, slamming me into the wall. I heard the crunch of broken glass underfoot. All of a sudden he had me by the shirt collar and I was pinned up against the wall. I struggled to break free, but his grip was strong and he seemed to fill the whole room. He pulled his arm back as if to hit me. "Lucien, don't!" I yelled. I closed my eyes and put up my hands to protect my face.

But the blow never came. Instead, I felt his grip loosen. And then he released me. I opened my eyes and saw him looking at me with disgust.

"Pathetic," he said, shaking his head. "I always knew you were a coward. I just never thought you would betray me." He spat on the ground and stormed out.

I looked down and saw that my hands were shaking. I went into my room and pulled the door shut and locked it. And then, feeling very pathetic and very much like a coward, I curled up on my bed and started to weep.

That was the moment when everything hit me. That was when I realized the enormity of all I was about to lose. Marcus would never look at me the same. How could he? He would tell Arthur. Of course he would. He had to. That meant no spring show at Marian Goodman—no future with them at all. My only hope was that Arthur would be discreet. If word got out more widely, it might mean the end of any chance I had at a real career in art. Even if I didn't get kicked out of Harvard, I realized my life at school was over. Any chance I had with Harriet—gone. Lucien would make sure of that. He would spin the story to make himself the victim. I would become a social pariah, a figure of contempt. People liked him more than me. They would believe him and not me. I would forever be known as the guy who stabbed Lucien in the back.

Lucien was right. I was a coward. I didn't have to give Lucien up right then and there. But instead I'd panicked and betrayed him at the first opportunity. How could I blame him for losing his temper? I deserved it. Maybe there was still a way to fix the situation. Maybe I could repair my relationship with Lucien. I drafted and sent a long apology text to him and followed it up with several more, hoping to make amends. He didn't respond and I fell asleep with my phone in my hand.

CHAPTER 22

I was woken several hours later by the sound of someone trying to open my door. "Atlas. You there?" It was Lucien. He tried the handle again. "Mate, I'm sorry, too. I don't know what came over me. I freaked out. Let's talk. Will you open the door? Please?"

"You're not still mad?"

"Atlas, come on, it's me. Look, it's all fine now. I took care of everything. You were right, okay? I get that now. You didn't have a choice. You had to turn me in. One of us had to go down for this. I'm sorry about earlier. I just lost it. Come on. Open the door."

"You promise we're all good?"

"Promise."

"Okay," I said. I unlocked the door and let it swing open. Lucien came in and wrapped me in an embrace. "I'm sorry," he said. "It was a moment of madness. Can you ever forgive me?"

"I thought you were going to hit me," I said.

"I *was* going to hit you." He laughed. "Hey, grab a jacket, let's take a walk. We have a lot to discuss."

I put on my coat and followed him out the door. We crossed the courtyard and passed through the Eliot Gate onto Memorial Drive. We took the footpath that ran along the bank of the Charles. Night had fallen and the river ran black beside us.

"I took care of the painting already," said Lucien. "It's officially withdrawn. And I emailed Marcus. I'm going to see him first thing tomorrow morning. He wants me to bring him a signed statement giving my side of the story. I'll write it tonight when we get back."

"What are you going to say?"

"The truth, I guess."

"About the other paintings, too?"

"Don't be silly. No need to make this worse than it already is," he said. "You can help me draft it if you like."

"Okay."

"We'll make sure it's consistent with what you told him. And that it puts you in the clear."

"Okay," I said again, taken aback by his sudden generosity. "Thank you."

"Don't thank me. This is my fault. I'm the one who fucked up. I'll handle the consequences. And besides, you were right. My family has excellent lawyers. I'll be fine."

I looked up at him.

He smiled. "I'll be fine," he repeated, as if saying it a second time might make it true. "I'm a survivor, Atlas."

Halfway across Weeks Bridge, Lucien paused and gazed out over the river.

"Do you remember our first night? When we came here with those girls and jumped off?"

"Yeah," I said. There had only been one girl with us that night—his girl—but I didn't bother to correct his memory.

"That was fun," he said. "We should have done more things like that."

"We had a lot of fun."

"We did," he said. "It's a shame it has to end like this. A real shame." He cocked his head to the side and I could see a thought forming in his mind. "Hey," he said. "Let's get fucked up."

"What—now?"

"Tonight. Yeah. I want to go out with a bang. Let's have a fucking ripper of a night. I can't stand this melancholy bullshit. It's depressing as all hell."

I couldn't help but smile. "Sure, why not?"

"That's the spirit," he said, turning back the way we came. "Come on, Judas. Keep up."

I remember walking back with Lucien to our room. And I remember him taking out the bottle of whiskey and pouring me a drink. I can't remember if he drank the whiskey, too, or if he had something else. I remember sitting down with him in front of a laptop to draft his statement, but I don't remember a single sentence of what we wrote. Instead, I remember only the heaviness of my eyelids and the feeling of being wrapped in a warm, drowsy darkness. I have a brief memory of being sick in a trash can. And I remember Lucien closing my fingers around a pen and feeling confused as I watched my hand scribble jagged lines across the bottom of a sheet of paper.

After that, I remember nothing.

CHAPTER 23

No one calls me Atlas anymore. It's been more than a decade since I last heard that name. My life as Atlas ended on that dark night in Cambridge—the night Lucien disappeared.

I still don't know exactly what happened that night. Lucien was long gone by the time I woke up in the hospital two days later with a broken sternum and three cracked ribs. What I do know about that night I've learned from others.

I'll begin with what I know for sure. I know that Lucien drugged me and that I had enough GHB and oxycodone in my system to cause respiratory arrest in someone twice my size. That's what the doctor told me, anyway. I know that security cameras capture Lucien leaving Eliot alone at 10:42 p.m. He's wearing a hoodie and he has a backpack on. He looks like he's heading to Lamont to study for a final. Six minutes later, at 10:48 p.m., he returns in a hurry. He bursts through the front doors and comes running down the hallway in the direction of our room. Fifteen minutes go by and then the camera footage shows the two of us together. I look blackout drunk. I have vomit all down my shirt and I can hardly stand. He's supporting my weight, guiding me down the hallway through the front door to the taxi waiting outside. I know that when we arrive at the hospital eleven minutes later, I'm barely breathing and about to go into cardiac arrest. I also know that before he slips away and disappears into the night, Lucien tells the nurse the exact drugs I've taken.

I assume from there Lucien went back to our room in Eliot, packed up all his belongings, and left. He must have gone in and out through a back door because he doesn't show up on the main security cameras again. In any case, by the next morning Lucien had vanished. There was no note, nor any clue of where he might have gone. He left his room spotless. It was as if he had never existed.

Of course, I knew none of this when I woke up in the hospital and saw my mom and Marcus standing at the foot of my bed, talking to a cop. I was awake but I was so groggy and out of it that I could hardly make sense of what was going on. I remember feeling like I was still in a dream state, the way you feel when you've half woken up from an afternoon nap and are on the verge of falling back asleep. I was confused about where I was and why there was a cop and why it hurt to breathe, but I was too tired to find out. When my mom saw my eyes flicker open, she yelped and rushed over. In her excitement she forgot about my broken ribs and squeezed me so tight that I cried out in pain. I spent most of the next two days sleeping.

It was Marcus who pushed to get the police involved. At first my situation was assumed to be either a substance abuse problem or a suicide attempt. But when Marcus learned that Lucien was nowhere to be found, he went straight to the dean of the college and told her she needed to call in the police department.

It took some time for the totality of Lucien's deception to come to light. The first indication that he wasn't who he said he was came when the police were unable to get in touch with his parents. The addresses he'd listed for them did not exist. The phone numbers were not in service. Lucien must have filled out the form wrong. Or perhaps they'd moved. I know this because during my police interview they asked me if I had any way of contacting his parents. I realized I'd never once spoken to them.

The police had a lot of questions about Lucien. Questions about his past, his family, where he'd grown up, and where he'd gone to school. I told the police the same lies Lucien told me. Only I didn't realize they were lies when I said them. I still thought all of it was true.

I told the cops other lies, too. Lies of my own invention. When they asked if Lucien had a motive to hurt me, I lied and said that I couldn't think of one. When they asked if I thought Lucien had drugged me, I lied again and said I wasn't sure. When they asked if I'd tried to commit suicide that night, I told them I didn't remember. I lied when they asked if Lucien had a history of substance abuse and I lied again when they asked if I'd ever witnessed him acting in a violent or aggressive manner. I lied for Lucien because I understood if I didn't that he could be charged with attempted murder, and I wasn't prepared to condemn him outright.

I couldn't bring myself to accept that he had actually tried to kill me. I convinced myself that it must have been an accident. I figured he tried to get me fucked up so I would agree to confess to everything but had used too strong a dose by accident. There was still too much that was unclear about that night: too many unanswered questions; too much that just didn't make sense. At worst, Lucien would have lost his place at Harvard, but for someone who was so brilliant and had so much wealth and privilege, was that really such a setback? Was that worth *killing* over? And if he'd really wanted me dead, then why did he take me to the hospital? It was only months later when I found the suicide note that I was able to make sense of it all.

By that point I already knew that Lucien had lied to us about who he was. I was back at home on administrative leave from Harvard when the articles started appearing in late January. The *Crimson* was the first to break the story. They published an article titled "Air of Mystery Surrounds Missing Student." *The Boston Globe* picked it up, too. They assigned a pair of investigative journalists to look into Lucien's past. The whole devastating truth about Lucien came out in a resulting series of articles published over several weeks that spring.

His name wasn't always Lucien. He was born John Blair, not in Stockholm but in Millerton, New York, a rural town of nine hundred people. He wasn't a Vanderbilt and he wasn't nobility. He never attended an elite boarding school and certainly not Eton. He did, however, grow up down the road from Hotchkiss and Kent, although he had neither the grades nor the money to attend them, and so instead he went to the Housatonic Valley Regional Public High School in Falls Village, Connecticut.

His parents—his real ones—were dead. His mother died of liver failure when he was three and his father, a pharmacy technician who suffered from depression, took his own life a little more than three years before John Blair turned up at Harvard with a new name and a new identity.

Once the details of his story were made public, there was a rush of interest in finding out everything there was to know about the boy who had conned his way into Harvard. For several weeks reporters emailed and phoned me with question after question about my former roommate. I refused to speak to them.

The Boston Globe sent a reporter to Millerton to interview former classmates of John Blair. By all accounts, he had passed through high school without making much of an impression on anyone. Several classmates had no recollection of him whatsoever. Those who did described a quiet, shy boy who kept to himself and was most often found reading in the school library. One joked his nickname had been the "invisible man." His former math teacher was quoted saying that John had been one of the most talented students she'd ever had but one she found frustrating to teach because he didn't apply himself. She claimed in terms of innate ability he was by far the brightest student at the school, but perhaps because of a fear of being singled out for the wrong reasons he kept that intelligence hidden from his classmates. Often he would turn in perfectly completed homework, but whenever she called him up to the board during class to do the same problems, he would feign ignorance.

John's closest friend was his father. And so when he committed suicide during John's junior year of high school, John had his own breakdown and dropped out of school. He told the administration he would return the following fall, but he never did. That was the last anyone from the school had seen, heard, or thought of John Blair until the reporters showed up.

I struggled to reconcile the friend I had known so well with the stranger I read about in the paper. The chalets and châteaus, debutante balls and private jets—those trappings of a charmed, fictional existence were replaced by the sad, mundane details of his real life. Lucien had been so talented, so outgoing. Far from shunning the spotlight, he had adored being the center of attention. The description of John Blair reminded me more of myself than it did of Lucien. How was it possible these two people—total opposites of one another—existed in the same person?

The *Globe*'s team pieced together what happened to John Blair after he left Millerton and how he came to be at Harvard. The day after his father's funeral John attempted suicide himself and almost succeeded. He was committed to the Hudson River Psychiatric Center in Poughkeepsie, where he was diagnosed with a number of mental disorders. It was there that he began inventing new identities and constructing his own private universe—a landscape of his dreams.

After he left the institution, John Blair sold the family house for $300,000, collected the money from his father's life insurance policy, and began the process of erasing his prior self and inventing a fresh one. He spent a year traveling around Europe, trying on different identities, each more outlandish than the last. At times he went by John Francis du Pont, a professional gambler and card counter on his way to the casinos of Monte Carlo. Then there was Misha Rublev, the son of a Russian oligarch (although he only used that one around people he was sure did not speak Russian), and also Jack Paris, an operative for the CIA. At other times he was an art collector by the name of Sir Godfrey Allenby. But more and more, he was Lucien Orsini. Over the course of that year he taught himself how to speak French, German, and Spanish. He changed his accent and the way he dressed. And he became fixated on the idea of getting into Harvard.

When he returned from Europe, he had his legal name changed to Lucien Alexandre Orsini-Conti. He took the SAT and came one question short of a perfect score. He had no intention of going back to Housatonic High but still needed a diploma, so he forged a transcript and claimed he had graduated from Eton at the top of his class. His three recommendation letters came from Eton's headmaster, a professor at Oxford named Simon Armstrong, and the director of the Royal College of Art. Only the letters didn't come from those people because Lucien wrote them all himself. Simon Armstrong didn't exist, and neither Eton's headmaster nor the director of the Royal College had ever heard of Lucien. But no one in the admissions office thought to check, in part because Lucien had been so impressive and so convincing in his admissions interview. Amid the 34,248 applications Harvard received the year we applied, Lucien managed to slip through.

In the beginning I refused to believe any of it. It wasn't possible, I thought, for *everything* to have been a lie. Even if Lucien had lied around the edges, there was no way he could be this John Blair kid. It was too much of a departure from the person I'd known. But each week brought the discovery of more and more evidence, and it became harder and harder to deny the truth. The *Globe* ran a piece about the wreckage that was his finances. By the time Lucien fled, he was dead broke and had $80,000 in credit card debt spread across five different cards. The safe-deposit box that Lucien told me contained $60,000 was empty. I realized that was why he put so much pressure on me to keep painting forgeries. That was why he tricked me into painting the Dufy and put it up for auction. The painting was his lifeline. It wouldn't have solved all his problems, but it would have bought him another few months.

I began to form a new image of Lucien in my mind—one of a desperate, scared boy who found himself in a hole he knew he would never climb out of unless he took bigger and bigger risks. In those frantic final months Lucien had had the frenzied tunnel vision of a gambler chasing his losses. He wasn't rational. Not at the end. He wasn't himself anymore.

And then one morning in early March I found the suicide note on my laptop and the final pieces clicked into place.

I found it by accident, going through my schoolwork folder. I was looking for a letter I'd drafted for the Ad Board when I came across a Word doc titled "dear marcus." I opened it out of curiosity, having no recollection of ever having created it. As I read, I felt a chill run through my heart as I realized the only reason I survived that night was because Lucien must have gotten cold feet.

dear marcus,

I'm sorry for letting you down. And I'm sorry for lying to you but I was scared, and I didn't know what to do. I panicked and said Lucien did it even though he didn't. He had nothing to do with it. I did it. I did it all. I'm sorry that I've been such a disappointment and a failure. This isn't your fault. I just can't take it anymore. I'm tired of letting everyone down all the time.

Mom, I love you so much and I'm sorry I couldn't be the son you deserved. I don't want to cause you any more pain. Please don't be sad for me. I haven't been happy for a very long time, and I think it is just better this way.

Goodbye,

Atlas

The police never found Lucien. Not that I really expected them to. He was too smart for that. And besides, in some ways it was better for everyone that they didn't find him. The whole saga was hugely embarrassing for Harvard. I'm sure the president and Board of Overseers wanted everyone to forget that Lucien had ever existed.

Five years went by and then five more, but I never forgot. How could I? I knew he was still out there. From time to time, I would sense his presence and I knew he must be close by. Once I thought I spied him in a crowd, watching me from a distance, but I was mistaken. Still, never for a second did I believe I'd seen the last of Lucien. He would come find me when the time was right. I was sure of it.

CHAPTER 24

A white sky hung low over Williamsburg, drizzling rain in a cool, gentle mist. He was standing on the pavement in front of my apartment building, dressed in a dove-gray herringbone suit with an ash-colored tie and a navy overcoat. His hair was a wavy, dark brown. Tucked beneath one arm was a black umbrella. His skin was dark with a tan that would have looked natural on an Argentinian polo player. I couldn't see his eyes, only the reflective lenses of his tortoiseshell sunglasses. It had been ten years since I'd last seen him and he looked nothing like he did before, but still I recognized him instantly.

I stared at the apparition, hesitant to speak—as if saying his name might somehow break a spell and cause him to vanish.

"Lucien?"

"Is there somewhere we can talk?"

"Sure."

It was a short distance to the waterfront, and we found an empty bench on a softly sloping hill overlooking the East River. The river was a dark, inky gray, and a dense layer of white fog lifted off its surface and flowed north against the current. Across the water, Manhattan was lost in a cloud.

Lucien stared straight ahead at the ghostly city skyline while I rummaged through the jumble of questions in my head. There was so much I wanted to ask, so much I wanted to know.

"Where did you go?" I asked. "After you left."

"Everywhere," he said. "Anywhere. I don't really remember. I just kept going."

"Tell me what happened."

"I didn't come to talk about that," he said. "I came to make things right." Lucien paused to take a breath. He removed his sunglasses and looked at me and for the first time I saw his eyes. They weren't how I remembered them: bright and vibrant. Those eyes had been replaced by a pair of faded bluish-gray irises. It was like someone had taken a syringe and tried to pull out all the pigment. His eyes flitted about. Always in motion. Never still. It reminded me of that restless, vacant look you see in the eyes of dogs at rescue shelters.

"I know I can't give you back what you lost," he said, "but I'm sorry for what I did and I'm sorry for what's happened to you." The apology felt hollow and rehearsed. I wondered how many years he had spent thinking about what to say to me. He continued. "I know life hasn't worked out the way you wanted it to, but I'm here to change that. I brought you something—"

"Why didn't you tell me?" I cut him off. "About John Blair—about who you really were? I could have helped if I'd known. Things didn't have to end that way."

He took a moment to think about his answer. "I did tell you. You don't remember the day the man shot himself in the Yard? We were with Gardner. In Greenough."

"I remember that day," I said, trying to recall the specific details.

"I told you about John then," he said. "But that's not who I was. Not at Harvard. At Harvard I was Lucien. Fully and completely. Whatever I told you about Lucien's past—that was my past. It was real. I remembered going to Eton. I remembered skiing in Gstaad. There wasn't any part of John left. Only what I told you."

"I don't think I understand you."

"The past doesn't exist. Not really. It's not something physical. It's not something you can touch. It's all up here," he said, touching his temple with a finger. "The past is whatever we remember. It's a story we tell ourselves about how we got to where we are. If you change your memories, you can change your past. And if you change your past, you change who you are."

"You can't really believe that."

"I can and I do," he said. "John's life . . . it wasn't a happy life. A lot of fucked-up things happened to him, and the memories of those things . . . he couldn't escape them. They turned him into a certain kind of person—a person I didn't want to be anymore. So one morning I woke up and I started remembering new memories. I gave myself a new past and I rewrote the story of who I was. I wasn't Lucien all the time. There were others, too. But Lucien was the one who came out the most. After a while . . . well, eventually I just started forgetting things about John. Big things. Important things. His birthday. The color of his house. By the time those newspaper articles came out, John was as much a stranger to me as he was to you."

"But, Lucien," I said, "that's called denial. You can't do that. You can't just magic away the past by pretending it never happened."

"Why not?"

"Because it did happen," I snapped. "Not just to you but to others, too. It happened to people like me. Think about what you did to me. Do you really believe that goes away just because you pretend it didn't happen? Well, it doesn't." I was becoming more and more heated. "And look, I'm sorry that you didn't have a great childhood. But guess what? That doesn't make you special. My dad died before I ever met him. That doesn't give me license to fuck up other people's lives. Bad shit happens to everyone. People get cancer, they get fired, they're abused, lied to, cheated on; they lose loved ones, go bankrupt, whatever. Tragedy is the one constant in every life. Dealing with it is part of what it means to be human. The real choice is: Do you let it destroy you or do you get on with your life?"

A troubled look came over his face. He seemed unsure of what to say. "You don't understand," he said after a time. "It's not like that. When I started forgetting things, it wasn't intentional. I wasn't in control of it. It terrified me. Memories just started disappearing. Not only bad memories; good ones, too. I was forgetting things that should have been impossible to forget. One morning I realized I couldn't remember my own mother's face. Some days I would sit by myself and spend hours trying to remember something basic about John's life. I just couldn't do it. The memories weren't there anymore. And it kept getting worse. Whenever I thought about him, I would discover I'd forgotten something new. It was like I had this book of his life and every time I opened it, a new page was blank. At first it was just a page here or there, and that was fine. It didn't seem like a big deal. But the blank pages started to add up. I'd return to the book and I'd find that whole chapters were blank. That's when I began to get scared. After a while I just stopped thinking about him because if I didn't think about him . . . if I never opened the book, I could pretend all the words were still there."

"And it's like that even now? The memories never came back?"

He shrugged. "I have moments from his life in my head, but it's impossible to know if any of it is real. Are they memories or stories I made up to fill empty pages? And the details I think I know of his life—how much of it is even accurate? Do I know those things because I remember them, or did I read an article about him and internalize a few facts about his life? I don't know. That life feels very far away now. Sometimes I doubt that it ever happened. Even if it did, I know that I was never supposed to be that person—I was never supposed to be John. I was always supposed to be someone else. I always *was* someone else."

I looked at him, completely lost for words. I suddenly felt very sorry for him because I realized there was something wrong with his mind—a defect that allowed him to confuse memories and dreams, to disassociate and live in a world of delusion in which nothing existed outside of the present moment.

I knew then that he could never go back. He could never again be the person he'd once been because he no longer knew who that person was. There was only one direction left for him to go, and that direction was forward. I saw his future laid out with sudden clarity. His life would be one of perpetual motion, a constant and relentless sprint. There was no endgame. Whoever he was now would not last. He would just keep moving from one life to the next, trapped in a labyrinth of his own design, cursed to endure an endless cycle of death, rebirth, and reinvention.

"I found the note," I said. "From that night."

"I thought you might," he said.

"Did you mean for me to find it?"

"No," he said. "I just forgot to delete it. I realized that the next day, but it was too late."

"Marcus, my mom—they never would have believed I wrote it."

"I know."

"You signed it 'Atlas.' I never used that name with them."

"You have to understand, I lost control. I had a complete breakdown. All the pressure, all the stress, everything was just spiraling. I couldn't sleep. I was having these crazy, dark thoughts all the time. It doesn't excuse what I did—at all. But I want you to understand that, at least. I wasn't in my right mind."

"You know, I never went back," I said. "To Harvard, I mean."

"I know."

"I had to withdraw. And then, when I applied for readmission, they wouldn't give me any financial aid."

"I made fools of them. You were guilty by association."

"I don't know that I really wanted to go back. I saw what that world did to you. And the way everyone turned on you when the truth came out. All those kids who used to suck up to you . . . you should have heard the things they said. The Pudding kids were the worst."

"Which ones?"

"I don't know. Henry Frank, Abi Zhao. People like that."

"What did they say about me?"

"Oh, you were a fraud, a cheat. That you didn't deserve a place at Harvard. People said you only snuck in because some idiot in the admissions office didn't do their job."

"They said that?"

"Yeah. Henry Frank was going around saying he always knew you weren't that smart and always had a suspicion that you were just plagiarizing everything. He said a lot of shit about me, too. Gardner told me."

"That guy was a prick. I never plagiarized anything."

"I know that. You deserved your place as much as anyone. More than most of us, to be honest."

"You really think Henry Frank would have gotten in without his parents' money?"

"No chance."

"No fucking way. Kids like that would be nowhere without their SAT tutors and private coaches and the admissions consultants that wrote their essays for them. It's all handed to them on a plate, but they forget that. They think they did it all themselves. They mistake their privilege for talent. I mean, for Christ's sake, Henry's parents donated a hundred mil to the ed school," said Lucien. He was growing heated. "That's what always drove me crazy: how unfair the whole thing was. They tell you that you can grow up to be whatever you want. But it's a fucking lie. It doesn't matter how smart you are, how hard you work. The game is rigged from the start by people like Henry fucking Frank. They distract you with these illusions of freedom and opportunity just so you don't realize that you're actually not free at all. And by the time you do realize it, it's too late. You've already spent your whole life trapped in this shitty little box, doing the same shitty job, thinking if only you worked a little bit harder, then things might be different. I saw what that did to my dad and how it destroyed him. And I decided I wasn't going to let that happen to me. That's why I did it."

"I don't believe in illusions anymore. I see the world for what it is."

"Yeah, well, it's a bullshit world."

"Did you read the articles about you?"

"Yeah."

"All of them?"

"Yeah."

"They called you a sociopath."

"I know."

"Are you?"

"Do you think I am?"

I took my time before answering. "No," I said. "I don't think so."

"I don't think so, either. No. I know I'm not," he said. "But . . ."

"What?"

Lucien lowered his eyes. I watched his chest rise as he drew in a long, slow breath. He shook his head. "Never mind."

"Tell me."

"I tried to convince myself that I was. I didn't call it that in my head. But I had this idea that I was a survivor. That's what I called it. And survivors do whatever it takes. The ends justify the means. I wanted to be cold and ruthless and to feel nothing. I thought I could be like that. I convinced myself I *had* to be like that if I wanted to survive. That night . . . it had to be one of us. I told myself it was you or me, and so it had to be you. But I couldn't do it. I didn't have it in me."

"That's why you came back for me."

"I wouldn't have been able to live with myself."

"I know."

"That's what those newspaper articles got so wrong. They made it seem like I had everything figured out. Like I knew what I was doing. They painted me as this pro, veteran con man with an elaborate premeditated plan to scam my way into the ranks of the elite." Lucien laughed. "There was no plan. I had no idea what I was doing. I was just a kid. Just a dumb kid."

"I never saw you like that," I said. "You always seemed so confident to me."

"Maybe I was for a while. But by the end I was lost, and I was terrified. I got carried away chasing a dream. And then it turned into a nightmare." He paused. "I'm sorry about everything I made you do," he said. "I didn't mean for it to go that way."

"I didn't do anything I didn't want to do. Not really."

"Yes you did," he said. "I pulled you along with me and I made you do things you never would have done if you hadn't met me." He reached into his overcoat pocket and pulled out a green jewelry box with a gold clasp. "Here," he said, holding it out. "This is for you. To make things right."

"What is it?"

"It's a new life. A new start. Whatever you want."

I shook my head. "I don't want a new life."

"Take it," he said. "This is how I fix things."

"I don't want it."

"You don't know what it is yet," he said.

Lucien undid the clasp and raised the lid. Inside the box, resting on a green velvet pillow, was a diamond and emerald necklace crafted in the shape of a snake. Two glowing rubies made the eyes.

"How did you get that?" I asked, stunned.

"It's beautiful, isn't it? It's very valuable." He closed the lid and tried to hand the box to me, but I refused.

"Take it."

"Not unless you tell me how you got it."

"Just take it," he said. "Sell it. Use it to change your life. Go back to painting, finish Harvard, open your own gallery, buy your mom a house. Do whatever you want with it. Just take it."

"I'm not accepting that."

"Why not?"

"I don't want a new life. I tried that once. It didn't end well."

"But, Atlas, look at you. All the talent in the world and you're doing *what* with it? Teaching first graders how to fingerpaint? Talk about a waste. You should be so much more than this. It's my fault you ended up this way."

"I'm okay with who I am."

"You were supposed to do great things. You were supposed to *be somebody*. Somebody great."

"Maybe I never was. Maybe that was just hubris and this is all I was meant to be."

"No. You were so gifted."

"I don't have it anymore, Lucien. Whatever I had, it's gone now. I can't get it back."

"Surely—"

"I've tried, Lucien. I've tried everything. But it's gone. I lost it that night and I haven't had it ever since."

"Oh, Atlas . . ."

"It's okay. I've come to terms with it." I pointed at the necklace. "But I can't buy it back. And that's fine. I'm fine with this life. It might not look like much to you, but I'm happy enough."

We were both quiet. I heard the dogs barking behind us and the rise and fall of leaves rustling in the breeze. There were still so many questions I wanted to ask him. I wanted to know where and who he'd been all this time. I wanted to know the different lives he'd lived since being Lucien. Who was he now? And how had he come to be here sitting next to me on a bench in Brooklyn with a million-dollar necklace in his lap? I wanted to ask. But somehow I knew he wouldn't answer if I did.

He glanced at his watch. "I should be going," he said.

I felt a sadness collecting in my chest as I realized I would never see him again. "So, is this it, then?"

"This is it," he said, getting up to leave.

"Lucien?"

"Yeah?"

"I forgave you a long time ago. I just thought you should know that."

He nodded. "Goodbye, Atlas," he said. "It was nice to see you again."

The rain was falling heavier now, and he walked away under the cover of his umbrella. I followed him with my eyes until he was just a blurred silhouette in the watery distance—a phantom vanished by the fog.

ACKNOWLEDGMENTS

This novel would not have been possible without the generosity, support, and kindness of so many others. Thank you to my incredible agents Alice Whitwham and Addison Duffy. To my editor, Edie, for her enthusiasm and belief in this novel. Thank you to Brian, Jonathan, Heather, and the entire team at HarperCollins. To Nicole for the countless hours you spent helping me become a better writer. Thank you to my mother, my father, and my siblings for your love, support, and guidance. To the early readers: Christian, Sam, Ann, Tyler, Aaron, Antonia, Elliott, Ron, Teddy, Nick, and Caspar. To Liz and Bret for all their help in navigating the agent search process, and to Nick for introducing me to Alice. To Lu Jinbo and Wu Tao for believing so strongly in *Lucien*. Thank you to Chris Meledandri for your encouragement. To John Myatt for speaking to me so openly about the years he spent forging art. Thank you to the authors of all the books I had to read before I was able to write this one—far too many to list here. And finally, thank you to all the extraordinary friends I made during my time at Harvard, who continue to inspire me and whose influence has left a lasting mark on my life.

ABOUT THE AUTHOR

Born in London, J. R. Thornton attended Harvard College, where he studied history, English, and Chinese, graduating in 2014. An internationally ranked junior tennis player, he competed for Harvard and on the professional circuit. He was a member of the inaugural class of Schwarzman Scholars, obtaining an MA from Tsinghua University in Beijing. He lives in Italy and works for AC Milan. *Lucien* is his second novel.